Lioness

Lioness

Emily Perkins

B L O O M S B U R Y   C I R C U S

LONDON • OXFORD • NEW YORK • NEW DELHI • SYDNEY

BLOOMSBURY CIRCUS
Bloomsbury Publishing Plc
50 Bedford Square, London, WC1B 3DP, UK
29 Earlsfort Terrace, Dublin 2, Ireland

BLOOMSBURY, BLOOMSBURY CIRCUS and the Bloomsbury Circus logo
are trademarks of Bloomsbury Publishing Plc

First published in Great Britain 2023

A catalogue record for this book is available from the British Library

ISBN: HB: 978-1-5266-6066-4; TPB: 978-1-5266-6067-1;
EBOOK: 978-1-5266-6063-3; EPDF: 978-1-5266-6065-7

2 4 6 8 10 9 7 5 3 1

Typeset by Integra Software Services Pvt. Ltd

Printed and bound in Great Britain by CPI Group (UK) Ltd, Croydon CR0 4YY

To find out more about our authors and books visit www.bloomsbury.com
and sign up for our newsletters.

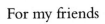

For my friends

1

Trevor turned off the alarm and rolled back to face me across the creamy hotel sheets. He gripped my wrist and held it on the pillow between us.

'I've got you.'

With my free hand I thumbed the sun-damaged skin below his neck. I thought of this part of his body, usually hidden by a shirt collar and tie, as mine.

'I'm going to be late,' I said.

It was our last day in Sydney. I was due to meet the real estate agent in Darling Point.

Trevor kissed me. As was my habit, I had got out of bed before he woke, to clean my teeth. Now he had my other wrist, and pressed them both above my head, against the padded headboard. His knee pushed between my legs. A memory of my neighbour, Claire − our last weird encounter − scratched at my brain but was erased by the morning smell of Trevor's sweat and his skin's heat as he moved on top of me. My blood rushed in response, and I shifted, arching to meet him.

'I've got to get up.'

'You've got to go,' he said. 'You've got to go to work.'

After all this time sex could still be a series of negotiations, small advances and retreats over territory. Yes. No. There. Briefly I floated out of myself to see us from above − the linen in the soft morning light, his tousled silvery hair, the thick curve of his shoulders, my blonde streaks spread across the pillow, one leg wound around his hips. The image took me to the edge of an orgasm, but Claire's face appeared again, distracting me. Go away!

I had a weird feeling of triumph when Trevor came, as if I'd won a fight.

'Now you,' he said.

'Later.' I got out of bed and stood naked in front of him, watching him look. 'I've got to go.'

We had come to Sydney so Trevor could meet an investor face to face, and I could scout locations to open my first Therese Thorne store in Australia. It was early December, and the city had already attained a heat we wouldn't feel back in Wellington even at the height of summer. The open air malls were strung with Christmas lights, the sea burned in electric glimpses between buildings and trees, and that stink of flying foxes hovered in the Botanic Gardens – the sort of hot smell you can't help sniffing for, like from a marker pen, or a pair of knickers kicked off onto the bedroom floor.

The Darling Point site was an empty retail space in a converted worker's cottage fronted by frothing jacarandas. The small, low-slung building was the last of its kind on a side street, off a road lined by grand hedges which afforded occasional views of wedding cake villas and airy modern developments. The estate agent's motorbike dominated the path that led to the front door, a sleek black insect that had waited outside all my viewings that week. I manoeuvred around it, sweating and nervous from the rush to get there, but inside, a respite from the heat, the space was quiet, and smelled cleanly of sawdust.

A wall had been knocked down to turn two small rooms – the front and back of the cottage – into one larger area. My sneakers squeaked on the floorboards as I circled the space envisaging my homewares here, textiles lining the exposed brick, ceramic treasures laid out on scrubbed wooden tables, ferns in macramé plant holders hanging from the ceiling. The window frames had been enlarged and paned with reinforced glass, and would be good for displays. A familiar pressure rose beneath my ribcage: I wanted it. I kept my expression neutral as I passed the estate agent. He pretended to be on the phone, but he was watching. I knew not to underestimate his baby-face, nor his compensating air of authority.

The back door led to a dark lean-to that must have been a kitchen, which I could use for storage. The windows looked out on a thin yard, an unappealing grey space that appeared wavy and distorted through the old glass. You couldn't tell what was out there. I had a queasy feeling, as if this cottage were floating through time, and I was stuck inside with the realtor. I turned back to the interior, imagining a family of Victorian settlers crammed in: thick black clothes, crying kids. Foreign heat.

'It's gorgeous,' I said. 'But is there much foot traffic?'

'It's an exclusive area,' the agent said.

'If I started here,' I said, 'and word of mouth was good, it would give a sort of cachet, right. Set me up to expand after a year or two. A department store tenancy, do you cover those?'

'Maybe,' he said. 'If that's the goal.'

It was. Therese Thorne Homewares had a flagship store in Wellington and boutiques in Auckland, Christchurch and Tauranga – the result of twenty-five years' work. The next step was to set up here in Sydney, where I would fulfil my ambitions and Trevor would retire to sail and play golf in the sun. We weren't quite ready yet – Trevor had to finish one final property development first, the big hotel project that was his last hurrah, and I needed to find investment to fund the move. If it weren't for my sharing Trevor's last name, the agent might have had me pegged as a tyre-kicker. But the real estate company had branches in New Zealand too, and they knew who Trevor was.

Trevor and I met in the 1990s, when I was not long out of university, having started in English Lit and ended up in Marketing. This was back when university was free. I was the first in my small family to go. At that time Trevor was a serial dater. He and Judith had been divorced a few years, after she had fallen in love with a friend, another mother from the tennis club. The other woman wouldn't leave her marriage but things between Judith and Trevor were now, they agreed, over. They kept the details close, or as close as was possible in those scandal-loving circles. Judith asked Trevor not to tell the kids about her affair, and he didn't, and he'd suffered for that when the children were young. Even now they were adults – my god, middle-aged – they still thought the divorce was his fault.

He had gone wild for a while after the marriage ended, leaving the four children – Annabel, Rob, Caroline and Heathcote – with their mother, while he travelled alone to Mexico, the Venice Biennale, sex parties in Berlin. When we were introduced in a café by a man I was pitching an idea for a stationery business, Trevor had recently returned from racing motorbikes in the Angolan desert. I'd never met anyone like him in my life.

I make it sound like I knew what I was doing, 'pitching'. In fact, I had met the other man, whose face I can recall vividly but not his name, at the hotel where I was a receptionist. I was twenty-two. Since graduating, my life had stalled. He was a regular business traveller and he kept asking me out for coffee till I said yes. 'But not a date-date,' I remember saying, and he laughed at me as if the idea itself was parochial. 'Of course not.' That was why I was trying to sell him on my idea. I didn't want to lose control of the conversation.

Trevor, who knew this man from school, swung a chair over from another table and made me tell him why I believed nice stationery was important, and I spoke earnestly because I really did think people should have pretty things. I told him stuff I never meant to, about the girls in my class with their glitter pens and scented rubbers, the longing those pastel colours had instilled in me, the orderliness they suggested, houses that were clean and cheery, how could anyone with a pom-pom on the zip of their pencil case come from a home where people called one another a dumb bitch?

4

He listened, is what I mean. And the man, the business traveller, watched him watch me, and the next day when he was waiting for his taxi before flying back to Auckland, he told me he would put in $2,000 for a proof of concept.

'By the way,' he said. 'You're a pretty girl but you'd do better if you straightened up that eyetooth.'

Feeling brave and rich, I called the number Trevor had given me to tell him that news, and ask if maybe he would like to invest in the idea too.

'I'm heading into a meeting, but I'll call you back,' he said. 'I'll be asking you out. You can decide whether business and pleasure mix. You can decide which is which, Teresa.'

I was still Teresa Holder, then.

I learned about his marriage on our first weekend away together, when we were recounting for each other, on that bed in his Martinborough house, our pasts. No – he told me his stories, but I didn't reveal mine. My life seemed trivial next to his. He was more than two decades older than me. I played the blank slate, which no girl is.

Another thing I found out, but not till later, was he'd sent his old school friend $5,000, more than double his investment, to clear the field. At the time I thought that was romantic.

A year after we met, *Therese Thorne* sold its first line of stationery into shops. That was the start of it all.

'What about *Therese*,' he'd suggested when we were designing a label. 'More aspirational than Teresa. And a last name is good too – creates a character the shoppers can identify with. But not Holder. How about mine?'

Soon after we launched, he suggested that I myself drop Teresa and adopt the name Therese. Therese was the homeware designer and bright businesswoman; Therese relaxed in white shorts at the beach; Therese got that wonky eyetooth straightened so that she could open her mouth when she smiled. Therese didn't worry about what Teresa's parents might have thought; they just needed to get the good seats at the wedding. First the brand had become Therese Thorne, then I did.

5

I left the killer baby realtor at the retail site and walked across to the Museum of Contemporary Art in the humidity, inhaling the lushness. The excited, wanting feeling in my stomach drove me on. It was wonderful to see new things, and everything pleased me: a little dog in a sparkly harness, trotting along like a busybody; a musclebound man who strode through the park, elbows out as if he were at a hoedown – I half expected him to veer over and sling his arm through mine, whirling me off my feet.

An exhibition by an artist called Pippilotti Rist had recently opened. I spent a long time in her room of hanging lights – a dark space lit by strings of organic crystal shapes that pulsed with soft, changing colours. It was like being in an underwater cave, or a nightclub on Venus. We all drifted around softly, like divers gawping at jellyfish. Jellyfish, I had recently read, would pack the oceans before too long. Or was it krill? Something that would survive at high acid levels and render the water viscous, unswimmable. In pushing that thought away I felt the blind poke of the morning's other unwelcome memory, from bed, about Claire. Like having a piece of food trapped between your teeth.

A woman caught my eye through the hanging colours and smiled as if to say, *can you believe this exists*. A thrill ran through me, the sound of a small bell.

As I was leaving the gallery I saw her again, now in front of a video installed in a bright corridor, and I slowed to see what she was looking at. On the screen, a younger woman in a blue dress, her hair in a high ponytail, sashayed down a city street, bearing what looked like a huge flower – a red hot poker perhaps. She looked as effortless as her cotton dress, enjoying the day. As we watched she drew back the flower like a weapon, gave a skip to get momentum, and whacked the driver's window of a parked car, smashing it.

The other woman glanced over her shoulder at me and I realised I had made a strange noise.

On the video the ponytailed woman skipped on, to another car, and did it again.

My phone buzzed in my handbag. It was Trevor.

'Just checking. Are you getting something for Judith?'

'Yes,' I said. There was time to go to the gallery gift shop. I already had the Christmas presents for his children and grandchildren.

Back at the hotel I released the shopping bags onto the floor with relief, my inner forearms striated with red lines where the handles had cut in. I had brought an empty suitcase with me and proceeded to pack it carefully as I waited for Trevor to return from his meeting.

The second bag was soon full, and I opened Trevor's suitcase to fit in the excess purchases – he always had space. As I tucked the grandchildren's stocking fillers down the side, my fingers met a small, hard object. It was a pill bottle – Viagra – something I didn't know he used. Had he woken too and left the bed in the early light of that morning, while I was cleaning my teeth and dusting sleep from my eyes in the bathroom mirror, to quickly pop one? Why didn't he tell me?

I put the bottle back where I had found it. This was our last night, and an old friend of Trevor's had invited us to dinner on his yacht. I was looking forward to the rolling twilight on the water, the city lights glimmering around us, being poured a drink on the deck. There would be crab and silver and white linen. I was good on boats, never seasick.

*

On the plane the next day it came back to me: a drab, functionary part of my brain was anticipating the climb up to our fourth-floor apartment with the suitcases, and I remembered the thing at the edge of my consciousness, about Claire. A week ago, I had been rushing down those stairs to get to work, and a floor below ours, outside her door, I ran into her returning home in her early morning workout gear. There were sweat marks on her T-shirt. I had said hello and she'd said in her smoky voice,

'Oh, Therese. I had a dream about Trevor last night.'

What?

She plunged a hand into her gym bag, feeling for her keys.

'It was so strange,' she said – almost as if I wasn't there. 'We were in bed.'

In bed? Even recalling this in the sterile plane, I flushed at the intimacy.

'Yes, and then—' She drew the keys from her bag's depths and held them aloft. 'Aha!'

'Then what?'

'Sorry.' A key in the lock. 'Never mind.'

'Claire.' I wasn't going to leave the landing until she told me.

She turned back to me. 'We were having sex. Like, it was really hot. I mean, intense.'

To my astonishment she maintained eye contact. Why was I the one blushing?

'And he pulled out a gun from beneath the pillow and held it to the side of my head.' She pointed to her temple.

A gun?

Now an air hostess came down the aisle offering landing champagne. Trevor shook his head. Trevor of other women's sex dreams. Sex play with guns? In our country only farmers and gang members have guns. Trevor was a property developer. I could feel him register the fact that I accepted the glass of gold bubbles, my third of the flight. Though I had been with Trevor nearly thirty years, I would never take business class for granted. Before we met I didn't even have a passport.

'What then?' I had asked Claire.

'Well, then…' Claire paused. Sun from the stairwell window lit up the silver streaks in her damp, dark hair. She gave a little shrug. 'Then I came.'

I stared at her. My feet were pinned. 'Excuse me?'

Alarm crossed her face, as if she'd remembered normal behaviour. 'Are you offended? I don't know why I told you that. I seem to have lost my filter.'

The change in her tone gave me back some control. 'All good,' I said. 'At least someone's having sex dreams about my husband.'

'Oh, god. We don't even know each other that well.' She had the apartment door open and the hallway beyond it gave off the chaotic vibe of working parents with a teenage child. Claire and I were roughly the same age, but my husband being so much older made it feel we didn't belong to the same moment in time. 'I'm so sorry.'

'It's OK,' I said as I crossed the landing away from her. If she apologised again it would make me feel like the butt of a joke. To show it really was all right I added, 'I hope you're coming to our Christmas party.'

'Oh – are you having one?'

'I left an invite in your letter box.'

'I'll ask Mick,' she said. Mick was her husband. 'He's in charge of these things.'

And she was swallowed by her hall.

The plane jolted, my champagne glass nearly snatched out of my hand by an unseen force. Landing in Wellington was infamously hairy, and even a jet like this could shake about in turbulence. The seatbelt light dinged on repeat. I drained my drink and tucked the glass into the seat pocket. Trevor was engrossed in the spreadsheet on his laptop, headphones on. We lifted and dropped, plateauing with another bump. I reached for his forearm and he unhooked his headphones. At the next bang of air, he closed the laptop. We held hands, our fingers interlaced, as around us people gasped and yelped in the shaking cabin. At the top of the galley the air stewards stared into the middle distance from their perches. If the plane crashes, I thought, it won't matter which class we are in. Another part of me thought, it will never crash with Trevor on board.

The next lift in the air – almost sweet, weightless – was followed by the sharpest drop yet, and someone screamed, and a woman behind us in the cabin started singing 'Amazing Grace'. Someone had sung that at our wedding. It was funeral music, a mistake, Trevor tried to talk me out of it but I'd insisted, twenty-three years old and it was the closest thing to classical music that I knew.

With my free hand I clutched the juddering headrest in front of me. My armpits felt slick.

'It's fine,' said Trevor, just as, with a plastic slither, the oxygen masks came down, prompting a general cry of terror. The panicked voices hushed for the captain's announcement that this was only due to a drop in cabin pressure and not to be alarmed, but to please put your own mask on first, and make sure it was fitted over your nose and mouth.

My fingers snagged my hair as I pulled the elastic over my head, and I felt a second's relief it fitted, despite a long-held fear that in a crisis I would be incapable of donning the mask – but what about the life jacket, I thought, as the pilot dragged the plane through the thick air and we tilted so that my window was filled with the sight of nothing but sea. We couldn't, in a matter of moments, be thrown into the raw, bobbing ocean, or worse, trapped in the cabin, sucked below the water – but we could, it was possible, anything could happen.

'Therese, look at me,' said Trevor, holding his mask away from his face. 'We're OK.'

I tried to take in the people around us. They couldn't all die. But already they looked like aliens or ICU patients, already the man across from me was on his phone, the mask around his chin, a steward waving at him, telling him to put the phone away. Who was he calling? Who would I call to say goodbye? Trevor was here beside me. I had no siblings, no children of my own. My parents were on the Gold Coast – my mother, in fact, was right now at a clinic recovering from a facelift – a facelift Trevor was paying for – now the plane shivered with a thin hard vibration that was somehow more terrifying than the great circular bounces and I stared at Trevor's hand to cling only to those details, nothing else. The liver spots. Those neat square fingernails. The hair on his knuckles. The wedding ring with a swirl in the metal. He kept the ring from his marriage to Judith in a small navy box in his underwear drawer. What would Judith say if he died, what would his children say – it would be my fault, I thought, my thoughts unhooking again, whirling out across space – I was killing Trevor, his work would go unfinished, his family would lose him, who would replace his vision, what would happen to the energy he brought to the world?

'Right,' said the captain over the intercom system. 'The northern approach is clear now. We're going to try that again.'

The calm in his voice was awe-inspiring, a greater skill than landing a plane. He continued talking, evenly, about landmarks and elevation. I wanted to give him my body with gratitude. Actually lie down on the cockpit floor and have him fuck me. Someone called out, 'Good on ya, mate,' and we laughed through our masks.

He did find another way, and we closed in on Wellington with nothing more than the usual buffeting. My shirt was soaked through under the arms, we were still surrounded by tubes and the dinging seatbelt bell, but we all knew we were going to live. I gave Trevor's hand another squeeze and pulled my mask aside to kiss him.

I forced my mind back to normal things. What had I been thinking about before the first jolt? Oh yes – Claire. Not that she was, as I understood the word in those days, normal. I knew her family only vaguely, as my downstairs neighbours, and of course Heathcote, Trevor's youngest, had the other apartment on their floor. Now I found I was oddly pleased she'd told me her dream; it was a little cotton stitch attaching us together. No one else I knew spoke like that. Was it acceptable? I didn't know. I was a woman without opinions.

The city looked incidental as we descended: a scattering of suburbs around the one-scoop harbour, nothing inevitable about it. A clutch of office blocks. The dense green of the town belt. I was on the wrong side of the plane to see the construction site of Trevor's hotel. I strove to see our building, where we lived.

Once I was down on the streets in the city again, I knew, the scale would revert to human size and I would forget how close it was, how like a small town. I didn't care. I loved living here. I loved Trevor. I loved the pilot and the stewards and the other passengers and I even loved the wind above that terrified me. There was another thunk and alarming jolt as the wheels dropped, but we hadn't yet landed.

2

The night before our Christmas party I stayed at our place in Martinborough, and headed home to the city early the next morning with the car boot full of cellar door wine and the back seat laden with armfuls of fresh cut dahlias, lilies and delphinium from the garden there, stems wrapped in wet tissue, the coolness of night still on them. Potted gardenias nestled in the footwells. The car was filled with so much scent I felt it infuse my skin.

Not long after leaving I passed a wild S of tyre tracks that ran off the road into churned mud. The tar seal was silky from the night's rain, and I was glad of the 4WD's grip. The river ran high beneath the one-lane bridge, tips of grass poking through the surface where it had risen up the banks. Out of nowhere, a swarm of bikers appeared behind me, the matt black domes of gang helmets above their blank stares in my rear-view mirror. They overtook my car with a quick roar as soon as I had crossed the bridge. I didn't recognise the patches on the backs of their jackets. I drove on into the air they had parted, but it took a few seconds to recall my thoughts. My plans for the night.

A mix of people usually came to our parties: rogue politicians from left and right, philanthropists, architects, civil engineers, property developers, maybe a visiting ambassador. Old satirists and their new wives, gallerists with favourite artists, Trevor's children, any non-weird city councillors and, occasionally, the Mayor. Wine merchants. Antique dealers. Actors. My hairdresser. A student we sponsored to study jazz performance at Julliard, who might be persuaded to sing. An old school friend of Trevor's I privately called Flat Tax because he could talk of nothing else.

I'd invited everyone who worked for the Therese Thorne brand, but had also thrown the staff blowout they preferred: dinner and drinks and karaoke, where, as usual, Emalani and Rebecca had goaded me to sing the dirtiest song on the playlist, and the sales girls did drugs in the loo then told me everything that needed to change about my generation, and I'd paid the bill for this self-inflicted Festivus. They were great young women, warm and talented; I loved to hustle alongside them during the rush. Although I was mortified they saw me as more Trevor's age than theirs, I couldn't blame them. Gen X, Boomer: to them, what was the difference? Still, after an evening with their young faces it was a shock to look in the bar's bathroom mirror and see my mother looking back.

Trevor had been forty-four when we got together. He was now in his early seventies. Through him, I spent most of my time with older people, and was used to feeling comparatively youthful, even since turning fifty. His friends were my friends – we took holidays with David and Sarah Russell, for instance, and went sailing with Matteo and Frank, or played cards with the Novaks. I had joined the women of our loose group on some of the Great Walks. I enjoyed it, didn't I? They appreciated life, those older women. They ran companies or schools and did their part for the community and they all breathed deeply of the clear air as we reached the ridge at Luxmore Hut and the views opened up. They were opinionated and worldly, and over the decades I'd grown comfortable with them. If at first I had gone overboard to ingratiate myself, to assure them I was not aware of their husbands' occasional stares, if I found myself compelled on those hiking trips to leap up and scrape the enamel plates and boil water for the coffee, if I did sometimes feel like a mascot, well that was on me. And there was no one to tell about it.

Over the Remutaka hill, now cell phone reception was steady, I made work calls, signed the head designer off on a scouting trip to Korea, and barely noticed the rest of the drive. Before long the harbour came into view, reflecting the pink still in the sky, warning of more rain. I refused to care. It would be warm and we could pull the balcony doors open and light candles in heavy glass lanterns and the rain could come down as hard as it liked.

The slow motorway traffic came to a standstill in the Terrace Tunnel. I wound the windows up against the exhaust fumes; the scent of lilies in the warm car was overpowering. I grabbed my phone and checked emails. A couple of people had written to apologise for not being able to make it tonight after all, citing family reasons. I replied *bring them!* and signed off with a kiss, the emails taking a while to send because of the weak signal in the tunnel. But as I wrote, another message came in:

Just checking the party's still on. Understand if not.

Was there a siren then, or did I imagine it? Or have I supplied it in retrospect, knowing what was coming next – does the siren sound come from the prop table of sensory associations that has already been laid out for me by the circumstances, the limited influences of my life? Wherever it came from, it's what I remember now. A blue flicker of light rotated along the wall from the tunnel's far curve, around which I could not see. A tuning-in feeling came over me, my senses honed as if at the sound of your own name in conversation across a room. I reached to the passenger seat for the paper I'd picked up from the gas station at the bottom of the hill, but hadn't yet read.

Trevor's hotel project was mentioned above the masthead. He wasn't named there but at the phrase *Council links trigger hotel enquiry* I knew. I turned straight to the business section. The article stretched across the top third of a page, next to a photograph of Trevor with his arm around a man of the same age – the councillor under investigation – both of them laughing. It had been taken somewhere outside: possibly it was lifted from social media. He had on a pale blue jumper I'd bought last winter. He wore it to please me but now I could see that it didn't fit well.

'Oh Trevor,' I said out loud. 'Oh no.'

I read the article in gulps; the words bunched and jerked so it took a minute to absorb. *Questions for councillor and developer over hotel development. Council to launch enquiry, construction to halt.*

I thought of Trevor's spreadsheets, his careful timetables, the domino effect. All those people who wouldn't have a job to turn up to on Monday.

The hotel plans, the article reported, had already caused controversy with rumours it would house a casino. Now there were questions about the speedy permissions process. An anonymous source alleged the council had favoured the hotel over an application to put social housing on the same cleared land.

This was the first I'd heard of social housing being in the mix. No way would Trevor scupper that. Hang on, I thought through my nausea, the enquiry was into the councillor who'd approved it, not Trevor. Maybe he would be OK. But then I got to the part that said construction would be on hold until the enquiry reached a conclusion. That could be months.

I made myself read the article again. The case against: Trevor and the city councillor had been at school together. The hotel plans had been green-lit indecently quickly. The usual decision-making process had not been followed. Meanwhile a fully developed plan for multiple units on the same site, which would meet the council's commitment to mixed public and private funding of social housing, had been one step away from approval, then passed over in favour of the hotel. The city suffered from a dearth of such suitable sites: the social housing project had gone cold.

The question to be answered, claimed the journalist, was if the councillor chairing the planning committee had taken some kind of kickback from Trevor? Or had he simply acted according to the old boys' unwritten code?

'That's two questions,' I said to the empty car.

The byline was not a name I knew. Ink from the paper had smeared onto my fingers. My other hand gripped my phone. Trevor voted Labour, or at least he used to; he would never ride roughshod over social housing plans, and if that part wasn't true, why should I believe the rest of the article?

I willed myself not to call anyone until I was calm. That help-less feeling – where's my dad – the hot need for someone to come and save me. More lights flashed further up the tunnel and I registered that horns were tooting.

After a few deep breaths I called Trevor. A long silence emanated from the line before the dial tone connected, but when he answered his voice came through clearly.

'Therese. Have you seen this nonsense?'

'Did you have any idea?'

'No.'

That was a bad sign, that no one had sent warning.

'Are you all right? Where are you?'

'I'm pretty frustrated. It's not a story. I'm just waiting on a call from Guy, then I'm onto the investors. Strictly speaking it's a problem for the councillor but the abatement's a fucking disaster and they've got to lift it pronto. Guy'll knock some sense into them.'

'OK.'

'Listen, a couple of years ago this wouldn't have warranted a second glance – business as usual.'

'Don't say that,' I said, paranoid that someone might be listening.

'Well it's a fact. This is how things get done. This is how they've always got done. He knows me, he trusts me, he pushed it through without the usual needless delays. But everything was in order.'

'Are you sure,' I said. 'You didn't, I don't know, buy him box seats to the football or contribute to his election campaign?'

He ignored this, or didn't hear. 'No one really gives a shit, they're all for the hotel anyway. They're just covering their own arse. And look,' he said, gathering steadiness, 'the council's not about to reverse their decision on the building permission. The thing's half up.'

His tone had shifted to mild irritation, as when the letterbox was jammed with junk mail, or the rugby hadn't recorded all the way through. So this was how we were going to handle it. I still felt dread. But I would follow Trevor's lead. Slow news day, storm in a teacup. The press, I thought, was a soft problem. It was the pause in the hotel construction that was a real problem. Like burning money.

'I'm stuck in the Terrace Tunnel,' I said.

'There's been an accident. Just heard it on the radio. You must be right behind it.'

'I'll be home as soon as I can. Should we—'

'What?'

'I think we should still go ahead with tonight, don't you?'

He laughed. 'What? Of course! I'll get T-shirts made with the headline printed on them to hand out.'

'Trevor?'

'Mn?'

'Did you know that, about the social housing development that was after the same space?'

'No!'

'I didn't think so.'

He'd worked on community projects himself in the past, on his own dime. But we were in a housing crisis now. That was the part of the article that cut through. And the chummy photo didn't look good.

I rang my brand manager. Denise was in Auckland and hadn't seen the news, but found the article online while we spoke.

'It doesn't mention Therese Thorne,' she said in that chesty rasp of hers: her breakfast was three cigarettes. 'Or you.'

'No.'

'Quite a bit about the need for better low cost housing in Wellington.'

'Yes.'

'Do you want me to do anything?'

'No, I just wanted to make sure you'd seen it. Maybe keep your ear to the ground? It's a worry for Trevor about the hotel but it'll blow over.' I had an image of the hotel being dispersed by the wind, girders and rebar flying away like so many pieces of straw.

'Shall I open a wee file. I'll update you if there's anything else. Oh, and I'd suggest you let Rebecca and Emalani know.' They were my PA and the Therese Thorne Homewares accounts manager, respectively. 'Nobody wants to feel blindsided by something like this.'

Something like this. You could never tell what Denise was thinking unless she wanted you to; she was good at her job.

While we were speaking, road cones had been put out and now a traffic cop came through the tunnel on foot, explaining that the accident area was nearly cordoned off and we'd soon be able to pass. Her uniform made me feel instantly guilty, as if I'd done something wrong.

'Thanks for your patience,' she said.

'Is everyone all right?'

'There's a medical team up there now.'

'I hope they're all right,' I said, but she had moved on. The crash seemed connected to the article. I knew that was insane.

I wound the window back up and put the air conditioning on high. The flowers would live.

The stony solidity of our building, the cool, quiet air in the foyer, reassured me for a minute as I carried the flowers in from the car. It was a four-storey former sewing factory that dated from the late 1800s and was originally owned by Thorne & Sons, who were ancestors of Trevor's. There was no lift, but we planned to move to Sydney before the stairs became an issue for Trevor; we lived on the top floor, the whole of which our apartment covered. The other apartments, which ran two to each of the other floors, were either rented or leasehold.

On the second floor I passed the padlocked door of the one that belonged to Annabel, Trevor's eldest, and her husband John. It was meant to be their bolt hole from Singapore, where they lived, but they never used it, and it sat cold, stripped of fittings, while Annabel hired and fired a series of architects to remodel the inside. Trevor's youngest son, Heathcote, had the free use of the one on the third floor, across the hall from

Claire, and sometimes lived there, but often let it out for the income.

Trevor wasn't in the apartment and his phone went to voice-mail. He was probably at Guy Benson's office. I put the flowers in the bath and took two armfuls of lilies to display at work.

The shop ran across the entire ground floor of a building that was a Trevor Thorne creation: the upstairs units had been sold off during the planning stage, but the open space at street level was always intended to house my flagship store. Before Trevor developed this building, my shop had to move around a series of rented spaces with difficult landlords, and the business kept losing traction. During the global financial crisis my rent rose while sales ground to a halt, and I nearly lost everything. In 2009, when his own business was still at risk, Trevor purchased this site and created the home for the store that I needed. The day we opened to the public, he surprised me with new letter-head stationery and a brass plaque beside the entryway: *Therese Thorne House*. He saved my career.

Just being outside the shopfront, now, soothed my anxious mood. It was gorgeous – steel-framed windows, cabinetry from recycled wood, lighting that could be angled to pick out a particular item. We filled it with pretty things. The furniture was for sale too, but sometimes people would simply come and sit on it to rest.

Over the years Trevor, his children, and then grandchildren had appeared with me in advertising campaigns, the seasonal newsletters and later in the website's blog. Therese Thorne Homewares portrayed an artfully imperfect life, illuminated by pontoon lights, outdoor candles and shafts of golden sun. It was fresh flowers cut from the garden, a jumble of sandshoes by the door, long grass weighted down by dew. Rugs, cushions, wall hangings in neutral colours. Homemade crafts, cupcakes, gratitude boards. It sold the fantasy of time to read poetry and handwrite letters to women who scrambled to make it through the day without braining themselves on a desktop paper spike, and mini versions of the same fantasy for their daisy-chained daughters. When I started it, in my twenties, I didn't know about the paper spikes. I still believed in poetry and handwritten cards.

Now I arranged the lilies in big vases, though there was barely any display space among the strings of Christmas lights and baubles. The girls teased me for keeping my sunglasses on – 'Big night?' – and I nodded and smiled. They wouldn't have read the business news. No need to explain.

I was quickly reviewing the week's sales figures when I heard familiar voices and saw two women I knew from Pilates cruising the scent table, picking up bottles, sniffing, replacing. Before I knew what I was doing I had ducked down behind the sales desk and was squatted there, staring at a tangle of cables and miscellaneous crap. One of the sales assistants tripped over me on her way to the wrapping station and I shuffled along to the end of the desk and rose slowly, as if I had just bent down to pick something up. I grabbed my phone and called Trevor, pretending to be talking as I smiled and nodded at the women on my way out the door – *busy sorry* – though once again he did not answer.

It was a shock to see the hotel site devoid of people or any activity, where only yesterday it had been ringing and grinding with the sounds of construction. Its layers of room shells and hallways were protected from the weather by white polythene. Ponderous cranes loomed, now still, above them.

The building sat on reclaimed land at the harbour's edge; two nineteenth-century warehouses, once used for customs clearance, as well as a winter skating rink and a tiny local museum, had been razed to make way for it. Perhaps because of the location by the water, the massive structure made me think of the cruise ships that appeared in the harbour overnight. Locals had started calling it the Hulk; it had taken Trevor's son Rob to explain that it wasn't a comic-book reference.

I removed my sunglasses to peer through a crack in the padlocked jib across the entrance way. Only days ago I had walked through it wearing a hard hat, surprised at the level of detail going up alongside structural basics: light fittings and switches hanging from wires beside doorframes and from the uncapped ceilings; a stand of full-grown nīkau palms growing from a square of soil that marked an indoor courtyard, while the lobby interior was unfinished and still looked like a concrete car park. Now a cordon roped it off, and although instinct had told me I'd see Trevor there, the place was empty. Who would look after the nīkau palms?

I checked the news website again on my phone, to see if Trevor's story was in the headlines. But the first item past the ad page was about the crash in the Terrace Tunnel, between a motorbike and a family car. The biker had died at the scene, and two of the family members were being treated for injuries. The bikers had been coming through the tunnel the wrong way, an eyewitness said, and the car had swerved to avoid them.

When I had finally exited the tunnel I had seen an overturned car, perched on the narrow shoulder outside the tunnel mouth, as though the laws of nature had been upended. But the driver couldn't have been going fast enough, in that rush hour traffic, to lose control and flip it, I'd thought – then I saw the sprawled motorbikes and the stretchers beside the ambulance.

Now I turned the corner towards the sea, and kept walking into the wind. A bit of grit flew in my face and I fished in my pocket for my sunglasses as protection.

3

The party invitation was for 6 p.m. I spent the rest of the day setting up the apartment, placing the gardenias, taking delivery of the canapés from the caterer, digging hardened puddles of candle wax out of holders and replacing them with fresh beeswax candles, polishing the glass doors and windows where they always got smeary, organising the food and drinks, the ice buckets, the side tables, moving chairs around into natural conversation areas, clearing away papers, magazines, CD piles, books, coats from the hall. Then I vacuumed. It gave me pleasure to clean a space so it looked as though I'd never been there.

At half past five I was showered, dressed, made up, with a rum and Coke in my hand. Trevor always teased me about the rum and Coke. 'You can take the girl out of the suburbs...' he'd say. He had got back from Guy's office and gone straight out again for a run, knees strapped. Now he was in his study.

We should have sat together before the party, as we usually did, we should have clinked glasses and counted our blessings, been grateful for what we had; we should have agreed on a breezy sentence in response to questions about the council enquiry or the newspaper article or the abatement. But he must have needed all his energy to pretend it didn't matter.

I sat alone in the tidy, gardenia-scented room, and stared at the residual floor dust picked out by the rich yellow light that slanted across the city below rainclouds that had been gathering all afternoon and which now finally broke. Rain came down in great uneven gouts, bouncing off the tiles on the half of the balcony that the awning didn't reach.

'Tropical rain,' Trevor called it, when he came in to close the windows. 'Don't usually get that here.' Its low din made any quiet, intimate kind of conversation impossible.

'Do you think we should cancel?' I asked.

'What, the party? Of course not. We talked about this.'

'Yes, but now I'm worried lots of people aren't coming. What if no one comes?'

He gave me a look of his I loved – a reassuring, crinkled smile. I felt my nerves settle.

'Of course they'll come,' he said. 'Look, I need to sort out this hotel thing as soon as possible. Keep the investors from freaking out – and find more, if I can. It's going to cost money just to sit in neutral for as long as this takes. I want to get it sorted before Christmas.'

'Christmas is days away. We're going to the Sounds.'

'Exactly. I need it done before then.'

I understood then that the party was work, for him. And he needed to work.

He went to close the balcony doors.

'Leave them,' I said.

I wanted the doors open to the evening, tropical warmth and rain and the spicy smells of flowers and the mulled wine set to a low simmer on the stovetop not because many would drink it but for its wafts of a boozy, clove and cinnamon perfume. A gesture to a wintry Christmas because we still made those, even though summer in December was all we'd known. But when Trevor slid the door back a sheet of wind slapped through the room, extinguishing candles and knocking over the Danish glass vase, which broke on impact, flowers splayed and water flooding the table.

I'd just finished clearing away the last shards of glass and delphinium petals when the doorbell rang and Trevor buzzed up the first guest. It was Flat Tax. And close on his heels, in a yellow party dress and wearing a black eye patch, came Claire.

She was with her husband Mick, a man I'd never had a serious conversation with. I knew he was a prop master on fantasy films, employed by visiting American production companies. As far as I could tell he had perfected a 'nice guy' stance that allowed him to retreat to some internal man-cave during social interactions.

What else did I know about Claire, really? That she and Mick had moved in to our building about four years ago with their teenage daughter Alex, after their oldest children, twin boys I'd never met, had left home. I had seen Alex often in passing, taking the stairs two at a time, alone or with friends, growing taller over the years, her girlish brown hair now pulled back to reveal an undercut, now short all over, now blue.

I knew Claire had worked first on film sets, then in fundraising, and had recently lost her job. And that she was a conversational minefield. That was all.

'Are we early?' Claire asked. 'Sorry.'

'No, you're perfect.'

When I returned with her drink she said, 'Ever since the role swap I have to trust Mick with our social lives, and he always gets it wrong. He forgot to tell me about this party – if you hadn't mentioned it the other day, I wouldn't have known.'

At this allusion to our last encounter, I felt myself blush.

'What do you mean, role swap?'

'Oh,' she said. 'We swapped who's responsible for what sort of things in the relationship. It's changed my life.'

'Do you mean like, who cooks?' I asked, but before she could answer another couple arrived and I had to go and greet them.

As I surveyed the small scattering of guests half an hour later, I had the feeling that not only Mick's, but everyone's conversation was simply a checklist of acceptable gestures. There was no oomph to the room, no guts, and I sensed that all too easily the few people who had come could drift out again and it would be as if the party had never happened. The exception was Claire, who was speaking to Flat Tax with secluded intensity, as if they were the only guests. The eye patch gave her a piratical air.

I ducked into the bedroom to check my phone. People blamed their absence on the rain – *so sorry* – along with crucial last-minute shopping, surprise house guests, sudden illness and, in one case, the death of a pet. *We found Farley under the house. The children are devastated, we can't imagine Christmas without him.* So sorry, so sorry, so sorry. Have a great time! Disappointed to miss it! If I don't see you before next year… No one mentioned the article, which confirmed its effect. Those were the ones who sent in messages at all. The rest of them simply didn't come.

I headed back to my guests and introduced a few neighbours to my hairdresser. I noted that she left as soon as it was decent to do so, and I couldn't blame her. I wished the others would leave too. I hated them for being witnesses. I hated Trevor's hearty laugh, ringing through the room. As he walked past me to get a drink, I asked how he was getting on. He kissed my temple. The Santa hat bobbled on his head.

I found Claire on the balcony, vaping. Outdoor lights shone up through the leaves of the larger pot plants, turning her yellow dress almost gold.

'What happened to your eye?' It was rude to ask, I knew, but I had to be rude to someone.

'Oh,' she said. 'Face work gone wrong.' She mimed injecting her forehead, and made a clicking noise. Again I thought of her dream about Trevor and the gun.

'Really?' I didn't know anyone who admitted to stuff like this.

'You know how it is, you work so you have the money but you look tired from working so you spend the money on not looking tired so you can keep doing well at work so you can make the money. Basically, capitalism came on my face.'

I laughed in shock. 'This is our second conversation about sex in a fortnight.'

'Maybe it's because I've gone off my antidepressants. I can finally have orgasms again. Sorry, I keep forgetting how to talk normally.'

She gave me an amused look – as if life was absurd and we should just enjoy it – and a surge of elation hit me. I glanced through the plate glass windows at my struggling party. I should be in there circulating food.

'Why did you go off them? The pills?'

'My youngest is leaving home,' she said. 'The only reason I stayed on them so long is the family liked me better that way.'

I stared, disbelieving – but she locked my gaze with her one implacable eye.

'Did they actually say that?'

'Yep.' Claire took a hit of her vape pen. 'It's great being a mum.'

'I've only got Trevor's kids,' I said. 'We've got adult children.'

'Sounds like a diagnosis.'

I didn't know what to say to that. Even after all this time, I was not quite on home territory with his children. For a start, I was much closer to their age than his, and often felt that around them I was cosplaying an older person. Over the years we'd made a lot of behind-the-scenes effort, but I behaved as though my eye was on my work and I was happy to let the family dynamics just evolve. Making things look easy isn't always a smart move. Maybe I should have done it the other way round; made the children feel like the most important thing.

There was Trevor now, walking around the party in his Santa hat, and his children weren't here – Annabel was in Singapore of course, but of the three who lived in Wellington not one of them had come – not Caroline, not Rob, not even Heathcote, who only lived downstairs. What was his excuse? They must have seen the news. Why hadn't they come to support their dad?

Even as I thought the question, I knew why not, although Trevor wouldn't understand it. He didn't know that the end of his first marriage, and his marrying me a few years later, would change his relationship with his children forever. 'People get over things,' he said. 'They adjust.' What he meant was, dynamics go back to the way they were. But the children could never be completely comfortable with him after the split. They treated us with a formality that was absent in their manner around Judith, despite the conventions of her class.

With me Trevor had both forged a new alliance and made himself vulnerable – he became a person they could criticise, he lived in a house that wasn't their home, they would talk to each other about him, not to his face. They blamed him still for their loss of innocence, as if holding onto that hurt would one day bring their family back.

'Anyway, now Mick's moving to Auckland,' Claire said, 'and Alex is going too. I'm going to be on my own.'

I had never lived on my own.

'Is it permanent?'

'No, he's going up for a job, it'll run most of the year. A new fantasy series about Atalanta, the hunter – hunt*ress*, they call her in the pitch doc. That's how they talk. They describe her as "a badass" and "the fiercest bitch in the classical world". Atalanta the girlboss. Like she wouldn't tear a studio exec to pieces with her hands.'

'Must have been a big decision,' I said, 'being away for work that long.'

'Well, it's not usually hard for us to make decisions,' she said, 'because I make the decisions.'

I laughed.

'But also, he wanted to do it. And I don't know that we're ready for the empty nest experience. Staring at each other in silence over the breakfast table. Maybe the distance will keep our marriage alive. Or you know,' she pulled on her vape pen, 'help kill it.'

I watched as Trevor poured wine for a woman who did political fundraising. He straightened up and met my eye through the glass, and gave me a rueful smile. I knew what he was thinking. He was the one with his hand out, now.

'I better go and help,' I said to Claire. 'The patch suits you, by the way.'

'Luckily,' she said. 'You should see what's underneath.'

Trevor was trying to draw Flat Tax into his study, where he kept an architect's model of the hotel. 'Come on, take a look.'

'Another time,' Flat Tax said. 'When I'm sober. I'll come back after Christmas eh.'

'You might want to get into this now,' said Trevor. 'There's going to be a rooftop pool. Members' club type thing.'

'Really mate. I'm cash poor at the minute.'

Trevor's eyes snagged on mine and I looked away.

I cooled my face inside the open fridge. Trevor didn't usually hit up old friends. I closed the fridge door, turned and bumped into Haimona, an environmental journalist who lived on the ground floor. He gestured to the glass in my hand.

'Is that a rum and Coke?'

'Would you like one?' I asked. 'Where's Leisha?' His wife was taking a break from the civil service to raise their young children, and exuded the manic intelligence of someone whose interest in world events was rarely allowed out.

Haimona selected a clean glass from the several dozen still on the kitchen bench. 'She's with the kids. We flipped a coin—'

'And you lost!' I laughed too loudly.

'...And I'm keen to catch up with Rob. Is he coming?'

Rob was Trevor's second eldest child. He worked for the Greens.

'Maybe? Rum and Coke. Right.'

I was aware of Claire coming in from the balcony, her yellow dress floating dangerously close to the candles burning on the coffee table. I overpoured the Coke. Dark liquid pooled over the bench top. Haimona helped me mop it up with kitchen roll.

'Sorry,' I said. 'I'm having a… reaction. To the day.'

'All good. Thought you might be a bit over journalists right now.'

'You've got to do your jobs,' I said, then couldn't resist: 'But there's no story there.'

He sniffed his drink. 'Haven't had one of these for a while. Takes me back.'

'Where to?'

He named the suburb I was from. 'We went to the same school, I think. You and me.'

'Really?' He would have been there a decade after me. 'How do you know I'm from there?'

'Is it a secret?'

'No, but.'

He laughed. 'Joking. I'm a reporter. I looked you and Trevor up when we moved into the building.'

He must have dug deep. The Therese Thorne website bio made out that I had appeared with the dawn one day, my head full of soft furnishings. I had the uneasy feeling of having been rumbled.

Haimona raised his glass and took a long pull, leaning against the kitchen island. He'd just filed a story on polluted waterways, he told me, and intended to get wasted. 'If you don't mind.' I topped him up and watched him cross the room to join the smokers on the balcony. I don't know what I felt – a kind of numbed wonder that for all the distance I had travelled, here was someone from that world, living a normal life in this very building.

It wasn't that I was on the run from my childhood. I had contact with my parents, who had retired to Brisbane, though my father remained a kind of stranger, as he'd been when I was a girl, and he was away on long-haul moving jobs. In his absence I'd built up an ideal father in my mind, but he was not that person. My mother shared a lease on a taxicab that she mostly drove at night. The shift work was hard but I think she must have liked the way the motorway led to the lights of the city, the inkiness and electricity. Some kind of glamour to make up for the hours. While she was driving I did homework and watched TV and put myself to bed, until I got older, and went to Donna's place. Mostly what I remembered about my childhood house, and felt again now, was the sparseness of the rooms, and the sharp smell of damp.

Just then another couple turned up. I went to greet them, and over the next hour was both relieved and embarrassed by the incoming trickle of guests. Each fresh arrival was a moment to manage: their surprise at the thinness of the crowd, hesitation on being offered a drink, the summer raincoats kept draped over arms, the phones and watches checked for the time. I felt horribly sober. The room was too big.

In the kitchen, facing into the open fridge again, I threw down a couple of tequila shots and waited for them to kick in. I never get wasted, I thought, as I stalked my empty party with heavy, uneven steps, I never cut loose.

Trevor said, 'I'm going to skip the toast tonight,' and I said, 'I'll do it. Give me the hat.'

I dinged the side of my glass with a fork. They turned to me – the neighbours, the antiques dealer, the acquaintance-level couple who worked at an arts festival, a smattering of others. As I looked at Trevor shaking the hand of a guest he hadn't yet greeted – his determination to be a good host, the vulnerability he couldn't allow himself to feel – a sense of clarity poured over me.

'Darling, come here.' I linked my arm through his, pulling him into my side.

'This man,' I said. '—I know it's Christmas and thank you for coming and season's greetings to you all, but I want to talk about love.' I squeezed Trevor's arm tighter. 'Love is what brings us together.'

Claire whooped and pulled out her phone. 'Yes!'

'Love, something I always say at my work—' I hesitated, wondering how many people Trevor had broached the subject of money with by now. 'Not to bring work into it, this is not a work do, this is friends, family—'

On Claire's wobbly cell phone video of this effort, you can see Trevor smiling down at his bare, this-is-my-party feet. You can see my face, bright and fervent beneath the Santa hat, and Trevor exchanging a glance across the room with someone near the camera. The tension sets in to his warm smile as I talk on, my voice getting posher and posher, about how success is all very well but adversity shows who your friends truly are, and what a true friend Trevor is, how no one knows the good works he does and the contribution he makes. How he's done so much for the city and I hope that will be acknowledged by the council in this – waving my hand in circles as though to pluck a phrase out of the air – hour of need. I actually say *hour of need*.

'Trevor is really generous with his time and expertise. He's always helping the younger generation, he's a wonderful mentor. And behind the scenes – I know no one talks about this but I think we should, it's important.' I wanted to talk about his philanthropy but suddenly realised he would hate it. I fell back on,

'We are very lucky. We are very, very lucky. And Trevor does a lot. And he'll never ask for recognition for himself. So I'd like to make a toast to him now. To Trevor!'

You can make out the individual voices echoing the toast. You can see me stand on tiptoe to kiss Trevor on the cheek, and step back to look into his eyes with a drunken, teary glisten in my own. Trevor turns to the room and says, 'This is how she gets me to do a Christmas toast, folks – here's to the back of 2017! Merry Christmas!' and you hear it come back to him, followed by low, masculine cheers. If you isolated the cheers, if those sounds were all you heard, you might be unsure if they were calls of praise or derision. At that the video stops.

In our ensuite I reapplied lipstick and dabbed on more perfume. Be quick. Don't think. Into the kitchen for another shot. Haimona was there.

'You made a speech.'

'Oh. It was that bad.' I knew that tactic, had used it myself at play openings and other public embarrassments. You wrote a whole opera! I saw your show! The useful statement of fact.

Haimona smiled. 'It was loyal.'

Much later I would be shown the video and realise I had not been expressing loyalty, but doubt. For now I was just grateful to Haimona for talking to me, and felt a sweep of regret that I'd so thoroughly abandoned my old life. He joined me on the plum-coloured velvet sofa and we reminisced, looking out across the room to our reflections sharpening in the long windows as the darkness outside deepened. Did he have this teacher, did he remember that? It was a drunken, elliptical conversation that I've largely forgotten but I do remember asking if he remembered a teacher who had always been kind to me and he said,

'Yeah, she was a bit of a racist. She reckoned she couldn't pronounce my name so she'd call me Simon.'

'She couldn't pronounce Haimona?'

'Pretty sure that was a cover.'

'Oh. I'm sorry. That's awful.'

He shrugged. 'She was loose with that wooden ruler. My mum had a strong word but she kept on doing it.'

'But that's illegal. Isn't it?'

He raised an eyebrow. 'Hey – did you hear back from Rob? Is he coming?'

I wondered what else I hadn't known or noticed, on account of how doting that teacher had been towards me. Her pet name for me was Little Floss.

We had gone to different secondary schools – he'd been sent to a sporty boys' college, and I'd gone to the big local co-ed – but we both remembered the tunnel by the quarry and the secret smoking spot under the sports field macrocarpas and the garage parties and nights spent getting high up in the gorse-covered hills. It sounded as if little had changed between my teenage years and his, but looking back I can see there were differences we didn't speak of, in trying to find what we shared, and that gradually these seemed to fill the space between us. It was a conversation that could have been intimate but really, we did not reveal ourselves.

When we fell into silence I realised everyone but Claire and Mick had left. Trevor said he was going to bed, and Haimona found on his phone a text sent an hour earlier from Leisha, who was over being downstairs alone with the kids.

'We're always the stayers!' Claire said. 'I was going to start the dancing. Is it too late?'

'Yes,' said Mick.

I tipped my head back on the couch and raised a glass to her. 'Thanks.'

Once Haimona had gone, Mick and Claire helped me carry the boxes of uneaten party food up the road to the night shelter. I handed over the boxes with a strange kind of shame. The air was soft and damp. Mick was knee-dippingly drunk.

Back in our building, making our heavy way upstairs, we heard the street door open and shut again and footsteps climbing up behind us.

'Wait,' Claire said when we reached her landing. 'I think that's Alex.' Her daughter.

Mick swayed: 'I have to lie down,' and fumbled his way inside.

The sound of talking got louder and Claire clutched my forearm and said,

'What if she's brought someone home? Wait with me.'

'Where's she been?'

'I don't know.'

Just before they appeared on the last set of stairs before the landing, I recognised the other voice. It was Heathcote. A clot of rage turned over in my gut.

'Hi darling!' Claire pulled Alex into a big, unreciprocated hug. 'What have you been up to?'

Alex was a gorgeous-looking girl, messy hair, jeans and sneakers, a tiny band T-shirt. She slid her kohled eyes sideways at her mother and said, 'Living my life.'

'We just met on the doorstep,' Heathcote said. 'Alex has been telling me what the cool kids are up to these days.'

'Ha,' she said, and disappeared into her apartment, Claire following.

All I could think about was why the fuck Heathcote hadn't come to our party, since he was in town, why the fuck he hadn't come to support his dad.

'Where have you been?'

'In Auckland,' he said. 'I just got back. Hello to you too.'

I clocked the cabin bag. 'Did you see the paper, about the hotel? Have you talked to Trevor?'

'Yeah, I saw it. Bloody councillors, they should be begging him to build that thing. He OK?'

This was where I called my own bluff. Of course he's not OK, I wanted to say, but my habit was to do nothing that would lessen Trevor in his children's eyes, and that force won.

'You know your dad. He'll be fine.'

'Great.' Heathcote wedged open his door with the cabin bag and said, 'I'll come to say hi tomorrow. I've seen a fucking cool house. It's a bargain, 1950s architectural classic, amazing investment.'

Heathcote didn't own the apartment we stood outside now, although it was his in all other ways: he took income off the holiday rents and used it as a crash pad when he was in town. In Auckland Judith had a family house he stayed in but I remembered, now, some talk of it being sold to fund a new place at the beach.

'A house? In Auckland? Where?'

He named an inner-city suburb. No way could a bargain be found there. And if by chance some last crusty bungalow was still standing, Judith's trust would buy it – but Heathcote wouldn't want something in the trust's name, I realised, he wanted a place of his own and was more likely to get that from his father.

'You've got a place to live,' I said.

'But it's not a home.'

'This place? It could be. Why not?'

He put on an Irish accent: his technique for avoiding scrutiny. 'Don't cockblock me here, Therese. It's a grand deal.'

And he leaned in, smelling of aftershave, to hug me goodnight.

Poor Heathcote. He had never settled to anything. He worked for Trevor briefly, around the time of the global financial crisis, but hadn't stuck to that. A series of ill-fated ventures followed: a boutique members' club, an online city guide. He was a walking battleground between a superiority complex and the inner voice that told him he was worthless, and he compensated for his lack of purchase on life with a studied loucheness, as if the family money was acceptable as long as he wasted it. His boyish haircut, receding now, his slim features and the tactical charm of his smile all belonged to a man ageing out of the role that had got him through so far. He infuriated me but, as with that goodnight hug, could disarm me as well. I could never quite forget the hurt, angry teenager he had been when I'd first met him, worshipping his dad but unable to forgive him.

As far as I know, the children never asked why their mother didn't remarry, or get a new partner. They didn't ask how Trevor felt when a project stalled for years, or when his business partner stiffed him in the early 2000s, or when the GFC threatened to derail us both, or when two of them skipped his investiture ceremony. One summer holiday I kept a tally of the questions they asked me that weren't requests, and it came to one: how was the temperature of the water.

Back in the apartment I turned the living room lights on and surveyed the party detritus, all the more bleak for there hardly being any. Despite his expert schmoozing Trevor had gone to bed empty-handed, there were no white knights here. The message from the community was clear: you cannot simply do what you want. I knew it wasn't orchestrated; there was a herd instinct at work. Nor did it matter whether Trevor had done anything wrong. Several of the no-shows would have done worse. The crime was being in the paper, and not even for a brazen, twenty-first century grift, but for something as old-fashioned as cronyism. That was a symbol of the old bad ways, and in rejecting him they raised themselves up.

I turned my back on the dirty wine glasses and went to the balcony, to sit on the chair Claire had sat in, her vape pen casually between her fingers. It was sad that people vaped now rather than smoking tobacco, leaving the smell to linger.

4

Trevor spent the week after our party with his phone glued to his ear. He chivvied the council, tried to placate the chief investor, and chased any source he could think of to drum up more money to cover what he called 'the spiralling costs of standing still'. He had to persuade everyone he spoke to that the enquiry would come to nothing and the abatement was a temporary blip; the hotel would soon be rising skywards again; it helped that he believed it. It was one of the things I loved about him, the relentless optimism, the faith that things would work out, if only you kept your eye on the prize.

I rubbed his shoulders and poured him stiff gin and tonics between my own work and the various tasks required for our Christmas holiday: washing the beachwear, ironing Trevor's linen shirts, folding, packing, shopping for suntan lotion, insect repellent, stocking fillers, food. I packed the Therese Thorne samples I'd set aside through the year to decorate the house in the Sounds – rose-pink lanterns, creamy bunting and painted wooden stars. I liked to glow the place up.

The 1860s homestead, a double-fronted, two-storey villa with wraparound verandahs on both levels, had originally been built by Judith's ancestors, and it was by her grace that Trevor and I went there. She had priority, though it fell to me to take everyone's preferred dates, arbitrate over clashes, and put them into the shared family calendar.

Every second Christmas and New Year we gathered: Annabel and her husband John came from Singapore with their children, three athletic blond boys who'd been summoned into life at regular two-year intervals, as if all Annabel had to do was snap her fingers; Rob, his partner Maria, and her teenage daughter Indy from a previous relationship, as well as their own child, a ringleted five-year-old who had everyone at her beck and call and divided her parents; and Caroline, who came with Andy and their two highly strung boys. Heathcote often brought a girl-friend and one year had turned up with an unexpected party of eight at the tail end of a week-long bender.

The house itself was called Heathcote – an ancestral name that had been passed on to the youngest son. Nowadays, though, everyone just referred to it as going to the Sounds.

Before we went, I baked and cooked what could be baked and cooked in advance. Rob and his family had recently become vegan. Caroline's boys were off sugar for their anxiety. Trevor had to watch his cholesterol and Annabel preferred to stay out of the kitchen, to avoid triggering the latent eating disorder that had dogged her since she was a teen, the oldest sibling bearing the brunt of her parents' divorce. It was simplest for me to take control, but Claire's comment about her role swap with Mick lingered in my mind. I knew there was another universe where women didn't do all this. However, this was mine, and I liked it. This summer more than ever, Trevor needed to relax.

Everywhere I went that week before the holiday, I feared running into someone who had cancelled on our party, but the jobs had to be done: I got my highlights touched up and a wax and a spray tan and a pedicure. Lying on the beautician's bed while she smeared hot wax on my upper lip I thought of Claire too, the click-click sound she had made when pointing at her eye patch. A sentence came to me: what you really want is Botox for the soul. I didn't know whose voice that was.

What *did* I know? – did I know, say, that this would be the last summer in the Sounds? The sheltered air that enveloped us there did hum with extra resonance. No internet reached us, no cell phone coverage unless you walked to the peak of the hill behind the house and raised your hand in the air as if to God. Several times a day Trevor's sons-in-law or grandchildren would perform the pilgrimage, and sometimes on a hike I would come across them in this strange tableau.

The days were hot and still, the thick water surfaced with glassy streaks, but when we took the boats out of the long arm of the inlet the sea feathered white, and on Christmas Eve Andy came back from kayaking around the point looking green and exhausted. 'Don't think the kids should be doing that.'

Behind the house, past the kitchen garden and the old barn, the remains of a wide driveway could still be made out through the grasses. There had never been sealed road access but horses and some delivery vehicles had once been able to make their way through on a track intermittently paved with local stone, the journey from Picton still taking intrepid cyclists the better part of five hours. Nobody drove that way anymore; supplies and houseguests arrived by the ninety-minute ride in a water taxi, or by yacht or helicopter, which landed on the dry and pitted lawn tennis court.

The villa and converted cabins accommodated us all, and the grandchildren pitched tents on the grass for fun. 'I love that they get to have a real Kiwi camping experience,' Annabel said, while the rest of us kept a straight face. We ate together at the outdoor table, the children either at a smaller one alongside or fed earlier and roasting marshmallows over a fire before bed. The sight of them turning their sticks in the embers, their faces glowing and bodies weary from a day in the sun, made my heart swell. It was every dream I'd had as a child come true. I still couldn't believe this was my life.

Bunting, strings of lights, fat outdoor candles in glass jars, tick, tick, tick. Booze cabinet housing ancient gin and sweet holiday liqueurs, tick. Beer fridge, crated wine delivery, tick. Kayaks, rowboat, paddleboards, fishing gear, boardgames, tick. Every year we had the argument about getting jet skis and a speedboat with which the younger generation wanted to water ski and biscuit, and as the grandchildren got older I could see that this concession would have to be made. John showed us photos of them all flyboarding in Fiji. Trevor would most feel the loss of the hush, the cicada-filled, beepless, paperback-page-turning, tide-sloshing silence.

I felt especially close to the Therese Thorne customers on Christmas mornings. Every year, standing at the floured kitchen bench before sunrise, gently kneading brioche dough, I would pause to think of those women and close my eyes (dangerous; once I fell asleep on my feet, hands in the sticky dough, and woke just as a string of drool escaped my mouth and landed on it). I would wonder how many were following this recipe too, and hope they'd been helped by our newsletter's tips for creating a magical day. As I sipped my coffee I would try to imagine where they were – in makeshift camp kitchens, or their in-laws' houses, or their own specially decorated homes. Children would wake, dogs might need walking, but if they were early enough, these women, if they got up in the dark, they would have the silence to themselves.

I set the dough aside to rise and checked on the living room. The pile of presents reached halfway up the tree – a wilding pine from the back of the property – and flowed out between the sofas in a landslide of boxes and mystery shapes. Annabel and Caroline wanted the children to open their presents one at a time, but they were dreaming. Nobody would.

The tradition was that the kids would demolish their stockings, then we'd all have a swim before breakfast. I dashed in and out of the water and ran to organise coffee, bacon, berries, pancakes, and bring the brioche loaf fresh from the oven to the table outside, watching in satisfaction as even Annabel tore hunks out of it, hair dripping over her towel. The trick was to keep people fed and relaxed – I'd learned at the first flicker of annoyance to pop a bottle of champagne and distribute it along with thimblefuls of schnapps, which I topped up through the orgy of present opening. *Be liberal with booze!* the Therese Thorne newsletter advised, but as I slugged more into Caroline's glass, I was suddenly stopped by the memory of Claire saying her family preferred her medicated. What did it mean if we had to be drunk to get through the day?

I wondered what Claire was doing now. What were her rituals?

One of Caroline's boys was saying, 'Mum, mum,' tugging her dress, nearly pulling it right down over her boobs, and I lifted him away to see what he needed.

'We've got a llama!' he said, waving a sharp-cornered card wildly so it scratched my cheek. 'A pet llama!'

'Have you? That's exciting.'

The card was from Rob and Maria and Indy, and explained that they had symbolically adopted a llama, in the name of Caroline, Andy and the boys.

'I'm going to have it in my room,' the boy said. 'It will sleep in my bed.'

'That'll be smelly,' I said, 'for the llama,' and he laughed and ran into the pile of wrapping paper, grabbing armfuls to throw into the air. I passed the card to Caroline, who glanced at it and said, 'What's this? A spa voucher?'

Rob and Maria smiled at each other, silently shaking their heads. I sometimes thought I'd like to spend more time with them, but they were a closed loop. One year, while Trevor and his children and grandchildren were playing beach cricket, I had asked Maria to help me with Christmas dinner and while she was peeling potatoes she'd said, 'Isn't this a bit like we're the help?' I'd been so angry at that I never asked again.

Judith had told us that Heathcote was having Christmas with friends in Auckland. The day after I saw him on the stairs, he'd spoken to Trevor about the house he was hoping to buy, and been frustrated when the answer came back: not now. He hadn't been in touch since then. Trevor accepted with resignation the silence that met his Merry Christmas texts and messages; another year it might have pierced him more, but for now Heathcote had to go to the bottom of the teetering pile of problems that were costing his father sleep. Trevor had neither got the abatement lifted nor raised more finance before we came away, and as he had feared, the main hotel investor was trying to pull out.

He pretended he was fine, but on the morning of Boxing Day I felt the bed adjust as he rose before dawn, and could sense the air settle once he'd left the room, as though his presence carried a field of electricity. I thought one of us ought to sleep, and tried to drift off again, angling the fan towards me. But it was a lost cause, and I found him outside in the starlight yanking convolvulus from the hedge. I asked if he wanted to talk about it.

'I might have to go back early. I've got to talk him down off the ledge.'

He turned his shoulder to me. I went to the kitchen to get on with the million invisible things that would make the day good. Caroline was sitting at the table, the kettle coming to the boil, moths batting the overhead light.

'Is Dad OK?'

I wasn't sure what to say. 'What's your take?'

'Both the boys came into our bed last night.' She spoke with her eyes closed. 'Sam's scared of the quiet, scared of the dark, mosquitoes, moths, possums, spiders, heat. I'm such a failure.'

'I asked them to give the cabins a thorough clean.' A local company set the place up for us every year, and visited regularly to maintain the grounds. 'Do you want to move into the house?'

'Then I'll worry about them crying and keeping you all awake. I couldn't do that to Dad.'

'He's not sleeping anyway. You'd be the excuse.'

'No thanks.' She was his favourite, and though it wasn't always a fun position, coming as it did with his laser-like but uninformed interest in her career at the design school, she wasn't about to give it up.

I pushed the plunger down on the coffee. 'Maybe they'll grow out of it.'

'I'm scared.' She opened her eyes, and to my surprise two lines of tears slid down her face. 'Has he done something wrong?'

'No! It's just an internal squabble with the council,' I said. 'Trevor says they're not even serious people. He's got caught in the crossfire, that's all.'

'So he hasn't done anything.'

The words *of course not* began to form but I hesitated too long, and her eyes flared, and she stroked more tears away.

'I'm sure he hasn't,' I said, as Trevor walked through the open verandah doors into the room, wiping his hands on his pyjama pants.

'What's the matter?' he said. 'Boys keeping you up? Thought they'd grown out of that.'

She shook her head, then quickly stood and flung her arms around him. 'Oh Dad.'

'Hey.' He hugged her, stroked her head. 'Hey. What's the matter?'

She pressed her forehead into his chest. 'I'm just tired. The boys.'

'We'll get them out on the water today. Bit of fishing, bit of sun, tucker them out.' He peeled her arms away. In her grey marl T-shirt and cotton pyjama shorts, her long streaky blonde hair falling about her shoulders, Caroline looked much younger than her early forties, and I had the fleeting impression that she and Trevor were actors playing their parts. The air sealed around us, as if we lived inside a snow globe, and a twitch ran through me, some huge finger giving our bubble a tap.

Trevor went upstairs and soon came the groan of the old copper piping that complained whenever anyone ran the water. Caroline, choosing to be reassured, went back to bed. Light melted into the garden, bringing soft colour to the agapanthus heads, now floating purplish-blue against the grey as though they were a trick of the eye. Two grown men, the sons-in-law, wearing diving gear, moved across the lawn like aliens and disappeared, swallowed by the water.

Ordinarily we relished going without internet access, but now, in the dead zone between Christmas and New Year's, the lack of outside connection made the bubble shrink around us. Trevor kept disappearing up the hill to make phone calls, and coming back angry. The board games, the book reading, the dinner prep to duelling playlists all took on a hyper edge. Trevor and I ignored the conversations in serious tones between the children and their partners, and pretended not to notice when they fell quiet as we shook our towels out on the thin strip of sand beside them.

Charades ended in tears, and the Post-it-note-on-the-forehead guessing game went on for hours, Annabel digging in as she stabbed wildly at famous people, though some wag had written *Annabel* for her. The sticky paper slid over one eyebrow and she took it off and reapplied it. Caroline accused her of cheating.

'What?'

'You looked at it!'

'I did not.'

'I saw you.'

'No you didn't, because I did not cheat. Marie Antoinette.'

'No.'

'Catherine the Great.'

'No. It's Maria's turn.'

'Did I fuck a horse, yes or no,' said Andy, who was drunk.

'Jesus Andy, the children.' Caroline kicked him.

While Maria was guessing, addressing her questions to the younger ones, Annabel spoke in a low voice to her sister.

'I can't believe you'd think I'd cheat.'

'Sorry. I thought I saw you looking. I was wrong.'

'Yeah, but that you'd even believe it.'

'Well if I saw it, I'd believe it.'

'But you didn't, because I wasn't.'

'No.'

'So you must have wanted to see that.'

'What? Annie, leave it.'

'It's not very nice to be accused of doing something you haven't.'

While this was going on Maria correctly guessed that she was a Powerpuff Girl, and peeled her sticky note from her forehead in triumph. 'Thank god!' The children crowded in to cuddle her.

Caroline stood, flush-faced, and said to her sister, 'I'm sorry! Stop painting me like some – I know you mean this is about Dad and I don't think he did anything wrong with that councillor. That's not what I said. Did I, Maria?'

Maria hushed a child and looked up at Caroline, confused. We all waited. When Annabel spoke, her voice was cold.

'Yeah, but you don't *not* think it.'

It was clear now what the huddled conversations had been about. Caroline swung towards Trevor, who was feigning disinterest over a crossword, having correctly guessed that he was Lord Nelson in the first round. 'Dad, I know it's just local politics bullshit.'

'Hey,' John said to her, in the tone of a brother-in-law who's seen it all. 'There's nothing to worry about. Therese got her shop, and the other units sold in time. The deal made money. The bank got it all back plus interest.'

My stomach lurched at the sound of my name. What did my shop have to do with anything?

I saw John lock eyes with Trevor then stare at the floor, frozen.

'That's enough.' My voice came out louder than I intended. 'John, that man, that councillor, has got nothing to do with my shop. So there's a pause on the hotel construction. Trevor's budgets always allow for delays. It's a political spat, not our problem.' John's stillness continued. 'And everything's going to be fine.'

Trevor met my gaze. 'Thank you, darling,' he said.

I grabbed the nearest glass to me and took a swig to counter the sudden dryness in my mouth. It wasn't like me to intervene like this, and the room felt seized with surprise.

'Right,' said Maria. 'Kids. Bed.'

Through the movement of their leaving, complaining and being shushed, I continued to watch Trevor. He closed his eyes for a few seconds, and slowly put his book of crossword puzzles down.

'John,' he said, 'have I ever shown you my old board from the sixties?'

'Your surfboard?'

'It's in one of the sheds here. Real tanker. There was an art to manipulating those beasts.'

I'd seen photos of Trevor then – before he and Judith were an item – his hair brushed thickly forward, plaid surf shorts, black Ray-Bans, an arm casually around a board nearly double his height. In one photo, black and white, he was topless, dragging the board out of the shallows, his smile not the immortal grin of the posed shots but introspective, entertained by his own thoughts. The sort of smile that made you want to know the person's inner life.

'I'd love to see it,' John said. 'If you want to show me.'

'We could motor round to Ward Bay,' Trevor said. 'Give you a crack on it. See if you can handle the size.'

It was only when I noticed how Annabel shone whitely, staring at the air between her husband and her father, that I understood this was one of Trevor's moves. To do with longevity. Survival. Squashing John, though I didn't know why.

'Of course in those days,' Trevor said, 'I'd have thought nothing of driving over the hills at six in the morning – three-hour drive, then surfing all day. Sleeping on the beach if it was warm. Or coming home at midnight then getting up the next morning to swim from here to the other side of the Sound.'

'We get it, Dad,' Rob said as he exited towards the hall. 'You're invincible. Night all!'

Andy said, 'Well the timing's not great for the council enquiry. In terms of hotel investors. With the change of government, people are gun-shy.'

'For god's sake,' Caroline said to her husband through gritted teeth. 'Read the room.'

I put a hand on his shoulder. 'Come on, Andy. Story time for the little ones. Let's go.' He wasn't happy about it, but he came.

*

The open acknowledgment of Trevor's predicament did not clear the air but thickened it. As the days went on, everyone seemed to be caught in poses. Two siblings seen in the hills behind the house. A cluster of grandchildren in a rowboat on the other side of the inlet. Even the wind beating in from the open sea seemed to pin the bunting static against the sky – the tide dragged back across the sand to expose mud, kelp and fish skeletons from the passing trawlers.

The children bickered with their partners, and with each other. I caught glimpses of Annabel's raised chin, or the way Rob stuck his tongue in his cheek when he looked away, and it was as though time collapsed and they were the disgruntled teenagers I'd met when Trevor and I got together – Annabel pretending she was fine, Rob wanting to escape, Caroline desperate to be asked how she was and bristling if you did. How could I soothe them, make things better? It had been beyond me then, and still seemed to be now. All I could do was the food.

Rob stomped down from the hill carrying concerned texts from Green Party officials, who had just caught up with the local council news, and paced around the property hunched over them, composing draft replies, until Maria shouted she was going to throw the bloody phone in the bloody sea. Caroline worried that more photos of her father with his cronies (her word) would appear in the press to be seen by her students and colleagues, which rekindled an old fight she had with Andy about not having taken his surname.

Trevor said they were all being oversensitive and it was why none of them except for John were any good at business. John had been forgiven for whatever his transgression was, and he and Trevor went surfing for a day and came back shining. 'I caught a couple,' Trevor said. 'This young fella's got the edge though.'

'Nah mate, you're a legend,' John said, throwing him a beer from the fridge.

I wondered if they were cooking up a solution for Trevor – John had plenty of connections – or were just enjoying each other, men cut from the same cloth. Either way it was good to see Trevor happy. Andy sulked, left out.

Annabel developed the habit of leading Trevor into corners by the elbow and asking him to go over his financial arrangements just one more time, as though he were dying. She'd be too locked into her ideas to notice anyone walk past them, to notice even that Trevor had stopped paying attention, wasn't listening as she told him there were better ways to structure the family trust, the investments, he could protect them with this and that and it was time to get real about off-shore, Trevor making those masculine noises he had learned from his own father, considering, weighing, yes, I see, staring out the window at the grandkids playing badminton, not listening to a thing. The game looked easy, but it took all your force to hit a shuttlecock.

I hovered in the hallway, watching one such encounter, wondering if I should intervene. Then I realised John was in the room watching them too. His face was lean, intent, as though he was lip-reading, then from stillness he leapt forward and inserted himself into the conversation, and Trevor suddenly came alive.

Indy, Maria's fifteen-year-old, was the easiest to spend time with. Her mother and Rob had got together when she was about nine, and swiftly acquiring a half-sister and extended family had turned her into a watchful girl. Sometimes I wondered what she made of us all.

Together we devised a treasure hunt, and taught Caroline's boys to make scones. Annabel's sons took the kayaks out. A biotoxin warning had been issued about the local shellfish, so instead of diving, John decided to train for a triathlon, going for everlonger swims, his Lycra-clad form moving distantly across the Sound. The five-year-old ripped up Judith's strawberries; Rob and Maria fought over whether this deserved a consequence or not. And then on the afternoon of New Year's Eve, when I was at an upstairs window spreading the bathmat out to dry,

Caroline came back from a shopping trip to Picton in the water taxi. Three more figures rose from the boat and splashed into the knee-deep water, helping her lift the bags to shore. One of them was Heathcote.

I found him in the kitchen, unloading booze and party food. Caroline was laughing at something he'd said as she arranged avocados in the fruit bowls. A bag of fireworks was propped by the verandah door.

'Therese.' Heathcote came and high-fived me.

'Hi. Your dad's out the back. Where have you been?'

He laughed. He was wearing a white shirt over swimming trunks, his legs brown, sunglasses that he now took off, revealing unexpectedly clear eyes. 'Long story.'

'Who are your—' I stepped onto the verandah to look for the people who'd come with him. Two girls, or very young women, were splashing each other in the shallows, long wet hair flying. One of them was filming the other on a small HD camera as she kicked her legs high, spraying crystals of water, and stripped off her T-shirt to reveal a tiny string bikini. The girl holding the camera looked familiar, but it was too far across the lawn to see.

'You little bugger!' Trevor stalked across the garden towards us. He was laughing, his eyes crinkled with delight.

We welcomed the New Year in with games and beach races. Heathcote and Andy rowed out to set off fireworks from the middle of the bay. Over the far hills an aura of colour from the Picton celebrations bloomed briefly and was dragged away by the wind. Heathcote's guests befriended Indy and brought her out before our bonfire with her face completely made up, daisies woven in her hair.

John let out a low whistle and Maria said, 'Do you mind? She's fifteen,' and he said, 'Oh come on, I wasn't—' and Annabel said, 'Don't forget Maria's a feminist, John. And so am I.'

'Hello?' John said, and I realised I was staring at him. 'Therese, what's up?'

'Nothing.'

A cry of pain from the verandah cut across the grass. Rob had put his foot through the rotten wooden boards and scraped a bad gash up his shin, and Maria and I ran to get the first aid kit, Indy forgotten.

The villa was a beast to maintain. The wood was vulnerable to the sea air, the paint peeled, the verandah palings and deck planks rotted, the windowpanes crusted with salt, birds nested in the eaves, spiders and rodents and wasps nested in all available holes and corners. We disinfected and bandaged Rob's leg under the kitchen light and poured him a shot of whisky with which to take the painkillers. He had never done well with physical pain.

'I hate this place,' he said, and to Maria, 'Let's go tomorrow.'

'But Indy's having fun.'

'I'm sorry,' I said. 'I should have had that board replaced.'

He turned his anger towards me. 'This whole kitchen will be swimming in water before too long. That new oven. That ludicrous fridge. That's what the family legacy's going to be, you know that. A rotting wreck with a few window frames above the water line. Seagulls in the roof cavity. If there's anything left for seagulls to live on by then.'

Maria made soothing noises while I put away the antiseptic and adhesive roll. 'Be good to get that checked by a doctor.'

Heathcote appeared in the doorway. 'Hey. The girls found a guitar in their cabin, it's not even out of tune.'

Beneath the sound of talk from the bonfire we could hear a few chords being strummed, a female voice rising.

'I'll carry you, brother,' he said. 'Come on.'

Propped between Maria and Heathcote, the whisky bottle dangling from one hand, Rob returned to the fire.

I watched them all, silhouetted around the flames, and wondered what the new year would bring. The Therese Thorne website suggested rituals involving candles and incense. Affirmations, cleanses, arranging your desk, changing the cushion covers. This year, I thought, a sage burning wouldn't cut it.

I was proud of how well Trevor was doing, and had the strong sense of holding a forcefield above the family, above all of us, so that this holiday could be a bubble in time. Here in the Sounds, every item was a talisman that kept us safe, that told us who we were: the rusty pushbike, the shells lined up on a windowsill, the sagging net on the tennis court. I knew what power these things had, even if the family, who had grown up with them, did not. It was my task to protect these talismans and add to them with my own – to mix the new with the old to rejuvenate it, keep it alive. But there was a cracking feeling following me around. It was there in the background, and I thought if I held myself tightly enough closed to it, it might seal over before anything split open. I wanted someone to tell me – Claire perhaps, I thought now, surprising myself – if the pressure was coming from inside or outside. If I didn't know where it came from, I couldn't know what was going to give.

I laid a kitchen chair on its side over the hole in the verandah, and fetched a bright sarong to drape over it as warning. I was tying this down to the chair legs, a torch propped beside me to light the task, when I thought to shine the beam down through the gap in the boards to see what was beneath. I slid the chair out of the way and lay on my stomach, my fist with the torch getting in the way of my gaze, so holding the torch awkwardly above me, trying to direct its light past the obstacle of my head and onto the hidden ground below, realising the hole would need to be much bigger for anyone to be able to look around properly. The air from down there was cool and musty. Perhaps I expected a glint of old silver, or a pearl handled knife. No. Nothing I could recognise. Only bare earth and the shadow cast by me.

5

I woke on the first day of 2018 feeling muffled, like there was seawater in my ear. Trevor was staring at the ceiling.

'Aren't you sleeping?' I asked. 'Is it the hotel?'

'It's just old age.'

'Do you want to go back early? We could leave today.'

'I can do everything on the phone. No one's in their offices anyway. Even in Singapore, John says, he can't get hold of his mates.'

'Is John thinking about pitching in?' I asked. 'Is that a good idea, getting family involved? You might open up a whole box of worms.' We had always agreed the flow of money would go in one direction, from Trevor to his children. Andy, his other son-in-law, had often wanted to invest in Trevor's projects, but Trevor thought he'd be more trouble than he was worth, and so it had been easier to make a blanket rule.

He made a frustrated sound. 'I hate this time of year, it's like you can get it up but there's nothing to fuck.'

'Excuse me?'

He was tanned, a white band on his wrist from the watch I had given him for his seventieth, which sat on the bedside table now, ticking. The man who used to surf all day, who could swim to the other side of the Sound. He propped himself up on one elbow and picked up a length of my hair, as if weighing it in his hand. He brought his face to it and inhaled.

'You don't fool me with that old age stuff,' I said.

*

The two girls with Heathcote were friends of his girlfriend, whoever that was. News that he even had a girlfriend was met with scepticism and teasing, and he wouldn't give her name, but the girls said no, this time it was serious. They said she was spending New Year in Auckland, where I presumed she and Heathcote had met. Perhaps she had something to do with the house he was so desperate to buy. They were very young, in their cutaway swimsuits. We were used to seeing Heathcote with younger women. It was actually impossible to imagine him with a woman of forty.

The girls kept to themselves, chatting and sunning, but when I passed the familiar-looking one on the stairs of the villa, a towel draped over her arm, it clicked into place that I'd seen her in our building a few months earlier, on the stairs, no doubt heading up to Heathcote's apartment. Her long dark hair had been wet then from a rainstorm, as it was now from the sea, and we'd exchanged a smile and a remark about the weather. She gave no sign of recognizing me here at the homestead, and I was reminded that I was part of the great formless mass of the middle-aged.

'There's a shower cabin just behind yours, if you're after some privacy,' I said.

'Thanks, but I'm going to have a bath.'

In an act of silent resistance I didn't say anything about the plumbing, the need to conserve water, or making sure to be done by the time the children would be needing their wash. Let Heathcote be the boring adult, let Caroline persuade her spray-phobic sons to stand under the garden hose to rinse off the salt. As I continued down the stairs, the pipes began their eerie song.

I grabbed my phone and went to the top of the hill to check for messages, wanting to be away from everyone. I craved proof that I existed, I wanted a flood of texts, DMs, a long roll of emails to deal with, but work was leaving me alone and there was only one text, from Claire, asking if I knew where Heathcote was.

Why was she looking for Heathcote?

I had one missed call, also from Claire. She had left a voice message.

'Therese. Hi.'

Her husky voice sounded so close. I felt acutely aware of the air around me, as though she was invisibly there, hovering.

'Just wondering if you could give me Heathcote's number. Or if you're with him, could you ask him to call me? It's about some people who've turned up at my apartment.'

In the little pause that followed, I felt a bit affronted. I wasn't Heathcote's secretary. Then she said,

'I know you're not his secretary. But I don't know how else to get hold of him.'

It made me shiver – that she'd answered my exact thought – a kind of predictive mind-reading.

'See you soon,' she said. 'When you're back.'

I saved the message and started down the hill towards the beach, letting the steep slope pull me into a euphoric run, my long strides catching air, a feeling I hadn't had since I was a kid.

I passed Claire's message on to Heathcote and he said, 'People who've turned up at her apartment? I don't know what she's talking about.'

'She asked if you could call her back.'

He nodded, as if he'd consider it.

There were other things to worry about. Andy's drinking prompted raised eyebrows; Heathcote baited Caroline by continually offering him a beer or topping up his wine. Annabel found nits in her youngest son's hair and made a performance of combing it out with the toxic shampoo in the middle of the lawn 'so as not to infect anyone else'. She 'strongly advised' the other mothers to check their own children, the implication being that they had passed the head lice to her son and not the other way around.

'I bet you twenty dollars,' I said to Trevor, 'that she'll get to the bottom of who is Carrier 1 before the week's out.'

But I admired her tenacity. Motherhood had made Trevor's daughters both more intensely themselves and more selfless. It was humbling to witness the automatic way they undertook revolting tasks, the unhesitating flow of love for their children, the patience and kindness they had learned. Alone within their families, they appeared ageless and free, and it was only when people were watching that falseness distorted a gesture as simple as wrapping a shivering child in a dry towel with an amateur dramatics hair toss, cooing loud enough for all to hear. That need to perform wasn't their fault, I think now; it was ours.

We had nearly three days straight of muggy rain and wind, rendering anything soft — towels, cushions, bedding, sofas — sticky and damp. Some of the time the families retreated to their cabins but there were eighteen of us for meals, and enclosed in the house it was impossible not to be aware of bodies: Andy's boozy sweat, the oil Maria put on her hair, Heathcote's aftershave, the rumbling of Annabel's half-starved tummy, the small children fidgeting and itching. Had John always had such a loud voice?

Sloughed wetsuits draped over the verandah railings like kelp. Grit and leaves tracked through the rooms. Caroline 'couldn't be fucked' organising a treasure hunt, effectively nuking the competition between the sisters — a god-level move. First there was a fight over rationing the children's DVD time, then a fight over what they would watch, then a fight over who got to sit where in relation to the computer screen, then a fight over the smell of the tea tree treatment in Annabel's sons' hair. When the rain stopped at lunchtime on the third day the doors and windows were flung open and eighteen people exploded outside and tripped over new banks and hollows in the sand to plunge into the churned, debris-laden sea.

After my swim I fell asleep on the rapidly drying beach and woke to hear Caroline and Annabel talking next to me, Annabel with her hand in the sand, clawing it in and out of piles with her fingers.

'None of the school parents are divorced. It's too hard when you're expat. What would I do, bring the boys back here?'

'Have you really thought about it?' Caroline's concern incompletely masked awe and a kind of delight. Perhaps this was one contest with her sister she could win – the battle to stay married.

In the pause that followed I wrestled with my conscience but didn't move, breathing slowly as if still asleep.

'I couldn't,' Annabel finally said. 'None of us could, could we? We know what it's like.'

Even with my head turned away from them I could sense the look cast in my direction, and their voices dropped. Although Trevor and Judith had broken up long before he met me, in their eyes I was still responsible. Once, on a holiday like this, I had walked into the kitchen to hear Annabel mimicking my voice, so different from her private school vowels, an event I had since striven to put out of my mind.

'Rob and Maria are doing my head in,' Caroline said. 'They have to get their parenting straight. I hate kids running around after 10 p.m.'

'I don't mind as long as they're not mine.'

Scritch, scritch went the sand. Caroline asked, 'Have you met someone?'

'No! No, it's not that. I don't know, sometimes I think the worst thing you can do with someone you love is marry them and have a family.' Scrape, scrape. 'It turns you into the most boring, uptight, worst versions of yourselves.'

'You're a great mother.' In this, Caroline sounded sincere. 'Your boys are great.'

'There's no way to say this that doesn't sound appalling,' Annabel said. 'But John makes so much money. It's oppressive.'

'Yep,' said Caroline, 'that does sound appalling.'

Her sister spoke searchingly. 'He's taking risks. I mean he always has, but the past few years, it's – like an addiction. He's obsessed with it, and we have so much, and there's the family money to start with and sometimes I feel like John's sort of – piling the money up around me so I can't get out. Like I'm choking on gold coins.'

'Give it away.'

'We do. Local hospitals, reading programmes, Club Rainbow Singapore.'

'Give more. Give enough away so you don't feel bad about it anymore.'

'Then I worry about the kids. Who knows what's coming in their lifetimes. They might need it.'

I felt a pressure in my solar plexus, and the strange urge to hit something, but kept still.

'Both my boys are in therapy,' said Caroline. 'That's eight hundred dollars a month.'

'Yeah, but Caro…' From Annabel's voice I could tell that eight hundred could leak from the money bucket every few weeks and there'd be plenty left. That trust fund came from their mother's side; I didn't know what it was worth.

Caroline laughed. 'You're the one who feels bad about it.'

'Anyway,' Annabel said. 'If the hotel really is falling over John's been saying we might need to help out Dad and…'

Caroline coughed, and in the pause that followed I realised she was silently pointing at me. Heat flooded me as if it were coming from the ground I lay on, playing dead. My first thought was, this will cause a fight. Then: Annabel thinks he is in that much trouble.

Caroline said, 'Dad can't be that worried about money. He's given Heathcote the deposit for a house in Auckland.'

My entire body tensed. I couldn't believe it. Trevor had said nothing to me about this.

'What?' Annabel said. 'What the fuck?'

'Yeah,' said Caroline, with the preening casualness of someone who has insider information. 'Heath just told me today.'

'He can't afford to do that!' said Annabel. 'He's insane.'

'Heath says it's an investment. I don't know, Dad's probably keeping his own money separate from the hotel. Maybe it's smart to throw it into a house.'

'What,' said Annabel, 'in case the hotel bankrupts him and creditors come knocking and want to take his cash?'

She was joking, but she also wasn't. She was furious. I was too. I didn't know how much longer I could play dead.

'The hotel isn't going to bankrupt him,' Caroline said. 'You're the one who said he's done nothing wrong.'

'That isn't the point. Fuck Heathcote. It's irresponsible. He should be thinking of what Dad needs, not just – buying whatever he wants and fucking his young fucking girlfriends.'

'I don't think young people have sex anymore.' Caroline liked to be an authority on the youth, in compensation for the fact that her students, year on year, stayed the same age, while she got older. 'It's all the medication.'

'Heath's not young.'

A pause, then Caroline said, 'Andy's on medication.'

'Is he? Then you shouldn't let him drink.'

'I don't "let him" – it's not up to me—'

'Well, you could—'

'Jesus Annabel, you're always—'

They were speaking with force now and it was impossible to fake sleep any longer. I was wondering if the best thing was just to leap to my feet as if I'd woken suddenly, when Annabel said, 'Is that John?' and the stark urgency in her voice drew me upright. It was obvious I'd been eavesdropping but neither of them paid attention – they were rising, making their way towards the water as if pulled by strings.

'Is he OK?' I joined them in the shallows, craning to see. John had kept up his triathlon training through the bad weather and was out in the deep water of the inlet now, a dark blob halfway to the hills on the other side – moving, fast, in the direction of open sea. That was his arm up in the air. Was he waving in triumph, or for help?

Now that we were upright the force of the wind was apparent, sheeting across the top of the water, sending spray into our faces. Trevor's daughters' long hair streamed behind them.

Within seconds, somehow Annabel had dragged a kayak from the grass and was in it, we were pushing her off, she was plunging the paddle this side then the other and we could see how hard she battled against the wind to get out to her husband.

Alerted by our silent surge of panic, children surrounded us, Caroline's boys wailing with anxiety. Her face, blurred and desperate, met mine, and I prised the kids away and brought them up to the house, gathering the others, counting heads, two, three, five, seven, all here, wondering if I should call Picton, my anger about Heathcote and his house still burning but irrelevant now.

Although the wind was plowing in from the sea, John had been moving fast in a shiny streak of water out towards the open Strait. We had seen his raised hand. I squinted seawards – Annabel had gained momentum; my god she was strong. I couldn't see John.

From the verandah I shouted for Trevor but he was down at the shore now too and Caroline and Andy were remonstrating, actually physically fighting over another kayak. She succeeded in stopping him from rowing out towards danger, and stalked away with the paddle in her hand like a confiscated toy. He kicked the side of the kayak, stormed up the short beach and stuck his chin seaward as though he had found a more effective vantage point and would bring John in by the power of will.

'Is Dad OK?' The eldest boy spoke for the rest of them.

'He'll be fine,' I said. 'Mummy's gone to get him. Who's for hot chocolate?'

I could not get a signal on my phone – for a flaming moment this enraged me too, as if not having signal was a lifestyle choice and in a crisis we should be able to switch it the fuck on. We're special, roared a voice in my head. We get to say when the phones work.

'I want to go,' said the boy.

'Your mum's got it sorted, darling.'

He pushed past me and barrelled down the beach to fling himself into Trevor's side. Together they stood and watched.

God knows what was happening out there. I yelled for Rob or Maria; Heathcote was first to appear and I said as calmly as I could, 'Go up the hill and call the coastguard.' I pressed the fridge magnet with their number into his hand.

'Maria's already gone.'

'Go and check? In case she can't get through.'

I hustled the kids into the living room and told Indy to find a DVD, promised them snacks and cocoa were coming, grabbed the binoculars and stood on the wind-battered deck. A single kayak was nearing Annabel's double; Rob, digging hard. The grey water swayed sickeningly through the lenses as I tried to get a bead on John. He would know to swim sideways through the rip. Perhaps at the worst the wind would push him into a far inlet and he'd have to wait to be picked up. I didn't like that now, as well as him, two of Trevor's children were out there in the gale, which was beating about the house: upstairs our open bedroom window banged and banged, and I tripped and scraped my shin on the stairs in the scramble to pull it shut. Wind still flew about the place, another window banged and I went searching for it, so many rooms and so many windows facing the sea. Through the crazy whistling sound rose the cries of children yelling and I shouted downstairs for Indy to check the milk on the stove. There came a massive bang followed immediately by a crash and I ran towards the sound and there, in Indy's room, the girls Heathcote had brought knelt huddled on the bed, mouths open at the window frame whose glass had smashed at the impact and fallen – I ran to look – onto the sloping roof over the verandah, half of it arrested by the guttering, half in large shards glinting on the ground. The eldest grandchild had turned at the sound and was heading back up from the beach to look, just as Indy stepped out from the verandah in her bare feet. I yelled, but my voice was dragged back inside by the wind.

'Could you not have shut it?' I shouted at the stupid girls before I ran, half-skidding, downstairs towards the verandah door, pushed through it against the wind and called to the children to be careful of the glass.

Back inside, wind continued to flood through the broken upstairs window, down the stairs where it swirled horribly through the rooms. I threw out the burnt milk and started again, panting, furious, beside the stove. When it had warmed through just enough for me to pour out the hot chocolate – I didn't want to look at the sea, I wasn't going to look at the sea – and deliver it to the children, I turned the element off and walked slowly back up the stairs. My shin was throbbing and blood had trickled down my leg.

'I think you two have stayed here long enough,' I said from Indy's bedroom doorway to the girls, who were slowly pulling on their clothes. I didn't wait to look at their faces but turned away, pulled the door hard shut behind me, and breathed in the stiller atmosphere of the upstairs hall, leaving the sea air eddying around inside that room.

I shut the living room door and told Indy to guard it and joined the others on the beach, handing the binoculars to Trevor. He looked a hundred years old. The kayaks, one yellow, one orange, moved now faster, now achingly slow. From time to time a sweep of sea spray blocked our view. A black blob that for several seconds had looked like John rose from the surface and spread its wings, a giant bird battling the current towards land. I still couldn't see John. But Trevor was there, next to me, the binoculars pressed against his nose, and I trusted that he could. A childish part of me had a flashing vision of a funeral, three blond heads bowed beside a coffin, Annabel in a veil – a stock image that had nothing to do with reality, and I shooed it away. It was followed by the shameful question, voiced distinctly in my mind, *what would be lost if John were to die?* With horror I pushed that aside too, took his son by the shoulder and said, 'Hey, they're watching a movie inside.'

He shook me off at first, then slipped a hand into mine and came with me towards the house.

We were on the verandah when Andy yelled from the beach, 'The coastguard! They're nearly there!'

'Wait,' I said. It was a risk, but now there was hope. 'Shall we watch the rescue?'

'Are they safe?'

'Yes.' Surely it was true.

The boy hesitated, struggling with something. I wondered if he didn't want to see his father rescued. There would be the story to tell at school, the danger, the near death, the survival. But also, perhaps, some vague humiliation. Fathers should be able to rescue themselves.

'Oh, let's go inside. There's cake in there,' I said.

He toughened: 'Cool,' and disappeared into the living room. I followed, to make sure he'd find a place around the screen without a squabble.

By the time I made it back to the beach the coastguard rescue boat was scudding towards us with John, Annabel, Rob and the kayaks all aboard. The children came to watch as they pulled into the bay, and as John and Annabel splashed out to hug and kiss their sons, wearing bright, laughing expressions over their ashen faces, saying, 'What an adventure!', the boy stood apart with his arms folded, taking a technical interest in the boat. 'How fast could that go, Granddad?'

'It's actually from an early America's Cup. They call it a chase boat.'

'Cool.'

'Dad!' Caroline said.

'What?'

'"It's actually from the America's Cup."'

'Well it is. He's interested. Aren't you?'

From the corner of my eye, I could see John lowering himself to sit, and then lie on his back on the ground. Annabel lay down next to him. I knew he was crying. His son kept his distance.

The man and woman operating the boat, local volunteers, waved the children onboard as they waded around them, patting the rubberised sides, pulling themselves up on the chrome handles.

'Go inside mate,' the man called to John. 'You want to get warm, get a hot sweet tea in you.'

Maria had blankets ready and patted them over John and Annabel, rubbing their arms and legs.

The man hopped down from the boat and handed John a half-eaten bar of chocolate he must have been given on the ride back. 'Here, finish this.' Maria helped him break it in half and give some to Annabel and they hunched over and ate like they were gnawing bones.

The grandchildren helped me pass drinks round and John sipped at his juice, slowly regaining control. The volunteers – the man's name was Sal but I didn't catch the woman's – said they couldn't stay long, but were persuaded to sit on the sand for five minutes and have a juice in lieu of a stiff gin. Trevor tried to give them some cash but they wouldn't take it.

'We can't, but you could make a donation online.'

'We do this for nothing, but money's always good for the upkeep.'

'I know a few of those America's Cup blokes,' Trevor said. 'If you're in need of an upgraded vessel. Could have a word.'

'Oh, right.' The woman nodded. I was suddenly conscious of the size of the house rising up behind us.

'Well,' I said. 'There's more chocolate up at the house? Cake? We're having a barbecue, are you sure you can't stay?'

'No, no. Thanks.' They seemed to think this was me ushering them off and stood, wiping sand from their trousers.

'You'd be very welcome.'

'There's actually a thing on up at the marae. Bit of a get together.'

'Sal's on hāngī duty,' the woman said.

'Oh, yum,' said Caroline.

'Yep, better get digging that hāngī,' said Sal, and he and the woman exchanged a glance.

'Thank you so much,' we all cried. 'Thank you.'

'All good.'

'We'll make that donation,' Andy said.

John had got to his feet and now thrust his hand out for Sal to shake. 'Thanks bro. I don't know what would have—'

His voice cracked and he wiped his eyes with the back of his hand. 'Thanks.'

'Pretty strong lady you've got there,' said the woman. Annabel was sitting with her knees pulled up to her chest, her face pointed out to sea, staring into the middle distance as though she'd just been in contact with something grand and terrible. A limit. Feeling our attention, she turned and gave an effortful smile. She clambered up to embrace the coastguards.

'Thank you,' she said. She was shaking all over.

'Yep, yep, all good.' Sal clapped John on the arm. 'Take it easy.'

The woman revved the engine. Sal hoisted himself onto the back of the boat and turned to the woman as she sped them out of the bay, exchanging words that were lost beneath the motor and the wind.

Maria announced a race to the kitchen for more cake, dragging Rob with her by the wrist, laughing as the children chanted cake, cake, cake. Andy had returned to his post at the end of the beach; Caroline, who'd clung to Annabel, sobbing, when she got out of the boat, watched him from the shelter of Trevor's arm, gauging whether to approach. John and Annabel disappeared to their cabin as soon as their saviours had left, the plume of water fizzing behind them.

That night was something of a bacchanal. The children were granted a joint sleepover in the largest cabin. We sat around the outside table long after the late sundown, drinking as if determined to run the place dry, Annabel between Trevor and John, eyes aglow and laughing at nothing, spots of colour on her cheeks. Maria sat with her arm twined round Rob who, it turned out, had very nearly made it to John when the coastguard appeared. Caroline must have spoken with Andy, because he'd shaken off any sense of outsiderness and joined us in this survival high.

'It's all going to be all right!' Trevor gripped me by the shoulders and squeezed hard, almost shaking me. He tilted his head back and roared at the stars. 'Do your worst! We're the fucking Thornes!'

I gave a supportive whoop, and hugged him. Now was not the time to raise the subject of him buying that house for Heathcote. I would do it tomorrow. Claire's face appeared then in my mind's eye – as if she was watching. As if she had something to say. I felt defensive, and hugged Trevor tighter.

It felt odd, loose-ended not to be preparing dinner, but Heathcote wanted to cook, and he insisted we all relax and let him do it. How could any of us relax? We had nearly lost John. We had hovered in that space between invincibility and total, devastating change. The taste of it was still in our mouths.

Heathcote pulled the speakers out through the living room window onto the deck and music spread through the night air and began to reaffirm a sense of safety, of some kind of mastery over nature. His guests, the twenty-year-olds, produced bowls of extraordinary salads punctuated with bright flowers and herbs, somehow fresher and more modern than the food with which we illustrated the Therese Thorne tableware in the catalogue. They moved around me with a punishing solicitude, as though I were a cantankerous aunt. I had no idea whether they'd any intention to leave.

We all drank too much, and the lights of the cabins shone yellow through the lengthy twilight, and the bunting flapped and candles flickered in the vestiges of wind. Citronella spirals burned at our feet. At one point I registered the dishes piled high in the sink and pressed an apron into Andy's chest, saying, 'Make yourself useful.' Then I was back outside and the sky was darker now; above the hills across the water, stars clustered. Somehow we were on our feet dancing, the girls in charge of the playlist, shaking themselves up against Trevor, Caroline, Rob.

Maria put the children to sleep; I saw Indy and one of Heathcote's girls at the end of the beach passing a burning orange tip between them, a cigarette or weed, and looked around for Rob to tell him to look after his daughter but the music had changed to an electronic beat and he was jumping up and down, shaking his hands above his head.

Trevor came to me, grinning, hugging, holding my face, 'God you're beautiful, you're so beautiful, how did I get so lucky,' and I danced with him for a while until he grabbed the other of Heathcote's girls, the brunette, and brought her into our circle. They laughed and he copied her arm gestures. I moved away to stand on the edge of it all, looking. Maria and Rob were floating upright together, swaying dreamily as the music doofed over them, and Annabel, Caroline, Andy and John danced in a tight hot quartet between the barbecue and the table.

The shadowy presence forming at my shoulder was, of course, Heathcote, and I said, 'Have you given them all an E or something?'

I was half joking, half fishing, but his cartoonish drawing back and tilting his head to one side confirmed it.

'Even Trevor?'

A pantomime shrug.

'You haven't given any to Indy, have you?' If he had done that, I would strike him to the ground.

The fake Irish accent came out again. 'You always think the worst of me.'

'No I don't.'

'Do you want any? Only I think I'm out.'

I doubted that. 'I'm fine.' I burned to say, *how dare you ask Trevor for that house*, but there was no point while he was in this state.

'So I hear you're chucking us out,' he said. 'Boss lady.'

'I'm not. No. It's not my place to, anyway.'

'That's what Bella said.' He gestured to the brunette who was dancing with Trevor. 'You tore a strip off them.'

'It was a bad moment. Of course you don't have to go.'

Trevor and the brunette pulled the other girl and Indy into their loop, and I watched Indy anxiously, wondering if she could sense the chemical edge to the night, but she seemed delighted, mocking Trevor's moves and calling to her mother to come and join them. Maria brought Rob with her and they became a loose heaving unit of arms, legs, shaking heads and raised, enraptured smiles. Indy jumped up and down between her mother and stepfather, happy.

A cool space opened behind me now – Heathcote had gone to join the dancers, wrists twining like the smoke that fluted from the chimney pipe above the patio fire. I wanted to hunker by that fire, to take a stick for each member of that family and crouch with the pile by my side, running their knobbled lengths through my palms, holding an end to the flames, brushing it – Heathcote, perhaps, or even Trevor – lightly back and forth in the heat and watching as it charred.

Ugh, who was that?

The night splintered and ran in short, fluid ripples – professions of love came at me from Trevor, Annabel, Caroline, the boys – John ripped his shirt off and gave an animal shout – Heathcote's girls kissed, hands deep in each other's hair, and Annabel pushed her way in to kiss the brunette too – Rob and Andy hugged and hugged, smashed beer bottles together, hugged some more – you're a good cunt, you're a good cunt – forever mate, forever – I looked around for Indy, suddenly panicking, and saw her through the living room window, in her dressing gown, watching a princess movie on the computer – my hand to my heart in dumb relief – Trevor embraced me from behind, murmuring in my ear, lips on my neck, you're so sexy let's go – and now John and Andy and Rob were naked, moonlit bodies leaping the hedge, running down the beach and into the sea, flinging phosphorescence – and Heathcote's girls in their bras and little boy short knickers, and Annabel, 'fuck it,' in her G-string, her stripped-lean muscles flashing as she ran – Caroline turning to me and laugh-crying, 'It's too cold!' – Trevor pulling me by the hands, 'Come on, come on,' reaching a hand out to catch Caroline, dragging us in until we were all throwing ourselves about in the shallows and if you looked at us not knowing anything we could have been half drowned people trying to make it to shore, tripping over our own feet, the seaweed, each other, just as we were nearly free of the sucking-back waves – where was Heathcote, was he watching, was he filming us – and later on the grass Andy stepped on a bit of window glass I hadn't caught and I was back in the kitchen with the first aid kit, back in my position.

It's funny, at the time that night seemed such an explosion of animal energy. But now, now that I can't see people dancing in my mind's eye without feeling, truly and in my own bones, the heaving pulse of moving with those other bodies, later, in Claire's room, the panting, wordless derangement that she could call up, the blow-out on the beach feels fake and tame. Now I've seen Claire, walking through us. Turning her good eye on us, then her bad. Now I've heard the pounding of her stick on the ground. Now I've bared my teeth and felt my skin split.

I spent the morning making coffee and toast and sweeping out the cabin behind the tennis court. Heathcote and the girls had left before anyone was awake. Apart from me. I heard the water taxi and stood at the broken window in Indy's bedroom. She slept behind me in her young girl's bed, her cheeks soft, breathing in a light snore. I watched the girls swing their multicoloured fabric bags onto the little jet boat, and watched Heathcote's white linen shirt shining like another window in the sun.

After that I went back to our room and sat on the edge of our bed, watching Trevor sleep. If he was going to have a comedown it would hit exactly when we returned to the city and got the latest update about the council enquiry. This was not the time to ask about Heathcote and the house and why Trevor thought it was a good idea to give his son everything he asked for.

I stood at the window and took in our view of the sea, the curve of the bush-clad hills rising across the water. I wondered who the coastguard volunteers were today. Who would go out too far, who would rely on someone else to save them, who would be caught by a freak wave and pulled off a rock, no one else aware it had happened for hours.

Trevor woke, and pulled the sheets back for me. I climbed in. My body fit into his hold. He pulled me close and started to shake. He was crying. Apart from at his mother's funeral and the girls' weddings I had never seen him cry. I pressed tightly into him, holding him.

'John could have died,' he said, and his voice broke and he cried audibly. 'Annabel – Rob—'

'It's all right,' I said. 'They're OK.' I kissed his warm shoulder.

The small children would be waking, and the adults, and soon I would make breakfast. Later in the morning the sound of the boat would draw near again and I would think it was Heathcote coming back, but it would be a photographer I'd booked to come and take candid family holiday snaps for the Therese Thorne website, booked a month ago and then forgotten to cancel, and she would disembark the water taxi to our nonplussed welcomes and, frozen, I would stare at the cold ash from the barbecue and the hungover adults and feral, nitty children in dirty T-shirts and synthetic track pants that were too short because all the cotton clothes hadn't had a chance to dry and the photographer would follow my gaze to a pile of gnawed chop bones someone had flung onto a corner of the lawn, to beer bottles with cigarette butts in them, to the gouges in the grass from a kayak that had been dragged up to the patio and sat covered with rotting seaweed in the sun, flies zigzagging over it and landing to crawl across the sticky outside table, and her eyes would meet mine and I would start, helplessly, to laugh.

For now, all that was outside, as yet unseen. The sheets were fresh and smooth. The duvet felt like air. I had the impression of lying, supported, in the palm of a giant hand. Trevor's long exhalations shuddered, and slowly settled. When he next spoke, he had control of his voice again.

'Can we give it an extra day?' he asked. 'Before we go back to town?'

Whatever would find us there.

6

A turd. That's what was at home waiting for us. The apartment door was closed but unlocked, so when I turned the key to get in, I locked it by mistake and took a second to realise what was going on before unlocking it again. I hauled the suitcases over the threshold. The apartment looked untouched, then a breeze lifted the curtains and I realised the balcony doors were wide open – and there was a brown mass in the middle of the rug I had brought back from a walking trip in Nepal. At first I thought it was a dead animal, perhaps a rat. Then I saw the flies on it. Then I smelt it.

'Careful!' I said to Trevor, who was behind me.

'What the hell is that?'

Before I could think, I had the rubber washing up gloves on and my hands out keeping Trevor at bay.

'Don't come any closer!'

'Is that a – did an animal get in here? What kind of—' Trevor stared at it, frozen.

A monstrous hybrid appeared in my mind, a huge, hairy possum, or feral cat, stalking the apartment, looking for a place to shit. Bulbous eyes, a striped tail.

'I think it's human,' I said.

'Have we been burgled?'

Trevor strode straight to his office, then through the rest of the rooms, checking for signs of things missing.

I picked up the shit with toilet paper and flushed it down the loo. The spare loo, not the one in our ensuite. I can still feel the sense memory of holding it in my fingers.

Trevor returned, incongruous in his holiday T-shirt and shorts, his hair thick with sea salt.

'Has anything been taken?' I asked.

'Not that I can see.'

'Is my jewellery still in the safe?'

'Yes.'

I checked the front door for signs of damage. Then I checked the balcony – for a second terrified someone was crouched there, hiding. There was no way anyone could climb up the side of the building, surely, without being seen. Had they come in this way and gone out the front door? Or had they come in the front door? But there were no scratches, no chunks taken out of the wood. A wild thought passed through me – that a spirit had done this – something cloudy that might lurk here still. But I said to Trevor in a calm voice,

'I should have kept it in a bag for DNA. If the cops take that sort of thing. Should we call them?'

'Nothing's been stolen,' Trevor said. 'There's no sign of a break-in.'

'Apart from that thing on the rug.'

Perhaps we had imagined it: a shared delirium. But no, there were the kitchen gloves in a plastic bag in the bin. There was the cleaning spray. There was the rug, rolled up in the corner. I would have to take it to get properly cleaned tomorrow. Exorcised.

'I'm going to call them,' I said, scrubbing my hands with detergent at the kitchen sink. 'I'm scared. They have to know for insurance, if we find something's missing later. And I'll email the residents' group, let everyone know. How the hell did they get up the side of the building?' The thought of a superhuman athleticism made me shudder. 'Maybe we should install pigeon spikes.'

'Wait. I don't want word getting around someone thinks it's funny to take a crap on our floor.'

He was sitting at the dining table, staring at the darker square of floorboards where the rug used to be.

'What do you mean? You think it was someone who – like it was targeted?'

'Why didn't they take anything, if it was a burglary?'

'Maybe they got interrupted.'

With a small jolt I remembered Claire's question for Heathcote, something about people in her apartment.

'I'm going to go and ask Claire, downstairs.'

'Don't tell her what happened.'

'Why not?'

From his silent shrug, I understood. It was like being bullied at school. The shame of the shit transferred itself to us. As if we'd done it, as if we were the ones who couldn't control ourselves, who were animals.

'Who would do it, Trevor?' Who were his enemies?

He shook his head. 'No idea.'

'We should at least tell the people in the building. They should know to be careful. Claire said some people turned up at her place, maybe she's been targeted too. Or it could be someone staying at Heathcote's? Maybe he's left a key to our place lying around.'

Trevor gathered himself, and grabbed his phone. 'Listen,' he said, while looking something up. 'There's that journalist on the ground floor. Let's not give him any fodder. You can say we got broken into, but you can't say what happened. I'm going to get CCTV for the foyer. Outside the building too.'

The wind was still coming in the open balcony doors, unsettling the air. But I didn't want to close them.

'The residents' group will want a say in that.'

'Fine,' he said. 'When they come home to a shit on the living room floor, then I'll listen.'

He showered, changed and went to his office, and after I'd unpacked and put a load of washing on I went down and knocked on Claire's door. I could hear music playing inside, and a sharp sound, like a hammer, banging in time. I wondered what she was doing. Who was there with her. I knocked again, louder.

My phone was in my hand – her call was still the most recent. I was about to press the call icon when the music got louder and I heard people whooping over the top of it. She would never hear the phone. I tried the door. It was open.

I had not been inside Claire and Mick's apartment before. It was a mirror image layout of Heathcote's place across the landing – both apartments were under half the size of mine and Trevor's penthouse.

'Hello?' I followed the music down the hallway into a living room.

The first things I saw were two fake stone lions mounted on plinths, either side of the sliding glass doors that led onto the balcony.

Claire was on her knees on the floor, a hammer in her hand. Two others were in the room with her, a dark-haired young man and a stunning woman, each holding one end of the plank that Claire was about to whack a nail into.

Could any of them have left the turd in my apartment? How on earth was I going to ask?

Claire leapt to her feet and turned the music off. 'Therese! You're back.'

Now that she no longer wore the eye patch, I could see her double-sided gaze. One of her eyes was warm, welcoming, but the other sat stonily in her head and looked at me as if from a long-ago place and time.

She introduced me to the young couple. They were Artan and Amina Xhina of Tirana, Albania, and they were her surprise guests. After we said hello they excused themselves to the balcony, where they shared a cigarette. The whole scene was so odd – their cosmopolitan air, the lions, the wooden boards laid out in a giant rectangle on the floor – I felt as if I'd walked into an art installation, or elaborate prank.

'I went to bed with a fever on New Year's Eve,' Claire said, 'and when I woke up in the morning, they were here. Amina's here doing some post doc thing in governance and Artan's her husband, he's in construction, town planning or something, I think he's just along for the ride.'

'How did they get in to your place?'

'God knows. Maybe Heathcote rented them his place as a holiday let, and gave my apartment number by mistake? They got the key from under the pot on the landing. But now there's someone else at his apartment, and I can't get hold of him.'

I explained he'd been with us in the Sounds, but had left before we did. 'I don't know where he is now. Maybe Auckland. I did pass on your message, sorry.' I felt guilty by association, as silly as that was, and a bit like I'd failed her.

She shrugged. 'It doesn't matter. I mean, I do want my apartment to myself. But I like these people. I never met anyone from Albania before. Reminds me there's a world out there.'

'The thing is,' I said. 'Someone broke into our apartment. In the last couple of days.'

'Oh no. Are you all right?'

'Did you see anything? It seems weird maybe, that these people have just arrived?'

She frowned. 'It wasn't them, Therese.'

'Yes, no, I don't mean that.'

'Don't you?'

Her stern eye was too hot on me. I couldn't continue. 'What are you building?' I asked, gesturing to the floor.

She smiled. 'Come and see. I'm having a dinner party tomorrow night. Bring Trevor.'

'Thanks.'

A movement caught my eye through the balcony glass. The young man – Artan – had lurched forward in his chair, and was doubled over, bracing himself with one hand on the railing.

'Is he all right?'

His wife stood, shielding him. I started towards them but she glanced through at us and waved me back.

'He's OK,' she called. 'Too many cigarettes.'

Claire had returned to her spot on the floor, and was sifting through a box of nails for the one she wanted. 'What's happening?' she asked.

Now Artan turned and waved a smile at me. Maybe he was fine.

'Nothing,' I said. 'I'll leave you to it.'

'Stay if you like,' she said. 'You any good with a power drill?'

Of course I wasn't.

That night I sent the email to the residents' group, telling them of Trevor's plan to install security cameras. Instead of being explicit about what had happened, I used the phrase 'suspicious activity'. The euphemism would haunt me for days: every time I went to the loo I would think, 'Here goes another suspicious activity.'

Eventually an email came back, direct to Trevor, signed by everyone in the group.

We disagree with installing surveillance technology. We believe it will adversely affect the neighbourly atmosphere in the building.

He was reading it out to me when his phone rang.

'It's Guy. Hang on.'

I stopped chopping parsley and watched his face, holding the green-smeared knife in the air. Maybe this was about the hotel. John was definitely investing but so far hadn't persuaded any of his Singapore friends. Apart from his contribution, Trevor had been unable to raise further finance. If the council were to at last lift the abatement—

'Good news?' I asked.

He shook his head tersely and took the phone into his study.

After a few minutes I turned the heat off under the pasta sauce. I poured a glass of wine, and waited, and thought again that the room looked naked and cold without the rug, which was still at the cleaners. I didn't like bare surfaces. When I'd drunk the whole glass and Trevor still hadn't returned, I went to find him.

The home office was an interior room that he kept dimly lit with a desk lamp from the Therese Thorne retro range, in a dark forest green. I had chosen the desk, and the sisal matting on the floor, and the black shelving that housed his file boxes. It all fitted my fantasy of what a man's study should be.

He was at the desk, looking at the architect's scale model of the hotel. Four little plastic humans stood in the atrium, tiny under its cathedral height, and one cardboard nīkau palm evoked the trees.

'Do you want dinner?'

Another headshake.

'What did Guy want?'

With dread, I thought perhaps the council had come to a decision against him. The hotel would never be built.

'He's just had word, and it's been confirmed... They don't like to let you know these things, but... Anyway, he's found out.'

'What?' I never saw Trevor lost for words. I didn't like it.

'There's another investigation. An historic one. He thinks.'

'What, have the council got nothing better to do—' I was swelling with outrage on his behalf when he said,

'Not the council. The fraud office. The SFO.'

Coldness swept me, as if the balcony doors were wide open, and the wind had moved all the way in. 'Why?'

'I don't know. I really don't know. They won't say what it's about before they're ready to lay charges. Oh, Christ. I can't believe I'm even saying that.'

He looked stricken. I couldn't stand to see it. The Serious Fraud Office? This was a witch hunt. Someone was out to take him down.

'Therese—' He gave a horrible moan.

This time it was me who said, 'Stop it, Trevor. There will be no charges. It's nothing. They'll find nothing because there is nothing. We just have to forget about it and live our lives.'

He focused on me then, and said, 'I'm sorry all this shit is happening.'

'Oh my god,' I said. 'You've got nothing to be sorry for.'

7

A terse little media statement appeared the next day: *The SFO can confirm that an investigation relating to Trevor Thorne Developers is ongoing.* We still did not know what they were looking for. I didn't want to think about it. Denise called, in brand manager damage control mode. I told her I'd have to talk later.

'Come and sit down.' I moved the pile of decorating magazines off the plum-coloured sofa and drew Trevor beside me, nestling into his side. 'Horrible things happen all the time,' I said. 'We just haven't had many of them happen to us.'

I could feel his heartbeat. He had never had a heart scare, never had cancer, never had a stroke. In the last few years such things had stopped being freak events in our friend group. We'd been very lucky.

'It will be all right,' I said. 'You're in a high exposure profession, you always have been. But I believe in you. You've got your integrity. Nothing can change that.'

'It pisses me off,' he said. 'It's such a waste of time.'

'Don't let yourself be dragged down by it. Let them do their job, whatever hoops they need to jump through, and we'll just keep putting one foot in front of the other. A year from now we will be in Sydney and this will just be that annoying thing that happened that time.'

He gave a small laugh and kissed the top of my head. 'What would I do without you, Therese.'

There was such comfort there at his side, feeling his soft shirt against my cheek, breathing in his clean, woody aftershave. The

thing I spent more time worrying about – even with his ongoing good health – was what I would do without him.

In the evening we dressed for Claire's party, and locked our door
behind us, drawn towards the music that was already playing at a
volume we could hear. I wasn't sure how we would be received
by her friends, or anyone else from the building who might
be there, but tried to jolly Trevor along, and in doing so, calm
myself. 'Come on,' I said, 'let's go and affect the neighbourly
atmosphere.'

The white noise of nerves rang in my ears, but worse than
that was following Trevor down the stairs, and seeing him hold
the banister for balance, and place both feet on each step before
moving on to the next one.

Claire greeted us at her door, a sparkling, high-heeled vision,
sheathed in a sequined dress. She hugged me. The smell of floral
perfume knocked me sideways – as if she'd upended a bottle all
over herself – and behind it, the whiff of fresh paint.

'I'm so glad you came.'

I supposed it was an allusion to the fraud office news.

'It's nothing,' I said, 'a wild goose chase,' and Claire nodded
and steered us towards her kitchen bench, where the drinks
were laid out.

A bunch of unfamiliar women milled around and for a
second I feared Trevor would be the only man here. Women, en
masse, made me uneasy. I didn't like the whole thing of 'being'
a woman any more than I liked being blonde, or average height.
I didn't like the special pleading, I didn't like the words 'gender'
or 'patriarchy' or talk of the female brain. It all just seemed like
someone else's doing.

Then the group moved as one to study the bookshelves at
one end of the room and I saw, behind where they had stood,
the completed platform – the thing Claire had been building
yesterday. Or would you call it a stage?

It was about six inches high and took up a quarter of the floor
space, projecting into the room from a wide end that abutted

the exposed brick wall. The way the light caught its slick black surface – the source of the paint smell – made it look like a hovering pool, oily and deep. It was set with trestle tables in a horseshoe formation, as for a wedding.

'What do you think,' I said to Trevor as he pressed a wineglass into my hand.

'Very witchy,' he said.

Was it?

It was hard to take your eyes off Claire, whose clothes had the air of a costume. Her lashes were thick and dark, her cheeks a clownish pink. A sociable smile shone from her face, and was convincing if you were on the side of her friendly eye.

I approached to ask what she needed help with, but the door opened again and she threw her arms around the new guest with a delighted, 'Hello you!' It was Flat Tax. I saw him clock Trevor, and paste a smile to his face before he crossed the room towards us. I couldn't bear to stay for the heartiness.

On the balcony, I joined Fern, a young woman who ran an art gallery across the road. She was in the middle of a monologue, addressing Claire's houseguests, whose names I blanked on.

'You know what that stage reminds me of? This exhibition I saw in Shanghai, in a massive gallery upstairs in a building that used to be a bank. There was a raised platform in the middle of the room – just like that – and the artist had replicated a playground on it. Climbing frame, slides, a seesaw – and kids clambered all over it, the children of these super wealthy collectors just playing while they drifted around looking at the rest of the art. Video work, very Nauman-esque.'

She registered my arrival and glanced past me into the room. Yes, Trevor was here too. It was clear from her face that she thought we shouldn't have come.

'So then my interpreter,' Fern went on, 'explained that this room, the gallery, used to be a location where they held show trials. And the platform was like, maybe an original part of it?'

'Do you think that's what's going to happen here?' I asked, nodding towards the stage.

'It would be funny, wouldn't it,' she said. 'Have you ever been to court?' Her eyes ticked with pleasure at her own daring.

'No,' I said. 'Have you?'

She shrugged. 'I've never committed a crime.'

'I suppose the people being tried in that room in Shanghai hadn't either.'

She ignored this. 'Did you have show trials in Albania, Artan?' she asked.

'Yes,' he said, 'of course.'

'Really,' she said. 'How awful.'

He exchanged a glance with his wife – Amina, that was her name – and Fern tilted her chin up as she brought her vape pen to her lips.

Across the room, Trevor was talking to Haimona. He shook his head emphatically and I could see that his nerves had metabolised into bullishness. Now his finger came out, the pointing finger, and Haimona clocked it too and took a step back. While Fern was mid-sentence, I excused myself.

'So sorry, I've just got to—'

I stopped by them as if casually on my way to the bathroom. As soon as I put my hand on Trevor's forearm I regretted it: he would feel patronised, and Haimona would easily decode the gesture.

In the peace of Claire's bathroom I exhaled. Everything about me felt put-on, fake. I bared my teeth at myself in the mirror and growled, then sat on the edge of the bath, wanting to climb into it and pull the shower curtain around me for the rest of the evening.

The bathroom rubbish bin caught my eye – it was full of cosmetics. Eyeshadow palettes, bottles of foundation, hair detangler, shimmering body oils. Some of them were barely used. I pulled out a compact, still laden with pressed pink powder designed to simulate happiness and health. The sticker on the back hadn't yet worn off, and out of habit I looked to see the name of the hue. When I first started my own line of homewares, I'd enjoyed naming the products myself, but that job had soon passed on to someone else. The blusher was called *rapture*. I put it in my pocket.

Claire called us to the tables and I found myself sitting next to Haimona.

'Are you OK?' he asked. 'I saw the paper.'

'Oh yeah,' I said. He knew where I was from. I didn't want him to think I had come all this way just to have it fucked up at this stage of life. 'It's nothing. We'll be fine. Thanks.'

He was still watching me with his thoughtful gaze, and I kept the cheery smile on my face as I raised my glass to him. 'How are you?' I asked.

'Waiting on a report from the new Climate Change Adaptation Technical Working Group. You know.'

'Right. What sort of thing will they say?'

'Hopefully something more than, we're all fucked.'

We sat in a brief silence, then he nodded towards the fake stone lions and said to me, 'What do you make of those? Reckon you could sell a few?'

'The lions? To be honest, not my style.'

'Strictly speaking they're lionesses.'

'Strictly,' I said. 'You mean it's correct to call them lionesses, according to...'

'The language.'

'Meaning that's what they really are. Something other than a lion. Almost a lion, but with an "ess" on the end. Does that make them more than a lion?'

'It's to differentiate them,' he said, standing to refill the water jug in the kitchen.

I watched him go. I knew words were his business but there were some absurdities, surely, we didn't have to live with.

I hadn't slept the night before, looping with the worry that someone might hack my customer database and send a mass email that outlined Trevor's sins, whatever they would turn out to be, even though he hadn't committed any, or had he, or hadn't he, or had he. Though I passed the olive oil and drank the wine and laughed and nodded I was half space dust already, as though the worst had happened but no one had yet pointed it out. It was like the impossibility of relaxing in nature anymore, of, say, looking at a full blue river without simultaneously seeing it polluted and gone, fish agape in the mud. The charred future inside every tree.

Leisha's voice cut across my thoughts. She was talking loudly to get Trevor's attention, and her voice was rich with drink. 'Hey Trevor,' she was saying, 'hey, what's with this idea of a security camera in the foyer?'

On his way back to his seat, Haimona put a hand on her arm and she brushed it off. Trevor had heard, and he zeroed in on her with his fuck-you smile.

'Security.'

'I don't want to live in a paranoid dystopia,' she said, 'and I don't want my kids to grow up in one either.'

Trevor laughed. 'It's for everyone's protection.'

'From what?'

Around them, the talk died away. The instinct to intervene charged through me but I was frozen. I stared at Haimona and he looked calmly back.

'I don't need your protection,' Leisha said. 'And if you put cameras in, I'll take them out myself.'

Someone said, 'Whoa, mama.'

'Then I'll take you to court,' Trevor said.

I could feel the floor of the stage stretch and part beneath me as if it were made of bubble gum.

'Will you.' Leisha leaned back in her chair. 'I saw you in the paper,' she said.

'Yes?'

I said, 'Leisha.'

I wanted to say more, but was struck mute. My face was burning.

'What about this building, seeing as it's one of yours?' The sweep of her hand clipped a wine bottle, which teetered until someone grabbed it. 'Are we going to be caught up in an enquiry here too?'

'What's she talking about?' the older woman next to me asked. 'Who's that poor man?'

Trevor looked down the table towards Haimona and with a big grin on his face said, 'Hey mate. Control your wife?'

'Trevor,' I said, laughing, why was I laughing, why would my face not move beyond this fatuous *oh you* headshake, 'come on.'

I couldn't even look around the table at the reactions but now, thank god, Claire was on her feet, tapping her glass with a knife handle.

'OK,' she said, utterly calm, studying the guests with her assessing eye. 'That's enough of that. There's something I want to say.'

Claire was speaking, but the only thing I could hear was the rushing in my head. Around the table, everyone's gaze was on her and I used that cover to check their faces. Aside from the red blotch slowly subsiding on Leisha's neck, there was no sign of a reaction to Trevor. In fact, they had all quickly cast him aside. And it dawned on me that no one here gave a fuck about him. He wasn't a power broker in this room – not even a villain. He was an irrelevant old man. A gnat. The idea was breathtaking. My hot shame cooled to such a desiccated state that I was nothing but a pulse with eyes. All I could say to myself was, *Duh*. I thumped with this new knowledge through the rest of Claire's speech, my ear at last tuning in when her sister – Melissa, we'd been introduced earlier – heckled with,

'Are you finally fucking off to Auckland?'

General laughter.

'No,' said Claire. 'I shouldn't make a big public spectacle of this. I should just quietly do it. But you know, if you've got a stage in your apartment,' at which people laughed again.

'No audience participation,' Haimona said. 'Please.'

'Too late,' Claire said. 'And anyway, I wanted to do this,' she gestured down her body at the tight sequined dress, waved a hand over her painted face, her hair, the table, the flowers and candles, 'one last time.'

A silence shook the room and she said, 'I'm not dying!' She wanted us to know that she wasn't ill, or getting divorced or moving town or going mad.

'The short version is, this is a goodbye to an old self. This self,' gesturing again. 'I'm just me,' she said. 'But I'm not that me anymore.'

What did she mean – was she transitioning? Changing her name? What was this?

'Sheesh,' said Haimona in a low voice. 'Are we in some kind of online stunt?'

He stared resolutely at his plate, as if embarrassed. He seemed suddenly young. Male. Incurious. I felt my gaze move slowly, as if weighted, from his fingers around the base of his water glass, to the end of the table where Claire stood. I met Claire's gaze, and she held mine. She might have been speaking only to me.

'I've been distracted by bullshit all my life.'

'Hey,' said her sister. 'That's no way to talk about our family.'

Everyone else laughed loudly.

'I've done terrible things,' Claire continued. 'Stupid, thoughtless things.'

Now she looked at two women I'd met as we sat down, her former colleagues from her fundraising job. 'I'm sorry. It's been so easy to believe one thing and do another. It's the story of my life.' I wondered what she was apologising for.

Trevor and I momentarily locked eyes. He winked at me, but I couldn't wink back. I felt as though I had one foot on a pier and the other on a bobbing boat.

Claire pulled at the bracelet around her wrist, and rallied.

'Every culture has stories about changing seasons,' she said, 'and the one for – I don't know how to pronounce it—' she looked at Artan and Amina.

'Dita e Verës,' Amina said.

'—originates with a hunter coming out of her cave.'

A woman near me coughed. 'Cultural appropriation, anyone?' she said in a low voice. 'Remind me not to throw a dinner party for my mid-life crisis.'

'You're too young to have a mid-life crisis,' I said, and shifted my weight away from her.

'Clearly I'm not a hunter,' Claire said, laughing. 'And obviously this isn't my myth, or my culture. I don't even know if I'm going out of a cave or into one.'

Part of me was with the disapproving dinner guest. Part of me could see the cave, smell its stony air.

With an effort I pulled my gaze from Claire and glanced around the table. The tutting woman had resumed eating, concentrating on the movement of her knife and fork. One of Claire's former workmates had gone bright red, her chin tucked into her neck, and the other was tapping at her phone as though noting it all in a text. Perhaps this was the sort of thing that got videoed these days – people embarrassing themselves in their own homes.

Claire ignored them. I wondered if she had reached that magical state, the ultimate consolation prize for ageing: not giving a fuck. She exuded a kind of clarity, as though the air around her showed things in higher definition. I realised the makeup, dress and pointed shoes were no more excessive than any woman here was wearing, myself included. It only looked like a costume on her because she wasn't acting any more.

'I'll try again,' she said, still standing, still smiling. 'Do any of you remember the story of Atalanta?'

A sharp yell came from another room and suddenly Haimona and Leisha were rising from the table, trying to untangle themselves from the bench and other people's legs, and their daughter ran in from the hallway, gulping with panic, finally getting out the words that her brother had eaten some bad medicine and he was going to die.

Later, it would strike me that Claire said 'do you remember' and not 'do you know' or 'have you heard of'. 'Remember', as if the story of Atalanta and the golden apples was something that had happened to us. And even as I asked myself, who do you mean by us, I knew that I meant women. I had read a version of the myth. I could suddenly smell the library carpet at my school, feel the comfort of the hours spent there with another kid (Donna, tall, blonde, with scabby knees; my dearest friend). See the illustrations of Cronos eating his children, the thrusting hooves of Poseidon's horses, Hephaestus's crooked back and Atalanta transformed into a lion.

I would have been around the same age then as Haimona's daughter was now. He comforted her on the sofa while Leisha squatted in front of their son, trying to hold his mouth open. The deadly pills had turned out to be contraceptives from a sheet the kids had found in the room where they'd been meant to sleep – Alex's old room, where Amina and Artan were staying. Half the sheet was gone but no one could ascertain how many the boy had eaten.

Fern had her phone out. 'On this parenting site they say go straight to A&E.'

'Poisons.com says there aren't any negative effects,' said someone else.

Leisha batted the air with her hand, fingers glistening with her child's saliva. 'Don't tell me what the internet says.'

'That's what it's for,' said Haimona. 'Leish. He's fine.'

'Look up boys and oestrogen,' someone suggested.

The boy's tears abated, and Leisha plonked him next to Haimona while she went to gather the kids' stuff from the bedroom.

'No hang on, they say go to A&E but everyone who's gone – wow, a lot of kids eat contraceptive pills – everyone who's gone says they were told to go home and wait and nothing happened.'

'Girls can have some vaginal bleeding.'

'What about boys? He's a boy!'

The voices held an edge of panic, as if there were something poisonous in the makeup of the pill itself, its hormonal combo. While they were fussing, Trevor scanned the bookshelves. The stage was empty of people. Claire scraped plates in the kitchen and it was like her little speech never happened. What about Atalanta? I wanted to know. What did she mean? Why were these people saying 'How many did he take?' and, 'Dogs get sick. If they eat the foil packet,' and 'Whose pills were they?'

'Shall we make an exit?' Trevor closed the book.

Together we said goodbye to Claire.

'Sorry to leave you with the dishes,' I said, which was a tiny lie, I know, but a lie that felt huge in my mouth after what Claire had been saying, about not pretending any more. Vaguely I wondered how many lies I had told that day. The phrase *including to yourself* sounded in my brain and I said, 'Shut up.'

Trevor looked at me. 'What?'

'Nothing.'

Claire leaned her back against the sink, giving me the full force of her doubled stare. 'Come and hang out,' she said, 'any time.'

Perhaps it was the running water but I could smell the cave again. I felt myself heating up. 'Yes,' I said.

Trevor was Skyping with Annabel in Singapore when I went to bed, her blonde hair shining through the screen.

I lay awake, my veins fizzing. I had seen Trevor's irrelevance. I had seen Claire's sharp outline. Our bed suddenly felt cloying and I threw off the sheets and paced around before falling asleep in the bedroom armchair, waking in the early morning with my shoulder on fire.

In the living room, Trevor was passed out on the plum-coloured sofa, the reading lamp beside him still on, the laptop open on the floor beside him. I tapped the keyboard and his screensaver image appeared, the same one as mine: the two of us outside our ivy-covered hotel in Brantôme, where we'd stopped on a walking tour by the river Dronne. The light was French and peachy. We wore straw sunhats borrowed from the hotel, and our glasses of champagne sparkled gold. How did I get there? Out of frame, a string quartet had been setting up to the left of us on the terrace. We were celebrating fifteen years of marriage, and were elated, as though we had completed an obstacle course and were breaching the finish line tape, arms aloft.

Although it was an easy walking tour, a couple of days later, in a forest near Villars, I'd slipped off the trail and broken my ankle. The pain had been bad but I couldn't remember it now – the rest of the trip was a blur, an ambulance to a hospital in Limoges, an operation involving a pin in my leg and a cast and a fortnight's wait before I was allowed to be driven to Orly and fly back to New Zealand because I'd had a seizure in the ambulance, possibly because of the potent French pain drugs they'd given me; Trevor, who hadn't left my side, organised a wheelchair at the airport and paid for an upgrade to first class. That was just before the global financial crisis hit.

In the screensaver image, we oozed what I had thought of as wellbeing, and now saw was wealth.

I thought, as Trevor snuffled in his sleep, we would experience such things again. We would wash away this time with a pilgrimage in Spain, or a music tour of the Balkans, or Hawaiian golf. People – his kind of people – liked Trevor. He had charm and warmth, he walked into a room with the expectation of finding pleasure there and god knows the world needed that, this positive life force, his cracking smile. But as I typed in his password and brought up his emails, automatically turning the volume to mute, and as I cast my eyes over the new messages and saw that nothing had changed, still no contact from former friends and colleagues, I thought that if the fraud investigation led to charges and Trevor was convicted, people would be unable to come back to us. Like friends who promise to be there through chemotherapy then panic-screen your phone calls. Even if he were cleared, they would be reluctant to accept Trevor as before, because what happened to him had shown them something about themselves.

The room's objects took shape softly in the very early morning. While the kettle boiled for tea I rested my head on the kitchen bench. That had started happening – levering myself up out of chairs with a hand to my thighs, holding on to bannisters, leaning on walls. Leaning! I had to put a stop to it. My thoughts were loose and circular and I couldn't get a grip on them. Trevor flew himself like a kite on a brisk sunny day and the wind was dropping away. The kettle clicked and in its wake I thought I could hear the sounds of Claire moving around downstairs.

My body took me to the bedroom, where I pulled on a sundress. Now I was in the hallway, tea in hand, and opening the apartment door. The stairwell light came on automatically as I walked down, still holding my hot tea.

Claire was squatting with a brush and shovel in her hand and stood as I gained full sight of her. I had the sense of a person unfolding from the ground beyond normal height – for a second she seemed terrifyingly tall. Then my perspective shifted back to normal, and it was just Claire, in her pyjamas. She stepped back, leaving a space through the open door.

8

'Artan and Amina are still asleep,' she said.

Her balcony doors were open, the lions guarding the muzzy air. The trestle tables had been broken down and stacked against a wall. The stage was empty.

She already had music playing, and as she crossed to the stereo she said, 'You get it, eh.'

'Get it?'

'What I was talking about last night.'

I wasn't sure. I said, 'Maybe?'

'Just say yes!' She turned up the music to blast level – I recognised the first bars of a stadium rock anthem from our youth, a slow-burn build to a banging chorus that was imprinted in my body's memory – and shouted over it. 'Say yes, Therese!'

'What about—' I gestured down the hall to where her visitors were sleeping.

'Don't worry about it. They're young.'

She stepped onto the platform and, as if she didn't care whether I was there or not, began to dance – casually, but meaning it. 'Come on!'

What the fuck? I thought, as my body slowly followed hers and started moving in time to the song. Of course I was self-conscious, but it would have been harder to resist moving, like being the weirdo at the sauna for keeping your clothes on. Soon enough my body fit inside the cheesy song and dancing to it was effortless. God, it was a relief to just move – I could feel the thoughts melting off me. I left behind the SFO and the hotel and the

Sydney efforts and the break-in and for the first time in forever, just moved. Claire caught my eye and we laughed.

The chorus hit right as sun struck the red glass on a high shelf, filling the room with orange light – its gorgeousness pulsed inside my skull and ebbed away. I was narrating my sensations in order to hold onto them and the feeling ran away from my grasp and the song sped up and I moved faster to get back to that pure blade of the moment, surfing forward on the crest of now into the place where nothing has happened yet – where we don't exist – a silver fishtail that flickered away from me and I plowed on, lumpily, trying too hard, till at last I felt so tired and uncoordinated that I let go all over again and was aware only of a floating sensation like a great weight had gone.

The full album played, it didn't matter if the songs were terrible or good, then the algorithm kept playing more of the same – that nineties mix of swooping vocals and driving orchestrations. My legs ached, I was breathless. Claire was lost inside it too. Our movements formed blurred arcs in the air like the afterimage from a long exposure photograph. 'Stage' was the wrong word for what held us, I realised – it was more like a zone. That word filled me now along with the music and the only other room was for the words *why not*.

By the time we stopped there were people in the street on their way to open up shops, and my sundress clung to my back with sweat. I lay on the platform, wiped out, but aware that although my body had changed so much since I was twenty, although my muscles were softer and I now wore an HRT patch as if I were a piece of labelled fruit, it was still me. Claire changed from her pyjamas into shorts and a T-shirt, and made some kind of herbal tea; it was delicious, liquorice-sweet. The sound of talking and laughter came from the visitors down the hall.

The family photos up on her fridge told of a normal domestic life – holidays and school graduation.

'Do you miss your daughter?' Speaking felt strange; so did the concept of daughter, and I felt a little panic at the ease with which familiar things might uncouple from their meaning.

Claire's voice was grounded though, as if she belonged to everything.

'Yeah,' she said. 'We talk on the phone all the time. Mick's there to keep an eye on things.' She told me how easily he had stepped into being the lead parent. 'All I had to do was get out of the way.'

I wondered – my usual way of thinking trickling back – whether things could be that simple, and if so, why weren't mothers getting out of the way in their thousands, why wasn't Caroline, or Annabel? But I didn't have kids, so what did I know.

Now Amina and Artan could be heard moving about – the day was starting in earnest. Phrases like, 'well that was fun' and 'lovely to see you' formed but I killed them in my throat. Before I returned upstairs to Trevor, I asked Claire if I could use the bathroom. I wanted to see whether all those cosmetics were in her rubbish bin or if that had been a drunken invention on my part. They were there. And another thing – her bathroom mirror was now covered over with a towel. Without being able to see myself, I felt somehow more private, as if no one were checking up on me. In her hallway an empty picture hook and rectangle of unfaded paint marked the spot where another mirror had hung.

Some women retrain, or take up volunteering, or fall in love with their best friend, or finally make partner or are squeezed out of the research lab they founded or become yoga instructors or raise surprise grandchildren or learn another language or dive into genealogy or run for local office or quit booze or drink too much or make other people's problems their business or give up altogether on other people's problems or cry themselves to sleep or can't sleep or divorce or remortgage or develop a cackle or get shingles or go into real estate or animal shelters or floristry or online activism or have to look for a new place when the landlord raises the rent, or get fired or roboted out of a job or have menopausal psychosis or family addiction crises or parents with dementia or home subsidence or violent kids or terminal illness. Claire threw out her makeup, plonk plonk in the bin. She sent her jewellery to her daughter in a padded envelope – *not even registered!* Alex told me later, when she was talking to me again – she stuffed all her clothes but her catering uniform, jeans and T-shirts, which she would also eventually ditch in favour of an old tracksuit, into recycling bags and took them to the charity shop. She gave away the expensive anti-ageing face creams and serums and hair masks and sprays, hundreds or even thousands of dollars' worth of what she now called chemical warfare.

'But doesn't your skin get dry?' I would want to know.

'This is what I'm talking about,' Claire would say. 'Dig yourself out!'

9

A week later, Judith rang Trevor. He put her on speaker, telling me, 'She wants to talk to you as well.' I was applying lipstick in the hall mirror, about to leave for work.

'How are you?' Judith said.

'Getting by,' he said. 'It's a pain in the ass but it'll blow over soon.'

'Will it?' she asked with the sort of low-key incredulity women reserve for their exes.

'Guy says they're pissing in the wind.'

'And how are you?'

It took a second to realise she was speaking to me.

'Yeah fine,' I said. 'All good.'

'It must be stressful.'

Trevor would want me to say *not really*, but I didn't want to lie and earn Judith's disrespect. 'Of course,' I said. 'It's taken over everything.'

'I can imagine.' Her voice betrayed a smile.

Trevor had once introduced me to a tall, sandy-haired woman in a chemist shop and we'd made small talk about the film festival and when she was called to get her prescription, he said, 'That's who Judith left me for.'

'Well,' Judith said now, 'I want you both to come over tonight.'

The invitation, on which she insisted, was to a fundraiser at her house, a three-storey colonial villa, on her steep street that looked over the Botanic Gardens and brutalist university buildings and the central city towards the curving promenade lining the harbour. She was spending her social capital on Trevor, and he was grateful. As usual, everyone arrived breathless from the steps up to the house, and the generous entranceway filled with soft exclamations and laughter at the climb.

The main reception room was softly lit, but dazzled with flares from silver and glass and the white catering linen. I was drawn, as ever, to the double bay windows, through which you could see yellow and orange lights wiggling in the dark water, white pontoon globes strung in the exotic pines on the other side of town. The yellows were echoed by the fire that burned powerfully in the large open hearth, despite the season.

Above the mantelpiece a portrait, in peachy oils, of Judith as a younger woman, cast a serene gaze around the room. The picture captured her in her mid-thirties, when she was already a mother of four children, the wife of a hotshot young developer, *a mover and shaker*, as she would put it – and, unbeknownst to anyone else, about to blow up her marriage.

Perhaps now is the time to say something about Judith. This house was the one she and Trevor raised their children in. The one where she fell in love with her tennis partner. Her own family homes had been Heathcote, the villa in the Sounds; a neo-Gothic affair that still poked its turrets into the skies north of Rangiora; a pre-war Christchurch residence with a stately rose-filled garden; and, on her mother's side, the Wairarapa: a mansion built on a sheep station from local wood and stone and decorated with imported carpets, curtains, rugs and antiques.

All the properties but Heathcote had sunk back into the earth, too large, costly and hard to heat to keep up, or in the case of the Christchurch house, cracked down the middle by the 2011 earthquake, and subsequently bowled. In the other houses curtains and carpets had mouldered, slate and stone were repurposed for descendants' drywalls and kitchen floors and cellars, furniture was auctioned off at times of need or disseminated to great-grandchildren who didn't know in which century or country it was made. Napkin rings and fish knives went missing from silver sets, christening gowns sat in tissue, a family Bible turned up in a charity shop.

Judith, as the portrait artist had captured, carried herself with a reticence that suggested she didn't need to flash her money around. When she'd married Trevor there still existed society pages that would comment on their difference in background, a class distinction that was meaningless to the vast majority of people, who would simply see them both as rolling in it. Trevor liked cars and travel; Judith was a patron of the arts, literacy programmes, medical research. She was one of the people I had studied and tried to model myself on when it came to spending Trevor's money, but I couldn't shake the feeling that with the contributions to scholarship funds and marine sanctuaries and so on we were somehow trying to buy something, or clear a debt that could never be paid.

Judith was not troubled by silliness like that. She got on with it. Here she was at her fundraiser drinks, introducing a leading paediatrician who made a short speech about a new hospital wing and the necessity for private philanthropy. A student string quartet started playing background stuff and the volume of talk rose.

I drank the wine and nodded at people – hello Flat Tax! – and in my peripheral vision noted Trevor shaking hands. Food began to circulate and through the crowd of familiar faces, carrying a tray laden with caviar-topped quail eggs, I saw Claire.

I felt an instant pulse of excitement, followed by a ripple of embarrassment. She looked across and saw me looking at her, and raised her chin in a wry greeting. She wore a white shirt and apron and a name tag like the other people staffing the party, but on her they could have been a sweatshirt and jeans. She looked natural, with none of the little signs of deferral that being in that role usually brought on.

We hadn't seen each other since the morning after her dinner party, the dancing on the stage – the *zone* – which now seemed like a dream. I had begun to wonder whether it had really happened. My life was orderly. I didn't do things like that.

The paediatrician was next to me talking to a social reporter and I positioned my body to look tuned in, nodding and making the positive affirmation sounds on autopilot as I tracked Claire doing her rounds. What did this gathering look like, I wondered, from her side of the tray? I had done this work, handing out samples in shopping malls and taking customer complaints behind a hotel desk and serving at office Christmas functions, back in the days when we shook packs of cigarettes out into a bowl on the centre of the table. I would never forget, decades ago now, the first event Trevor took me to – a party for art gallery patrons – when I realised I'd gone from being the one with the name tag on, offering the tray, to being the one with a glass in her hand, reaching for a strange cheesy morsel.

Claire paused to offer food to Trevor's group and I watched him pop a quail's egg in his mouth and pluck a paper napkin from the side of the tray and nod at what another man was saying, wipe his mouth and scrumple the napkin and put it back on the tray. He didn't see Claire. She moved on.

I waited for her to reach us but another server, a young woman with a visible tattoo at her cuff, arrived first, and the paediatrician's perfunctory statements to the reporter dried up as he turned his focus onto her.

'You're too interesting to be working in a kitchen,' he actually said. 'What do you really do?'

She didn't bridle – that was the genius of interesting, I thought, as opposed to pretty – and told him she was an art student.

He read her name tag. 'Lucy,' he said. 'That's a very juicy name.'

The reporter raised an eyebrow at me, then leaned in.

'Therese Thorne?'

'Yes.'

'Is Trevor here?'

Before I could say anything, he looked around the room and spied him. 'Excuse me.' He patted my arm in apology and moved towards my husband.

The paediatrician watched the waitress's mouth as she spoke about developing her final folio for an exhibition. She named a television franchise about the lives of wealthy people.

'My piece is a supercut of the people who work for them, like gardeners and drivers and stuff. A lot of the time you only get shown their legs, but sometimes they get cameos. It's like, a film about money with all the rich people cut out of it.'

The girl continued, not so much to describe her work as to explain what it meant, using the leaden art school speak I was familiar with from conversations with Caroline.

The paediatrician took the tray from her hands and put it on a nearby table, and she laughed and said, 'I'd better keep working,' and he cocked his head to one side like a sad puppy. Picking up the tray again, the waitress flicked her eyes at me. I don't know what she wanted to see.

'Come back,' the paediatrician said, and watched the girl move away, a rectangle of blue light flashing through her apron pocket as her phone registered a message. Her benign facial expression didn't flicker, her body a neutral machine.

He turned his gaze back to me, gave a cursory smile, and walked off. For god's sake, Therese, why were you still standing there? I looked around for Claire but couldn't see her, and went to poke my head in the door of the kitchen. A caterer opened the wall oven door to remove a tray of gougères. A fleck of gold foil from an emptied sashimi platter lifted in the draft of heat, catching and turning under the halogen strip above the bench. I was light-headed from the wine.

'Can I help you?' the caterer asked, and I said, 'Is Claire around?'

'I'm here.'

She was behind me, and squeezed past to deposit a clutch of empty wine bottles by the outside door.

'Hi,' I said, feeling an urge to help out, but reluctant to enter the working domain of the kitchen for fear of getting in the way. 'How's your night going?'

'How's yours?'

'Fine,' I said. 'It's a good cause.'

'Yeah,' she said, 'agreed.' She began to arrange the gougères on a clean serving plate.

'So is this – what you do? Catering?'

She nodded. 'For now.'

'I'll leave you to it.'

She glanced at the caterer, who had her back to us, and said, 'I'll find you.'

I nodded with a kind of relief at this dismissal, and turned to leave.

'Therese,' she said, and I turned back and she threw a pastry at me, a silly small missile flying across the room. I caught it on instinct and put it in my mouth and laughed at her with my mouth full. Suddenly elated, I went to stand by the ridiculous summertime fire, brushing crumbs from my dress.

Outside, the wind picked up, and the candles near the bay windows leaned their flames into the room. The social reporter took a photograph of Judith and another donor, the paediatrician in the middle with his arm around them both, and the flash hit the varnish on the oil portrait of Judith, decades younger, behind them, for a second lighting up the ridges and whorls on the canvas, a strange figure seeming to emerge from the lines.

Just before the second photo was taken Judith took a firm step to her left, away from the paediatrician, and he quickly dropped his hand. I tried to tell from her face: had he groped her? Squeezed too hard? But her expression was unreadable.

I crossed to the windows to look again at Judith's magnificent view, and as I passed Flat Tax he said, 'You're very quiet tonight.'

'How are you?'

'I'm all right. But how are you? How's Trevor?'

'He's bearing up.'

'That sounds ominous,' he said, with a smile. 'Oh!' He had spotted Claire, and beckoned her over. She turned her warm eye to him.

'Hi,' she said. The silver tray she was holding projected spangles of light up over her throat. 'What brings you here?'

He was on the board of a charity that supported the hospital. As well as the new wing, they were fundraising for another MRI scanner.

'Don't you think,' Claire said, 'that if we had a high enough wealth tax in this country you wouldn't have to do all this fundraising?'

He laughed.

'I'm serious.'

'So,' he said, 'are you a friend of Judith's too?'

'No.' She smiled and raised her tray. 'I'd better keep going.'

I said, 'Stop for a sec.'

'People are hungry.'

'No they're not. They're full.'

'I can't stop till the tray's empty.'

I took another cheese puff. 'Delicious.'

'That's only one,' she said. 'There are eight left.'

I turned to Flat Tax. 'Help me.'

'You're on your own. I've got to go and shake some money out of people.'

'Claire used to be a fundraiser,' I said, partway through my third pastry. I knew I would regret eating them but it was worth it to make her laugh, and I could see she was trying not to.

'Any tips?'

'OK, first,' she said, 'identify the tribe to which your donor belongs. Everyone here will have a personal reason why they're interested in healthcare, beyond the altruistic.'

Flat Tax took a pastry.

'Thank you,' I said.

'Find out what they want. Show them what they're going to get. Connect their personal experience with the greater good. Ask them a minimum of three times, then when they've given you the money, thank them a minimum of three times.'

'It sounds simple.'

'What would be simple,' she said, 'is redistribution of wealth.'

'Oh, communism,' he said before he left us. 'That worked so well in the past. Farewell, comrades.'

'There you go.' I had finished the last pastry. My great achievement. 'Your tray is empty, and I feel sick.' I took it from Claire and put it on a side table. 'Now I want to show you something.'

'What?'

'You have to wait and see.'

I drew Claire with me through the living room's large double doors into the hall. The wide entranceway, which smelled headily of tuberose, Judith's signature scent, was empty apart from a fully laden coat rack. I climbed the stairs and checked to see Claire was following me. She hesitated at the bottom, one hand on the newel post.

'Come on.'

'Do you know this house?'

'Yes,' I said. 'It belongs to the first Mrs Thorne.'

'You like saying that,' she said.

Off the second storey hallway, a row of bedrooms and two bathrooms looked onto the hill, and on the left side further living areas had been arranged to make the most of the view.

'My god,' said Claire, peering in a doorway. 'The bedrooms have got their own fireplaces.'

'There's a whole other floor,' I said, beckoning her to the stairs that led up to it. 'This way.'

But as we neared the office by the end of the hall I recognised a raised voice – Trevor – and automatically looked in, Claire right behind me, mid-exclamation about the grandeur of the house. Trevor looked stilted with anger, and I felt like we were a couple of naughty schoolgirls stumbling into the headmaster's office. He was standing by the window, and on the chaise longue facing the night view, his back to the door, sat Heathcote.

'Hello.'

Heathcote turned, with the cat-like ease of someone who has just scored a point.

Trevor recovered quickly. 'Claire,' he said. 'I didn't know you were coming tonight as well. We could have shared a cab.'

'I'm with the caterers,' she said, glossing over the way he'd ignored her downstairs.

'Well,' Trevor said, as if covering what must be an embarrassing situation for her. 'It's a small world.'

Heathcote said, 'Is there anything left? I wonder if you could bring us a plate. Dad's had to escape from a pesky hack.'

Claire ignored him and went to the window to give her attention to the harbour – a sense of the hugeness of the night rode into the room.

'God knows what the man expects me to say,' Trevor said. 'I don't know why the SFO are so interested in me. The sad fact is there are some bad egg developers and we all get tarred with the same brush.'

'Hello Heathcote.' I hadn't seen him since the Sounds. The only mention Trevor had made of his children lately was to report they were all freaking out about the investigation. His son-in-law John, I knew, was especially worried about the money he had put into the hotel. 'What are you two talking about?'

There was a slight pause, and Trevor gathered his expression into a relaxed smile and said, 'Nothing,' at the same time as Heathcote said, 'Real estate.'

'Are you staying here?'

'Yeah, my place is rented out at the moment.'

Claire turned from the window. 'Do you know anything,' she asked Heathcote, 'about why my apartment was listed on a holiday let website?'

'No,' he said. 'Not by you?'

'Yeah, they had photos and the address and everything. But the money went to an offshore account.'

'Some kind of social media scam? You should be careful what you post.'

'I don't post anything.'

'Ooh,' he said. 'A purist.'

She turned back to the window – I could see her expression reflected in it: fuck you.

'I'd better brave it again.' Trevor stood. 'Come on Heath. Time to do our bit.'

Heathcote said, 'I think Mum's the one doing her bit for you.' He winked at me, which triggered a reflexive smile I immediately regretted.

'Are you coming down?' Trevor asked.

'In a minute,' I said. 'I want to show Claire the telescope.'

Heathcote paused in the doorway and said, 'I don't suppose there's any pinot noir left downstairs?'

'Go and have a look,' said Claire. Her voice had a lid on it.

We waited in silence for a few seconds until we could hear the hallway was empty. She was still looking out the window. There were things I wanted to say about Heathcote, about my family, but I didn't want to be disloyal.

An open door further down the hall led us up small wooden stairs to an attic room whose front wall was all glass, where Judith kept a fat white telescope trained on the planets and stars. This was what I wanted Claire to see.

I turned the light on, and the window reflected the telescope and two people already there – the paediatrician, and Lucy, the art student waitress.

He stood behind her in the classic position, as a PE teacher and snooker-playing boyfriends and even once a hairdresser with an erection had stood behind me, his front pressed into her back, knees either side of her legs, arms encircling her. The girl was stuck between him and the telescope. He was speaking words I couldn't hear into her hair.

I felt embarrassed, and didn't know what to do. My mind formed the words, *he's the guest of honour.*

'Lucy,' Claire said, her voice coming out with all the force she had suppressed before with Heathcote. They turned, but didn't move.

Then, more softly, Claire said, 'You're needed in the kitchen.'

The man didn't move away from the girl as Claire crossed the room towards them. She put a hand on his arm and gently extricated the girl, saying, 'Excuse me. And also, I wanted to talk to you about fundraising. For your exhibition. I've got some tips.'

The man turned to gather all the air in the room into himself and give a humungous sneeze. I marvelled that so much sound could be expelled with so little self-consciousness.

Lucy slid out from behind the telescope. 'Coming.' She looked Claire, then me, right in the eye. 'It's amazing,' she said. 'I'm glad I saw it.' Her gaze said she didn't want our help. We worried over nothing. We were weak.

Too bad, Claire's expression said. You don't have to be grateful.

Our eyes – the eyes of older women – tracked her as she left the room. I felt a pang for the girl's animal youth, her certainty, the freedom of what she didn't know.

We caught each other's gaze again and both grinned, shaking our heads.

The paediatrician asked, 'Do you want to see Jupiter?'

'No,' Claire said, turning back to him. 'Wait. Yes. I do.'

He made space for her and held out an arm to invite her to the telescope.

'Turn the light out,' he said to me.

Across the dim room I watched him looking as she bent her knees and pressed her hands to her thighs. It was childish, but I wanted to be the one showing her.

'Therese,' she said, 'come and see this.'

The paediatrician made way and I bent down to the eyepiece. It took a few seconds to get my bearings and then there was the planet – dizzyingly visible. I could see the red spot.

'Nearly 600 million kilometers away,' the paediatrician told us, 'about as close as we can get.'

'Imagine if it was called Juno,' Claire said to the paediatrician. 'Or Mother.'

'Huh,' he said. 'Creepy.'

I laughed, and the planet wavered in and out of focus.

The three of us returned together to the living room, the man between Claire and me as we descended the stairs and crossed the foyer with its spiced rose smell. At the threshold of the reception room I reached for Claire's arm, to hold her back, and the man re-entered the crowd and made straight for the young waitress.

'Do you want to go for a drink next weekend?' I asked her. 'If you're free?'

I was nervous to ask. It was hard making new friends at our age, but I knew I wanted to be friends with her, for that comment about the planet's name alone – for the wild dancing, for the things she had said at her party, for knowing how to handle that paediatrician. I felt that she was ahead of me on a pathway – a path whose direction I didn't even know, that I'd barely stepped onto – and that if I could run to catch up with her, if we could move forward together, I'd be able to see something that was veiled to me now.

She regarded me, taking her time, and I felt my pulse hard in my throat.

'I'd like to,' she said. 'Yes.'

'Great.'

'We should—'

The next thing she said was lost to a loud crash from the far side of the living room. We spun round, together, to see that the oil painting of Judith had dropped from its hooks straight down, still upright, onto a chiffonier which housed burning candles. The impact sent uncleared champagne flutes and plates sliding forward to smash on the floor.

Claire ran straight towards the kitchen while I hovered on the edge of the room, watching with everyone else as the painting teetered in slow motion and finally face-planted onto the candles and abandoned dishes.

Judith said, 'Trevor!'

He and another man moved to lift the painting. Before they reached it a flame appeared through the canvas – so quick! – opening a hole as it burnt, peachy zigzags licking and rising. Judith snatched the glass of red wine the paediatrician was still holding and threw it at the invisible back of her own burning face. I realised I was clutching Flat Tax's wrist. Claire came out of the kitchen with the fire extinguisher and calmly covered everything in its spray.

Much later, when we were in the Martinborough house, where I was hiding out after everything had truly turned to shit, Claire told me about the rest of her night. By then, I understood that other people – her husband, her sister – knew her far better than I did, and I wondered why she confided in me about her transformation. Lots of women she knew had more experience of spiritual things, had been Facebook witches for years. I was a materialist. Fern would say, a bourgeois pig.

But though her family loved her, and though Fern could talk with authority about binding spells, or killing her ego (not entirely successfully, if you asked me), I was the one who sat at Claire's feet and listened as she told me what finally led to the change in her. Who asked questions, who made her slow down, who wanted to know. I was the one, when we were all deep inside the pounding rapture she had stirred up, whose cells dispersed – who disappeared, so that Claire entered me.

You know how we say we devoured a story, and also that we were consumed by it? Eating and being eaten. It was like that with Claire, for me.

10

The paint had burned in the most delicious colours, pinks and creams, and the burn hole left in the middle of the younger Judith's chest, if anything, enhanced the portrait. But it was the dot of planet that we had seen – Jupiter, or Mother, whatever you wanted to call it – that had plunged into Claire. She wanted to be out in the night underneath that sky.

Outside the house, she realised she was still wearing her white cotton apron. She untied it and bunched it into her bag, which she slung over both shoulders. The house was halfway up, or down, a steep street that led downwards to the Botanic Gardens and the shiny purple sea, and up to a pathway between houses that nestled against Te Ahumairangi and its swathe of the city's green belt. Her feet and legs ached. She made her way up, towards the path. A fresh surge of energy came over her and increased with every step she took away from the party.

The houses at the top of the street were dark, and she had a moment's pause before making her way along the cut-through, bordered with wooden fences on either side, into the trees. The lichen on the fence boards glowed orange and pale green in the streetlight, its short tendrils curling like fur caught in sun.

At first she used the torch function on her phone, but its light was weak and claustrophobic, and a few meters into the trees she turned it off and stashed it in her bag, pausing for her eyes to adjust. The moon cast pathways through the pine branches. Night sounds: rustling, things turning over, the milky one-two call of a ruru, birds that had been around in her childhood and were now again rising in number. She didn't have to go far for the occasional traffic noise to fall away. She supposed she should be scared, and waited to see if the feeling would come over her. Instead, she felt a kind of charge rising up from the ground, through her feet, up her legs and cunt and round her hips, into her stomach, up her back, her ribs, her lungs, her heart. The heart was thumping, but not from fear. As she walked on, a bank appeared up one side of the path, titiwai clustered beneath its overhang like another galaxy.

She had done women's studies papers at university. She had been at university when women's studies was something to do. She had sat next to the one guy in her tutorials and thought about kissing him either because he was funny and smart enough to do women's studies or out of a sort of desert island theory. The point being she knew it was binary and essentialist to associate women with nature. It was reductive to separate nature and culture and technology and to believe that the structures by which she lived were laws of the universe. Of course, yes, those things were inventions, but also they were real and this was the system that had made her and whose air she breathed and without which the great question was whether she could exist, so yes, she did feel freer here in the bush at night where she was meant to not go alone, where she was meant to stick to the path.

And of course they were all looking for something because it was tiring trying to change the material world, it was so slow, and she had to do something while she was waiting for old men to die.

There she was, that night, the great nameless planet in its place above, gravity holding her feet while some force from deep in the ground charged up and through her. She regarded the fact of her missing fear with mild interest, as though it were a piece of paper slid in front of her while she was on the phone. She had been more afraid walking on a country roadside in the middle of the afternoon, as a passing ute slowed down and the men in it stared. More afraid in a suburban fast food chain, when a man broke off from threatening his girlfriend to come swinging for her. Out of her depth in a choppy sea with Alex, aged four and unable to swim, pushing down on her shoulders. Those were physical fears, notable because she was lucky, because there had been so few of them in her life: of course there had been other kinds. But this, now, picking her way through the bush, the path knotted and uneven beneath her, felt so good because she was meant to be afraid and she was not.

The air was cool, but the hill and trees shielded her from the most cutting wind. Through the wholesome smell of dirt and rotting leaves, she occasionally got a sharp remnant from the party: smoked fish, pastry grease, charcoal from the hibachi grill that she'd crouched over on the patio, turning skewers. She put her hand out to touch tree bark, the dry curves of dead nīkau fronds, slippy kawakawa leaves. Time was uncountable but it didn't seem long before the lights of the city began to appear through a clearing and she turned back into the bush, unwilling to give it up yet. She kicked over bottles and cans of RTDs, heard people's voices, men more interested in each other than in her, and walked faster away from all that, trying to get lost.

From the daytime world she remembered a predator fence but as she looked for a place to sit, she did wonder about rats, she did feel a tightening of her skin, something close to fear. Once she was on her back amongst the leaf litter, looking up through scraggy branches at the night sky that was dulled by light pollution but still so available, she'd stopped worrying. Now, at last, she could give her full weight to the damp earth. Insects, worms, creatures – it was all okay. The chill rising through her from the ground felt hot somehow, the space between the branches was a pool to stare down into, her aching muscles were a pleasure.

Time slipped its noose. For a while, hours, minutes, she sat listening – scurrying, rustling, the distant burn of traffic, police or ambulance sirens of which there were always a surprising amount in this small city. Her ears attuned to smaller and smaller sounds. A few raindrops fell although there were barely any clouds. The soft splat of the waterdrops landing spread a circle of soundwaves to encompass her, to join her with everything else that was here. Sitting with her forehead to her knees she closed her eyes, and walked into the darkness to the sound of her breath.

The space was huge. It smelled of wet cave walls. Without looking up at it she felt the implacable force of the planet above her. Embers glittered along the edges. The soles of her feet tingled and she pressed them into the earth. The harmony of gravity held her safe while an incredible sweetness drew up from beneath the ground and through her, while her wrists tingled and her hands and head wanted to float away, disperse into molecules. The air was perfect, the ultimate sustenance, and she was breathing it and being breathed.

Her ecstasy lasted all night, through walking, taking paths towards electric lights, passing, stopping to stare at the details of the leaves held in their pulsating glow. Through holding her hands to a tree. Sitting on a wooden bench, the gravel path, in the long acidic-smelling grass. She jumped. Leapt. Ran. She felt ridiculous of course but only fleetingly, because it didn't matter, she was alive, who cared? Emotions visited her as if rising from that ground and taking their turns – she realised she'd been pushing back at grief, for god knows what, anything, nothing, and let it in and through her, feeling the muscles of her face distorted, her throat swelling with all her regrets. But there weren't even things, specifics, they didn't matter, it was a feeling of a new self coming through, finally, up from the earth and pouring like liquid fire through her body, burning everything it replaced to smoke.

When the morning light came, she felt as though she'd only been there for minutes, and also that she'd aged 200 years.

The houses below Te Ahumairangi rippled as she passed them, down the hill into the city. Willis Street was empty. Traffic lights changed colour for no reason. The smell of sea air blew in from the harbour. A street cleaning truck circled its brushes in the gutters and a man unloaded boxes full of frozen chicken to the fast food place on the corner by the bank. Claire walked down the middle of the road. When she reached the apartment building, she floated up the stairs and unlocked the door. Elsewhere in the building, other humans were dreaming. She stood beside the lions and felt bolts of joy shoot through her, her body moved without instruction as if in an act of worship to a nameless force, the disparate pieces of self that were scattered about the room, the building, the city, and her past returned to her and reconnected into a seamless whole.

11

I had been coming home every day in trepidation. I dreaded trying the front door handle to find it already open. Whenever I left the living room I closed and locked the balcony doors. I couldn't shake the image of a strong-limbed creature scaling the side of our building to enter and soil the rug. The afternoon after Judith's fundraiser I was in the bedroom changing, thinking I was alone in the apartment, when Trevor walked in and I screamed.

'That's it,' he said. 'We're getting security.'

Although he wouldn't admit it, Trevor had been convinced by Leisha that it would be an act of war to install CCTV cameras, so he rang the security company that was in charge of the hotel development and asked them to send one of their guys.

The man who turned up, Jesse, was strikingly good-looking, with dark blond hair and green eyes that could have been lined with makeup, his lashes were so thick and black. He sat on a stool in the building's foyer and sweltered in his mandatory uniform of black jumper, black polyester pants, and thick-soled black shoes, an outfit that couldn't disguise his elegance or the ever-present amusement on his face. The effect was sort of rockstar-policeman-stripper. He felt to me like a good guardian spirit.

Everyone quickly took to Jesse, who could chat easily and made quick, funny sketches of passers-by to leave in our mailboxes. He took requests from Leisha and Haimona's kids to fold drinking straws or advertising flyers into ingenious shapes. A few times when I walked past he was chatting with Amina and Artan.

The trio brought a kind of glamour to the place: elfin Jesse, Amina with her brooding looks and shining hair, and Artan, who dressed in a European manner that stood out in the New Zealand summer: rolled up shirtsleeves, hard shoes. He carried himself earnestly, as if he might one day run for office.

When I saw them there, I felt something of the shifting gear I'd felt in Claire's zone as we were dancing – a sense of the world expanding, of openness, possibility, even joy. I would stop and say hi and return to my apartment refreshed, and would drop my usual habit to keep working or read the terrible news on my phone or straightaway cook dinner. Instead I'd sit on the plum-coloured couch – on the floor sometimes – and let my thoughts drift, looking at all my much-loved things, the plants, the coloured glass candle holders, the way the evening light fell through the balcony doors, and feel that I was beginning to tune in, that there were big forces out there, and not all of them were to be feared.

Claire got called up for a solid block of catering work, and we had to defer our drink. We struck up a pattern of texting back and forth every few days, sharing comments on the news or describing funny things we'd seen. A language began to form, our own way of using punctuation and emojis. The texts looked like weightless bubbles but I spent several minutes composing mine, aiming to make her laugh. The sight of her name flashing up when I was in a meeting pierced me with excitement, and I wouldn't be able to fully concentrate until I'd read the text. When I passed her apartment door my breath held itself high in my chest – I was in a state of constant anticipation.

It was Jesse's third week in the job when Trevor met me at the shop after work one day and we walked home together, across the little park a few buildings down from ours. The place hummed with late summer twilight, design school students eating takeout on the steps, a couple of big dogs on leads sniffing each other, the smell of exhaust fumes from the traffic crossing town.

Jesse, who was meant to be at his post in our foyer, was there, sitting on the grass and splitting a beer with Artan.

I felt queasy as we neared him – quick, I thought, run back now and we'll pretend we didn't see! – but he didn't get to his feet. He moved as if he were in control of time. A pull on the beer, a swift suck of cigarette smoke, a glance over his shoulder at Trevor, which I saw when I looked back once we'd passed.

The building's foyer, without him in it, seemed especially open and vulnerable. Trevor crossed it and climbed the stairs in a large silence.

Once we got in the door, he took out his phone.

'What are you going to do?' I said. 'It's OK, I'm sure he was keeping an eye on the building from where he was.'

He ignored me, and called the security company, not bothering to take the phone into the other room, and told them in his clipped deal-making voice that Jesse was sacked, he was dropping the contract and would not pay it in full.

Then he got online and ordered CCTV to be installed.

I texted Claire that night – I forget about what – and didn't get a reply.

I knew it wasn't me who had sacked Jesse, but still felt a twist of shame when I ran into Claire, Amina and Artan in the foyer later that week. She was clearing her mailbox and her house guests were waiting at the bottom of the stairs with bags of groceries, comparing pieces of paper. It was the first time I'd seen her in person since the fundraiser at Judith's. I didn't know then about the night she'd had after that, and how it had affected her – but she seemed even more vivid, as if illuminated by a key light while everything else in the foyer was slightly out of focus.

'Hi,' I said. 'Hey. How are you?'

'Hi Therese.'

I couldn't tell how to read her face.

'We're around this weekend,' I said. 'If you're still up for getting that drink?'

'Check this out.' She held up a torn piece of note paper. 'Jesse left it for me. I think he's done everyone.'

It was a little pencil sketch of her, looking straight out from the paper. He'd really got her – the ambiguous gaze, at once warm and intimidating, that held you so that you barely took in her other features, the flat hair, the slightly crooked teeth.

'He's good,' I said. I pulled my mail out of the box not knowing what to expect, but a picture was there, with the real estate ads and the dentist's bill. He'd done me and Trevor together.

'Let's see?'

I held it out to her and watched her study the image: as drawn by Jesse, I wasn't looking at the viewer but was in profile looking at Trevor, whose gaze was frontwards, somewhere beyond the frame. I was smiling at him, you could only say adoringly, while he frowned into the middle distance. I didn't look old, at least, but I didn't look much of anything: catalogue model blandness was the overall impression. No distinguishing features.

Amina said, 'See you upstairs,' and Artan said, 'We'll get the cards ready, loser. And the beers.'

'Deal for Murlan. I'm going to get you this time,' Claire said.

'What's Murlan?'

'A game they taught me.'

'How are they getting on?' I asked. I was covering the air with words. Recently I had become aware of a certain simpering expression I adopted without thinking: a don't-hit-me smile. It was on my face now.

'Amina's nearly finished her course. It's their last week,' she said. 'They really liked Jesse. We all did. Why did you fire him?'

I felt sick, and at the same time relieved she had brought it up, that she hadn't just written me off.

'I didn't,' I said. 'Trevor did.'

'Why?' She breezed over the distinction as if it made no difference. Didn't it?

'Well, he was in the park and the door was wide open. Anyone could have walked in.'

'He told me he could see the building from where he was. It's been really hot, I think he could take a few minutes outside, don't you?'

'Hang on,' I said. 'Why are we arguing? I didn't want Trevor to fire him.'

'Couldn't you stop him? He could have talked to Jesse first. You know the pay's minimum wage and they just cut him off. He's not even been moved to another job, he's just out of the company.'

'I'm not in control of what Trevor does.'

'Did you ask him not to?'

'It was too late.' I was blushing deeply, furious with her now. What was this regressive view, that my husband and I were one unit, that we thought the same and did the same?

'Did you talk to Jesse?' she asked.

'When?' That was a stall, and we both knew it.

'When it happened. Or since.'

I hadn't talked to Jesse. I hadn't gone downstairs and found him. I hadn't said, come and sort this out with Trevor, let's make it work. I had said, 'Trevor, did you really have to do that? Ring them back and say you've changed your mind.'

And when he'd replied, 'I'm not going to change my mind,' I'd let it drop.

Now, to Claire, I said, 'No. I didn't talk to Jesse. Have you?'

'Yeah.'

'Is he OK?'

'Well, he's looking for work.'

He was in the park, I wanted to say again. He was drinking a beer. You didn't come home to a shit on your rug. You're not Trevor, you don't have the Serious Fraud Office investigating you, looking into old deals, emails, stuff you can't even remember doing it was so long ago. You don't feel the past being dragged behind you like a giant scaly tail you can't get rid of.

I said, 'Well I hope he finds something.'

She gave me the worst kind of look: disappointed.

I pretended my mailbox needed checking again, so she could go up the stairs ahead of me. I was still standing there sweating, hot and embarrassed, when Leisha came home with her children.

'Hi Therese,' she said in a cool voice.

'Hi.'

I couldn't stick around to see her children discover Jesse's drawings of them, and hear how much they missed him. The cameras would be installed next week and I wouldn't want to face her, or Claire, then either. I had the urge to be far away, in the misty garden at our Martinborough house, and the thought crossed my mind that I could hide out there. Hide! No. I wouldn't hide. I left the building and went to pace around the park to walk off this horrible feeling. It seemed to be full of people who felt at home there.

I told myself that night that by morning the encounter with Claire wouldn't feel so bad, but it wasn't true. At work I bumbled my way through a video call with potential investors. The location I loved in Darling Point had gone to a short-term lease arrangement, and as soon as I had the backing I'd be able to leap in with an offer. I felt my future coming for me, a future in Sydney, with strangers, where we could start again.

The call wouldn't take off though, it was dead, we had no chemistry. The investors were Sydney-based – I couldn't tell if news of Trevor's investigation had reached them. I showed them mock-ups of the boutique, I amped up the charm wattage, but the investor was a woman a bit younger than me, and I couldn't discern what she wanted.

Eventually she said, 'Look. Your brand is profitable. It looks lovely. But lifestyle shops like these are a dime a dozen over here. What's so special about yours?'

The grin on my face felt painted on, like a clown's. I don't know what I replied – opportunity space, growth mindset, some such word salad.

Afterwards I said to Rebecca, my PA, 'I think she just called us basic.'

She folded down the projection screen, boot-faced.

'We'll find someone else,' I said. 'There are more on the list.'

'I'm getting engaged,' she said.

'Oh – congratulations!' I went close, thinking to hug her, but she slid around me to put away the ambient mic.

'Yeah, he's going to ask me soon.'

Did this mean she was already engaged, or was there an engagement to become engaged? Was Rebecca one of these people, like Caroline had been, who needed a choreographed proposal, witnessed by everyone they knew and including a treasure hunt? I thought of Atalanta and her golden apples, the distractions rolling to tempt her in the dust. These days she would have found 'marry me' carved into the skin of one, and all her friends would have jumped out of the bushes crying.

'How exciting!' I said, and took her for a drink, and we had several cocktails and at the end of the night Rebecca's elbow slipped off the table and she said didn't I know her dream was to move to Sydney and run the office there? Didn't I know that? She'd told her fiancé, her soon-to-be fiancé, that this was their future. He had been looking into the job market there.

'I thought it was your dream too,' she said, outside now, tracking her Uber's progress on her phone. 'I thought it was what you want.'

'It is.' I squinted, trying to keep the traffic light colours from swooping.

I heard people on the stairs now and then, but didn't see Claire or her houseguests for a few more days. Maybe it wasn't long: it felt like weeks. She didn't text me; I didn't text her, for fear of there being no reply.

The next time I saw her I was with Trevor, we were heading to his lawyer's office to sign some documents, and she was on her way to the catering company. The three of us walked down the stairs in silence, and I felt homesick, like I'd been so close to something, and it had gone away.

Outside the building she waited at the curb to cross the road northwards, and before we headed west I said, 'Have a lovely day,' the words meaning nothing but the fact of speaking them, having some kind of sound traveling between us, vital.

'Thanks,' she said over her shoulder as she crossed. 'Go well.'

Go well? Ugh.

Trevor took my hand. Guy Benson, who usually paid house calls, had requested that we meet in his office.

'Death by a thousand cuts,' Trevor said.

He wanted to remove himself as a beneficiary of the family trust: this way, if his assets were to be frozen, the trust might be exempt and the children would still have access to their funds.

The risk was that this prophylactic act would be seen as evidence of Trevor's having something to hide, as Guy had warned him, but it wasn't in Trevor's nature to wait things out. Rather than idle in traffic he would pull a U-turn, change lanes, dive down a side street and take the long way to any destination, not to save time but to keep moving.

I had helped him dig out a suit that was over a decade old, because he'd recently lost weight. Guy Benson's 'old-womanish' concern for appearances gave him some fighting spirit. He was not unhappy.

We walked through the unusually hot April morning across town to Guy's offices, clinging to the small shade beneath awnings. Trevor's black shoes shone. Rubbish sweltered on the kerb. The refuse workers were protesting job losses with rolling stoppages in one neighbourhood after another. I had seen people from the northern suburbs drop their bags in our street in the early morning, when it was their turn. Now it was ours. We crossed the road to get away from the smell, but it followed us.

In the streets and cafés of the central business district we ran a high chance of running into someone we knew. We were early and I drew Trevor into a small outpost of a bakery chain under the pretext of getting something for his grandsons' dessert the next night – Caroline was bringing the boys around. We bought paper cups of scalding brown water and stood at the window counter, facing the street, while we drank.

A rubbish truck pulled up right outside the window and the barista ran to the door with stuffed polythene bags held high and the rubbish collector put a palm out like, not today. The barista pleaded. The truck blocked the daylight and there were Trevor and I reflected in the window. I was wearing a jumpsuit with a cut that mimicked the rubbish collector's overalls. It was silk.

Trevor read the paper. The business pages bore news of a convicted fraudster's lost appeal for name suppression. (*Fraudster* was the paper's jaunty choice of word.) The man was pictured in court, in his suit and tie, managing to look startled and defiant at the same time. It pressed on me urgently, the need to get Trevor to speak, but I barely knew what to ask.

I'd noticed that when Claire sat down, she leaned forward with her elbows on her knees, legs wide. I uncrossed my legs, swivelled on the stool away from that reflected Therese, and tried it now.

I hoped the stance would unlock my words, too, but my mind was dry. I couldn't even formulate the thought that he was withholding information from me about the fraud investigation – but it was there, wordless and insistent, nonetheless. How could I tell him I didn't believe there was nothing for them to find? Why did I say *confused* instead of *suspicious*, or *baffled* instead of *angry*? – it wasn't like saying serviette instead of napkin, which Trevor had trained out of me. It wasn't like saying toilet.

The barista came back with one rubbish bag he'd been unable to offload and jammed it into the bin by the door. He stalked to the counter and sucked at a smoothie with rage.

Now Trevor was on his feet, smoothing his suit jacket. He made a thing out of checking his phone and folding the newspaper. I hooked my bag over my shoulder and from my vantage point by the door tried to see him as a stranger might. An older guy, comfortable in a suit, though he still thought of himself as a *maverick*, expressed here by his haircut and the casual relationship between collar and tie. You would think he was well off (the shoes, the fingernails), and preoccupied. Yes, older. Not just in the euphemistic way of that modifier, as if it were one thing to be older, but an insult to be old – older than the version of him I held in my head.

He shoved the newspaper as far as it would go into the over-full bin near the exit.

'Hey,' called the barista. 'There's an empty bin right there. Recycling.'

'What?'

'The paper goes in the recycling bin.'

I tugged the paper out and a half-full coffee cup came out with it and splashed across the floor.

'Shit.'

Trevor handed me some paper napkins. I dabbed at the streaks that spattered my silk jumpsuit and the floor. The server approached wielding a mop.

'Are you OK?' he asked.

'Yes. Sorry about the mess.'

'It's all right.'

Trevor was on the other side of the door, holding it open for me.

'I didn't mean to yell at your dad,' the barista said.

That hadn't happened in years. I used to correct people.

'Oh. Thanks. I'll tell him.'

'People keep trying to sneak their home rubbish into our bins.'

'People are terrible,' I said.

'Yeah.' He applied the mop forcefully to a mark on the lino-leum that might have been part of the design.

Guy Benson kept us waiting in his plush brown reception room. Someone had decided that charcoal and chocolate were masculine colours, and that flecked orchids, which spoke of determination and skill, were an acceptable sculptural touch. The lift dinged, announcing another arrival, and through the smoked glass doors a familiar figure walked towards us, clutching to her chest a massive brown paper bag.

'Oh,' I said. 'It's Judith.' I put a hand on Trevor's arm.

Then she was in the room and we were standing and saying hello and leaning in for the double kiss. A little pale pink sticking plaster clung to the bridge of Judith's nose.

'Can I carry your books, miss?' Trevor joked. It was almost possible to see the schoolboy in him still, or to see them as the couple they'd once been.

'Ha ha.' She plonked them on the couch and sat down.

'This is a coincidence,' I said.

'Oh?'

'What have you been buying?' Trevor asked at the same time as I said,

'Who are you here to see?'

'What do you mean? I'm seeing Guy,' she said briskly, 'to sign the papers.' And then, 'I've picked up some classics to read to my mother. I thought I had them at home but can't find them anywhere. You don't have them, do you? Austen, Dickens, that sort of thing. Weren't we given a set?'

'My god,' said Trevor, 'the pages would be yellow by now. Maybe in the Sounds, but I don't think so.'

Damp pages, buckled covers, that's what I thought of. The papers. Why was Judith here to sign them?

'The new editions are a good price but the font is tiny,' she said. 'I had to order special copies. Anyway, Mum enjoys me reading them to her. Her hearing's sharp as ever.'

Judith's mother would be in her late nineties; it was at least a decade since our last encounter at a family wedding. She lived in a retirement village that had been one of Trevor's earliest developments.

'Sorry?' I said, looking at Trevor.

'We've added Judith as an executor. She needs to sign off removing me from the trust as well.'

'Of course,' I said. But I hadn't known Judith was an executor. Or had I not paid attention?

'How is Margaret?' he asked, taking a coffee that had appeared on a tray.

I also took one from the young blonde woman; her hair swung as she stooped to offer them.

Judith shrugged. 'Mum's remarkable. She's frail but her will is strong as ever. Keeps everyone on their toes.'

Margaret would be a thinner, beakier version of thin, beaky Judith, propped up by pillows and issuing edicts from her bed. She had the same ability, I remembered, to greet the world as if from the prow of a sailboat, letting it all glide by, what a pretty view. You never felt quite seen by Judith; perhaps this was what motivated Trevor as he reached into her bookshop bag and weighed a copy of *Great Expectations* in one hand, a college student now, talking to the cool girl on campus; he wanted her to notice him.

'Is your painting going to be restorable?'

'The art gallery conservator thinks so.'

With a double handclap, Guy Benson materialised in the doorway. Don't ever mess with short men, was something Trevor liked to say. 'Come through, come through. Sorry to keep you waiting.'

In the office kept aside for meetings such as these we sat around a black lacquered table that reminded me of Claire's zone. I was squeezed between Trevor and Judith, as if they were my parents at a school conference, and Guy sat across from us, curly-haired and alert. He had an energy that I could almost smell.

Trevor said, 'As you can see, I plan to sign my share in the trust over to Heathcote.'

Heathcote's name was already typed in. This would mean, effectively, he had double anyone else's shares. Trevor hadn't mentioned this plan to me. For some reason, I thought of the money he had paid my putative investor, all those years ago, to go away: $5,000. The electric light above the table emitted a hum.

On my other side, Judith was reading too.

'Trevor,' I said, 'are you sure?'

He leaned past me to address Judith, and I shrank back to clear the sightline.

'We agree he hasn't taken off. But he's no dope. He's got good ideas. The others will be fine, they're set up. This is a backup for him. A boost to get him started.'

Judith nodded her head, a tiny bit of her sadness about Heathcote leaking out.

'I'll tell the others,' Trevor said. 'And if for any reason I need access to the money...'

Guy Benson made a small noise in his throat and Trevor stopped talking.

'Therese?' Guy said.

'I know my perspective is different,' I said, 'but maybe that's useful?' I struggled to suppress another rising inflection. 'The kids should be treated the same. It doesn't help to be singled out. Heathcote's been given a lot.'

'But they're not the same,' Judith said. 'People have different needs.'

'You're always saying it's not a level playing field,' Trevor said to me, and then to Guy, 'You know, we have the odd political barney.'

'Trevor,' I said, 'we're not even on the playing field. We're up in the members' box with a crate of champagne. Heathcote's got a smear on his binoculars lens, that's all.'

I had raised my voice, and for a moment no one spoke. The light buzzed as if it were zapping a fly. I could feel the silk jumpsuit get damp under the arms, at the crotch, behind my knees.

'That was very poetic,' Guy said. 'Trevor? Judith? We could put this to a vote, happy to do whatever you want.'

I could feel Trevor looking at me. I wanted to climb over the table and grab Guy by the face and push him down through its shiny black surface, plunging into the zone, to fight him there. Judith was signing the papers.

12

And then that evening, she texted: *I've got a favour to ask. Understand if you can't do it. C.*

I made myself wait half an hour before replying. But I didn't fool myself.

Sure. I'm free now.

I thought she would phone, but a few minutes later there was a knock on my apartment door. I floated to open it. There she was. She raised a hand in greeting. I wish I could describe how the smallest gesture she made was rock solid: she had achieved the art of living in the world as it was.

'Do you want to come in?'

'No, I've left the rice on downstairs. Therese, I feel bad about our – the whole Jesse thing. I know you and Trevor aren't the same person.' Her gaze shot over my shoulder, and I said,

'He's still at work.'

She nodded.

'And you were right that I should have contacted Jesse. I think I felt shy.'

'I get it,' she said, 'it's easy to confuse being polite with doing nothing.'

'Ouch.'

She laughed. 'Too much?'

'No.'

On the wall beside me, the front door bell sounded. I remembered that the cleaned rug was being delivered this evening – it had been ready for weeks but I'd been reluctant to have it back in the apartment, until the evenings got cooler and Trevor asked why the floor was so cold.

'I have to get this,' I said, buzzing them up. I still hadn't told her the exact details of our break-in.

'I'll keep it quick. Here's the ask.' Artan and Amina were leaving for the South Island the next day, but Claire had been rostered on a catering job and had to take the work. Would I have time to drive them to the ferry terminal?

'Of course.' I was a bit disappointed it wasn't something more. 'So you're going to have your place to yourself at last?'

'I can't wait,' she said. 'You'll have to come over. We'll do the thing again.'

'The zone.'

She looked at me, considering. 'Is that what you call it? I like that.'

'Come to the zone,' I said in a silly, woo-woo voice.

She laughed. The homely smell of boiling rice drifted up the stairs. A sense of belonging suffused me.

Amina and Artan were packed and ready when I picked them up from Claire's. She had already gone to work. Her collection of things, the lions, the glass, the other bits and bobs from film shoots, looked even more motley without her energy there to hold them together. I wanted to linger in the apartment, but we had to go.

On the way to the ferry terminal a car behind tooted and I looked in the rear-vision mirror to see a man furiously smack his steering wheel then make a throat-slicing gesture at me with his hands. I wasn't about to speed up: I could see that Artan was looking pale in the back seat. Apparently they'd been clubbing for their last night in town with Amina's cohort. They were headed south to travel around for the final month of their visas.

'Do you get seasick?' I asked. 'Are you going to be OK?'

'I'm fine.'

I was reminded of the first time I'd met them, when he'd had that attack of cramp out on Claire's balcony.

'Great day for a sailing.'

We reached the terminal right on time. Rows of cars waited before the giant mouth of the ferry. Artan and Amina hoisted their backpacks onto their shoulders beside the raised door of the car boot.

They waved, and set off over the stretch of windswept asphalt to the check-in area for foot passengers, and I slammed the boot and got back in the car and reversed in order to pull onto the road. As I checked the view out the rear windscreen, I saw Artan's backpack drop out of sight, and I realised he'd fallen. Amina followed him down then rose, one arm up like a flag, then disappeared again.

For long seconds, as I braked and got out of the driver's seat, I lost sight of them, until I'd rounded the car and there was Artan revealed across the tarmac, on his knees, the backpack lurching off to one side. He hadn't just tripped. He couldn't move.

While Amina waited with him in the back seat I pushed to the front of the queue to get a refund for their ferry tickets, and was given a claim form and angry looks from waiting passengers.

'He's not well enough to travel right now,' I said. It was clear this wasn't just a hangover or a bug. We should bypass the GP. What was I doing in this ticket queue when he needed to be in hospital?

Out in the road a truck honked and I ran towards the car – I'd parked at an angle right across the entranceway, and vehicles were backed up. Artan's eyebrows were stark against his face; he was slick with sweat and had been sick on the ground.

'His pulse is very fast,' Amina said. She continued talking to him in Albanian.

It crossed my mind to find a plastic water bottle somewhere in the car and wash the vomit away but then I saw that it was streaked with blood and we had no time.

I drove as fast as I could to the hospital, a drive I would barely remember making, Amina holding Artan in the back. At some point at a traffic light I phoned work and said I'd be late. Artan was sick again on the floor of the car.

'Amina. Are you OK? We'll be there soon.'

Clutching Artan's hands, Amina met my gaze in the rear-view mirror and looked away.

Outside the A&E entrance I ran to find a wheelchair. An orderly helped Artan into it and they disappeared into the Emergency Department with Amina in tow while I went to park the car. In the footwell behind the passenger seat Artan's vomit looked dark and gravelly and I made a rough job of wiping it out with the tissues from the glove box. I lugged their backpacks with me across the car park.

They were in triage, and Amina was struggling to communicate; her English had evaporated. He'd had stomach cramps, I told the nurse, once, maybe more times, I didn't know for how long. I was dizzied by the form that asked for contact details and whether you were a resident or citizen. Money, I thought, this means something to do with money. I wondered if they were insured.

The nurse made notes while I explained about the collapse at the ferry terminal. Artan's face was spongy. His T-shirt was soaked, but he said he was freezing cold. We were sent to wait on the plastic bucket seats that lined the walls, opposite a poster saying hello in many languages but not in Albanian, and I thought how far they were from home. Artan took small steps to the chairs with Amina and me holding his elbows, lowered himself into a seat and hunched over his stomach. We shared the space with a couple of listless kids, an old man with blood soaking through tissue on his head, a massive teen in rugby gear nodding off in the corner, his arm strapped. As Amina stroked his forehead Artan's breathing slowed, his exhale careful as if trying to cool a burn, but he shook.

In the bathroom I splashed my face with water and tried to dry it with the harsh waxy paper hand towels that moisture slides off. I phoned Claire, and it went to her messages.

Artan was called for an X-ray. An orderly wheeled in a bed so he could lie flat. Amina and I held the sides as we travelled a complex route of corridors into a lift that expelled us on the opposite side from the one we'd entered, followed more painted arrows through massive hydraulic doors and into another waiting area.

Artan's X-ray was followed by a CT scan, which showed what the problem was – a ruptured ulcer.

'But he's so young,' I said to the doctor. I thought only people Trevor's age suffered from those.

She shrugged. 'It happens,' she said. 'Has he been under stress?'

How could I know? These people were strangers to me. Amina squeezed Artan's hand but would not meet his eye. We followed the orderly and the wheelchair to a ward where Artan was admitted to wait for surgery.

He was pale against the hospital pillows, and there was something emasculating about the wide neck of the hospital gown. When the orderly left Amina drew me into the corridor and said, 'I can't stay here.'

'He'll be all right.'

'I don't want to be here.' She turned to stare down the hall. 'I hate it.'

'Come on. Let's get a coffee.'

I ducked back into the room to collect their backpacks, just in case he was taken for the operation while they were out. Artan's eyes were closed.

In the café I bought Amina a piece of cake – she hadn't eaten all day – and tried to keep her talking. I poured the tea and it slopped everywhere from the loose stainless steel teapot lid, and I mopped it up with a paper napkin, my brain flashing, as it always did, with the word *serviette*, followed by *lounge, settee, pardon*, as if I might short circuit and blurt them all out in a great flurry. For fuck's sake, Therese, concentrate.

Amina pulled a large pair of sunglasses from her shoulder bag and put them on, generating stares from the other patrons. The effect was incredibly glamorous, and I said so.

She said, 'I like to dress up. Why wouldn't you?' The shield they offered seemed to give her strength.

She sipped her tea and told me about an exchange trip she'd been on, as a teenager, to Kansas. She had got off the plane wearing a full face of makeup, a gold miniskirt and six-inch heels, expecting to encounter young women as spray-tanned and glossed as the ones she had seen on American TV. But she was met by a host family who told her she would have to go to church, that she couldn't wear makeup, couldn't smoke.

'God they were boring!' she said. 'Their music, their clothes, sweatshirts, mom jeans.' Her host parents had been hardcore Christians terrified she might be Muslim. 'Sure, my family is, but we don't practise. Anyway, so what? They were just prejudiced.'

'What did you do there?'

'I lasted two weeks.' Amina shrugged, her eyes hidden. 'I don't like being told what to do.'

I could see that. Although she then told me she was here on her dying father's instructions. It had been his wish that she find a way to travel as far as she could. That was why she'd chosen New Zealand for her study, though it was also of interest, she said in her formal, politics student diction, as a welfare state with widening inequality. Her father had come of age, she told me, when Albania's borders were closed and its citizens forbidden to leave, and once the country opened up, he'd been so busy running his shoe factory that he'd never gone further than Italy and Greece. Amina cried, comfortably, when she talked about him.

'I hated seeing him sick,' she said. 'I never want to remember him like that.' She pushed her teacup away. 'Everyone loved my father. All the factory girls, the workers. He made them proud of what they did. And he wouldn't take any shit, you know? A very strong man. I think he would have been disappointed in this city. It's so modest.'

I laughed because it was true. Trevor was a big fish in a small pond. Her father sounded a bit like him.

'I only saw him cry once,' she said. 'Artan cries at anything.'

'Does he?' He'd been brave that day, I thought, in terrible pain on the other side of the world from home, trusting his body to the surgeons.

'One of my father's workers was caught sleeping with someone and had her eyes put out by her own father. My father had to deal with the family. Artan wouldn't be able to handle that.' She stared at me from behind the tinted lenses.

'My god. That's terrible.' I thought not many people would handle that.

'I know.'

She remembered her father motionless at the kitchen table for hours, this man who hated to sit still for even a haircut, who was always at work or drinking coffee with his friends or playing with his children in the park.

'What happened to the girl?'

Amina shrugged. 'Someone looked after her. I don't know.'

Outside the day was darkening and the fluorescent overhead lights seemed to harden. A cold wave of gloom came over me. I closed my eyes and tried to imagine.

I left the café to try Claire again – no answer – and called Rebecca at work. I wanted to care about room scent and which width of corduroy to choose for the beanbags that were coming back in style, but the details wouldn't stay in my mind. In a hospital you can't help but be aware of souls hovering. The maze of halls and hydraulic doors became some kind of dizzying limbo.

While Rebecca and I were talking I wandered through the lobby, past the surreal white grand piano, and around the parking lot, then in another entrance and down a hospital corridor before realising I had gone the wrong way. When we finished the call I found myself at the paediatrics wing, and as I studied the hospital floor plan on the wall beside its doors, they opened and the guy from Judith's fundraiser walked through with three student medics in tow. He gave a half double-take as if he got a vibe but couldn't place me. I watched him go. On that night of the fundraiser, I thought, I'd made a choice, and it had connected me now to being here at the hospital, when I barely knew Amina and Artan. If Claire hadn't been at that party I would have smiled and nodded and made small talk all night, drawing men out, flattering them in the way that had become second nature. I wouldn't have bothered to go upstairs to look through the telescope. There would have been no one to show.

For a second, I saw this tiny dot of Earth as if from Jupiter, zooming in through space until the colour appeared in the oceans, finding water-bound New Zealand and this speck of city and the cell that was this hospital and the atom inside it that was me. I could see just how little and light my life was, how easy it might be to move in a different direction from my old habits. I circled back and walked and walked until at last I recognised a mural that was definitely just around the corner from the cafeteria.

When I reached the brightly lit space, with its soft rock in the background and too-small tables occupied by humans suppressing their emotions, Artan's backpack was leaning against a chair, and Amina was gone. So was her backpack.

I gave it five minutes. Perhaps she'd gone to freshen up in the loos. I asked if anyone behind the counter had seen her. No. Ten minutes. I watched the entranceways for the dark gleam of her hair, but there was no sign. I called the number Artan had given me and heard it ring from the side pocket of his backpack. I didn't have a number for his wife.

Claire's phone was still turned off.

Some things couldn't be outsourced, I thought. You didn't leave a man from the other side of the world to come out of surgery alone. If I left, maybe Amina would come back – she might have gone looking for a shop, or for better food – but no, I understood in my gut that she would not return. The last ferry sailed at 8.30 p.m. and I knew – I just knew – that Amina would be on it. I knew because if it were me, if I were a young woman without children who had the chance to start over again, I might want to be on that boat too. But I would never do it.

13

We got Artan home the day after the operation and set him up back in Alex's room. Claire hadn't expected to be playing nurse, yet here she was. Amina wasn't answering her phone, and had made her social media private. We thought she might have changed her SIM card. Artan slept and talked to his family in Tirana and apologised for being in the way.

'Just recover,' Claire said. 'It's fine. I hope someone would do the same for my boys.'

When we were unpacking Artan's stuff for him, I found the pieces of paper with the sketches Jesse had done. He'd captured Amina well – the glowering capability with which she met the world – but the image of Artan was something else. It looked as if it had been done from life, not from a memory, and perfectly got his sweet and slightly troubled gaze. In the picture he looked beautiful. It was the sort of portrait that could only have been made by someone who was entranced by him. I smoothed both sketches out and put them next to his bed, with the jug of water and his phone. The pictures told the story of a triangle – the couple, and the illustrator. Whatever the private reality of Amina and Artan's marriage was, this felt connected to her decision to leave.

I'd missed a call from Trevor, and took my phone to Claire's balcony to ring him back. We had spoken that morning but my own universe seemed remote, an ongoing hum of work and the tension of the SFO investigation that it was easiest to move through on autopilot.

He answered in a warm, happy voice I hadn't heard for ages. 'Therese. Therese. It's back on, beautiful. It's all back on.'

'What – the hotel?' His mood was infectious – I could feel myself smiling, excitement rising.

'I knew it, I knew it would come right. We're on!'

As if by exerting his will over the family trust Trevor had restored his own mojo, he'd at last been delivered good news. The council enquiry into the hotel building permit reached a conclusion; they found no wrongdoing, Trevor's councillor friend was exonerated, and the abatement was lifted, overnight. Official word would follow. Work could begin again.

I looked down onto the street, at the tops of people's heads. Beautiful humans! I pushed all my weight against the balcony railing, wanting to shout, 'He did nothing wrong! He's free!' then spun round to see Claire in her living room, on the other side of the fake stone lions, watching me.

'I have to go,' I said. Screw her judging eye.

When Trevor got home that night, carrying a bottle of champagne, he scooped me into a huge hug and swung me round. 'You've got to know how to celebrate, Therese!'

I'd put makeup on, I was wearing a dress. I lit the candles, we drank the fizz, a sliver of my mind thought of Claire downstairs looking after Artan, the pain he'd be in from his stitches, it imagined Amina facing her freedom in a bright South Island landscape of mountains and lakes, I pushed away the image of the girl she'd told me about whose father had – no, I pushed it away – I looked at Trevor over the candles, I clinked his glass with mine, here was my life, thirty years of my life, I loved him.

His joy, his energy rushed through the apartment – it lifted me up – he juggled four phone calls at once, hauled investors back on board, he called Annabel and John and told them over speaker that their money was safe, strapped his knees and jogged alongside the project manager between home and office and construction site – he persuaded the building team to leapfrog over their next scheduled job back onto his – he rebooked the cranes and told the interior designer and greenswoman and half a dozen other contractors to stand by, he drank the protein shakes I put before him at six in the morning and he ended the day with poached chicken and greens and camomile tea because the legacy gig was back, Sydney was around the corner, and he was planning to live forever.

Suddenly I found him more attractive – I'm not proud of this but it's true. Every action was imbued with purpose, and this to me was sexy. The first fuck was hot, urgent with relief and a sense of order being restored. But it was that very thought – *order is restored* – that stole through my mind as I lay, my nerves shimmering, over him, which caused a problem. It became a march; I heard it when I walked around the apartment, when I watched him in his study from the doorway. Order is restored, order is restored. I became aware of our patterns, and every move towards sex after that seemed rehearsed and unspontaneous. It was too familiar of a language. He put his thumb in my mouth and I thought, who wants a man's thumb in their mouth? My usual ability, to find the performance of sex itself erotic, disappeared into the realisation that for decades now our sex life had effectively been both of us fucking me. Fucking Therese.

I longed for the simplicity of the Martinborough house, the weekends spent there during my thirties, before the sickening brake-screech of the GFC put paid to weekends for a while. The house where Trevor had taken me on our first trip together. We had arrived in the dark on a Friday night, and in the morning I had woken early – still Teresa, then – and walked through the wide, light, cedar-panelled rooms and out to the misty, park-like garden in astonishment. I had known people lived other lives, but never been inside one like this. As I ducked beneath dripping chestnut and dogwood leaves (I would learn later what they were), the inescapable feeling came over me that I was a burglar – or that the place itself was stolen. Whatever it was, the sense of not belonging was deep, queasy, and intoxicating.

Joining the curved path, I followed the sound of rushing water through a garden of flowering herbs down to a tangle of trees and a river – the other side was a steep bank; the electric fence of the neighbouring farm could be seen beyond it, and I recognised the rank smell of sheep. My legs were streaked and wet from the long grass when I got back to the house. Trevor was at the kitchen bench slicing bread – white T-shirt, blue pyjama bottoms. I crossed the slippery deck, wanting him.

Now, I pushed myself away from my husband as he stroked my thighs, and sat on the edge of the bed, looking out the window to the security lights in the office buildings across the road.

'Therese.' His hand was hot against my back.

'I forgot to take the compost out.'

'What?' He laughed in disbelief. 'That's not very sexy.'

'Sorry.'

It was feijoa season, and the bucket under the sink gave off their particular scent of citrus and talc. Trevor would break them in half over the sink, suck out the seeds then turn the pieces inside out to scrape the gritty flesh with his teeth. I walked barefoot to the ground floor and shook the torn green shells into the community compost bin.

I climbed the stairs with the empty bucket and paused outside Claire's door.

Claire had ripped her mask off in one yank and gasped, her face stinging in the cold air, raw but free. Mine was still stuck tight; even finding it had been like feeling for the end of a roll of Sellotape. I had hold of its edges now, but no matter how much I tugged at them I only yanked myself, staggering, forward.

I went back upstairs.

Heathcote called from Auckland, having heard the good news. Trevor put him on speaker while he set the table.

'I've discovered a super cool new bar here. It's going off. Just the artsy kids now but that'll bring the suit money. I reckon they'd be perfect to set up the bar in the hotel.'

'Put them in touch,' Trevor said.

'Will do,' said Heathcote. 'And if it works out – finder's fee?'

'Sure.'

'Yeah, and on that, the roof on my place up here needs a bit of TLC. Auckland rain is the worst.'

'Hang on.' Trevor screwed his AirPods in and switched the speaker over.

Caroline, Andy and the boys came to dinner, the kids running into the apartment full tilt, Caroline crying on her dad's shoulder, 'It's such a relief!'

After we'd eaten, I set the kids up in the television room with an anime, hanging out with them for a while, mesmerised by the beautiful images. Absent-mindedly the youngest one, Sam, stroked my hair as he watched, then pulled the long gold chain from around my neck and draped it over his shoulders. I squeezed his ankle and he leaned on me until the next exciting part, which brought him to his feet, boogying around.

When I came back to the living room, they were already a bottle of wine in. Trevor was red-cheeked, expansive.

'This is the problem with you lot,' he said. 'Always too worried about what's coming next.'

'Who's you lot?' Caroline asked.

'Your generation.' His gaze swept all of us. 'Do you know how much I'd be getting done if I was your age? Fuck's sake.'

Andy said, 'To be fair, there's a lot to be anxious about right now.'

'Get up and do something about it! We had Cuba, nuclear war.'

Caroline shook his shoulders as she went to get another bottle from the kitchen bench. 'It's not a competition.'

'This new generation,' he said, 'the ones younger than you, they're the ones who have it tough.'

'They do,' she said, 'and it's all your fault.'

'Hey.' Andy nudged her with his foot.

'Anyway,' she kicked back at his foot, hard, 'they give me hope.'

'As long as we don't rely on them to do it all,' I said. 'We need to change ourselves.'

Caroline eyeballed her wine. 'It's hard to change when you've got a freelance husband and two children who need driving to music and swimming and therapy.' She sat on the floor and stretched out her legs, and said, 'I'd love to change but there's no time.'

'You have changed,' Andy said.

'Well, yes, for the worse.' She laughed. 'I used to be fun. Rebellious. Now we're just straightos.'

'I wore a skirt,' he said from the other side of the coffee table. 'When we first met. Doc Martens and a tartan skirt.'

Caroline spoke to his departing back. 'Well, I used to sniff glue. And have boyfriends in gangs.'

When I'd first met Caroline she was sixteen, in a runaway phase. I took her for an abortion once; we didn't tell her dad. It made me feel close to her, having been by her side through that intimate thing, but perhaps understandably she drew a line under it, as if it had never happened.

'Was that rebellion though?' Andy was in the doorway. 'Or just you know, Marie Antoinette?'

'Fuck you.'

'You have to be joking when you say that,' he told her, and left the room.

'Hey,' Caroline turned seamlessly to her father, 'could you guys have the boys next weekend? We're going to a wedding out of town. It's in a forest. I wish I'd got married in a forest. Maybe we can renew our vows in a forest and Andy can wear a dress and I can wear a suit.'

'Who's getting married?' I collected the pudding bowls to take to the sink.

'Two of my colleagues. Amazingly that's still allowed.'

Trevor laughed. 'Red card from HR.'

'You can talk, you guys getting together, that was practically a Me Too situation.'

'What?' I said.

'Well, if you look at it now.'

144

'Steady on,' said Trevor. 'I was never her boss. An investor, that's all.'

I scraped the plates. 'Caroline,' I began, taking a second to control my voice. 'That is out of order. We were in love.'

'No offence,' Caroline shrugged. 'Things were different then. I had a fling with a lecturer. Some bitch wrote graffiti about it in the loos but I honestly think they were jealous.'

'Glad I didn't know about that at the time,' Trevor said.

'You didn't know a lot, Dad.'

Trevor frowned at his daughter as if she were impossible to understand. Even across the room I could see her eyes fill with tears, and she turned her chin away.

'Excuse me.' Trevor picked up his laptop. 'I've got a call booked with the Philippines.' He kissed his daughter on the top of her head and crossed with Andy as he exited the room. 'See you in a week or so.'

Andy shut the hallway door behind him. 'Their film's getting scary. We should go.'

'All right.' Getting to her feet, Caroline tipped over a little and shot a hand out to save herself on the back of the sofa. 'So, can you? Have the boys?'

'Of course,' I said. 'We'd love to.' Trevor and I did love being with them – they were sweet, their anxiety didn't stick to us, and they opened up another city, one of playgrounds and ice creams and tiny things to notice as we walked at the boys' pace down the street.

Sam wanted to be carried down the stairs, so Andy hoisted him onto his back. Seeing that Caroline was unsteady I offered to bring the bag of toys, tech and acceptable food they travelled with, and staggered under its weight.

'Don't judge,' Caroline said.

Claire's door was open a crack.

At the bottom of each flight of stairs we waited for the eldest boy to backtrack and step down them again on different feet, swapping his left for his right to even things out.

'What are you doing with Heathcote's apartment?' Andy asked. 'Now he's got his Auckland house.'

'I don't know,' I said. 'Maybe I should reach out,' I said, mildly appalled to hear myself use the phrase 'reach out'. It made Heathcote sound like a disgruntled customer, which in a way was true.

Caroline nudged Andy. 'That's not a great idea.'

'Ow,' said Sam. 'Mum, you hit me.'

The block was buzzing with Friday night, people clustered in the doorways of bars and restaurants. I waited with Caroline and the boys on the street while Andy brought the car round.

'Caroline,' I said, 'is there anything I should know? About Heathcote? Something I've done?'

'Just leave him for a bit. Let him cool off.'

'From what?'

The boys spun in circles on the footpath, hyper, and Sam whacked into a passer-by. Caroline grabbed him into an embrace and said, 'Are you all right, darling?'

'Sorry,' I called after the young man who'd been knocked.

'Therese,' Caroline said. 'Children have to be free to express themselves.'

'Yeah, but there are other people in the street.'

'You can be a free spirit,' she told her son, and said to me, loud enough for him to hear, 'We're trying to get them not to worry so much about their behaviour all the time so it would be great if they don't get a constraining vibe from you.'

'It's a narrow footpath,' I said. 'He hit someone, you say sorry, it's no big deal.'

'Exactly. It's no big deal. Hey,' she said, tugging the necklace off him, 'where did you get this?'

The boy grabbed at it when a horn beeped and Andy pulled their people mover into the bus stop. He looked at me with pleading eyes and I nodded.

'You can take it.'

'Quickly, boys!' Caroline rushed them on as the back door slid open.

'I'll see you next weekend,' I said, passing her the bag.

'The thing is,' she said, buckling a giant child into a NASA-level car seat, 'it's not your place, is it.'

'What isn't?'

'The Sounds. It's not for you to say who can be there and who can't.'

'What are you talking about?'

'Besides,' she said. 'I thought it was your M.O. to say nothing.'

I took a step back, and stumbled over the kerb. By the time I'd righted myself the passenger door was closing and I was staring at my own funhouse reflection in its street-lit sheen. 'What the fuck,' I said to no one.

I knocked on Claire's part-open door. It wasn't even the zone I was after – just someone to bitch with. But when she came down the hall I saw her eyes were red, and realised she'd been crying. It wrong-footed me; I didn't think of her as someone who still needed to cry.

'Sorry. Is it a bad time?'

'No, Artan's at Jesse's. I've finally got my famous solitude. Turns out it sucks.'

We sat in her armchairs, the platform dormant on the other side of the room. She told me that Alex had been going to come home for a week but had just decided not to.

'Can you go up there to see her?'

'She doesn't want me to! She's 'establishing her independence'. She 'needs to separate'. It's like talking to a self-help column.'

For years I'd been addicted to those, but lately – a sign of the times? – the advice had got harsher until it was fully scorched earth: divorce your parents. Chuck him out. Tip your desk. What were the afflicted meant to be left with? I knew passive aggression was a bad thing, but couldn't see that active aggression was much better.

'You must miss her,' I said.

'Yeah, the hardest part of parenting is not doing it. The twins always had each other, it was different. I mean, I miss them, but there's something else bound up in the way I miss Alex.'

'Is it a mother daughter thing?'

'When she was little she used to get homesick on sleepovers. I think that was to do with fear, not for herself, but that something would happen to us. This is a bit like that.'

'You're afraid for her.'

'Not that I could ever say. I'd be 'undermining her agency'. Basically child abuse.' Claire stood and stretched. 'She's probably right — we were too close.'

I felt a pang of envy. Or jealousy. Or both.

'Anyway, she's having a ball. Staying with some rich friend, she's not even paying rent. Working in a bar. Living the dream — her dream, not mine.' She smiled. 'I hate the fact she's got her own mind. Did you ever want kids?'

The question took me by surprise. The idea of having my own children with Trevor had always seemed too complicated — as if it would overbalance something. He said early on, been there, done that. And I'd only wanted him. 'No,' I said. 'Not at all. I know that's not very normal.'

Claire raised an eyebrow. 'Don't worry, there's nothing *normal* about having a child. It's one of the most uncanny things you can do.'

The platform pulsed in my peripheral vision — that was what I wanted now — to lose myself. But that moment Claire's phone rang and she shifted her quizzical gaze away from me. Her tone, when she answered, was one I hadn't heard before.

'Hello darling. No, of course I get it. It's fine. It's fine. I love you too.'

It was a week after that, a bright, cool Friday afternoon, when I was in the museum with Caroline's children, that Guy Benson phoned me and said, in a voice thin with shock, that charges against Trevor and two other men, for mortgage fraud relating to the Therese Thorne building that housed my flagship store, had just been filed.

14

My store? My name? Mortgage fraud? I left Caroline's boys clutching the handrail in the museum's earthquake simulation room and walked to a quiet spot in the exhibition, pressing the phone hard to my ear to take in what Guy was saying.

These were the charges: back when Trevor was developing the building that would house my store on the ground floor, he (and the finance director and a lawyer on the project) had allegedly lied to the bank about the presales of the office floors above. They had secured the bank loan with false documents on the basis of those sales. This happened years ago, in the wake of the financial crisis, when, as Trevor used to put it, 'everyone else was running out of the burning building, so I ran back in.' The buildings, everywhere, on fire.

I had a memory of something John had said in the Sounds. The way he'd watched Trevor, as if looking for a chink in his surface. Had he known about this? But I didn't believe it. Other people did this kind of thing – of course I'd heard stories – I'd heard worse. Not Trevor. Not outright lies.

'Where's Trevor?' I asked Guy.

'He's with my assistant. We're running down the details as fast as we can. He says he'll see you back at home.'

'It's not true?'

'The thing is,' Guy said, 'whatever the exact details of the timeline, those units did sell later. The bank got their money back.'

'But falsifying documents? He wouldn't do that.'

I was staring, blankly, at a life-size model of a dinosaur. People began to file out of the earthquake simulator.

'It's all going to be fine.'

I couldn't see the boys.

'What could happen?'

'I have to tell you that in other such cases,' he said, 'where there has been a guilty verdict, there have been custodial sentences.'

'Prison.'

'Not maximum security.'

'How long?'

'That's not going to happen.'

'Guy. I will fucking Google it. Just tell me.'

I was walking around the exhibition now, looking for Sam and his brother.

'Ah, I can think of a couple of chaps... three or four years?'

'Three or four years?' I wanted to be sick.

Guy said, 'I'm getting him the sharpest fraud lawyer in the firm. And Therese—'

'What?'

'Trevor absolutely denies doing anything wrong. It's important you know that.'

'OK,' I said. 'I trust you.'

'Good.'

I didn't trust him. I said it because I wanted him to feel obliged to save us. He hung up and a muffling like the seawater from the Sounds rushed into my ears. My mind skittered over the news.

Where were the boys?

The earthquake room was filling up with the next viewers. I crossed through it against the crowd, bumping people, and came out through the entrance, still not seeing the boys. I called their names.

They weren't by the volcano projection, or under the giant eagle. The exhibition wasn't that big or crowded, but displays and information boards were placed at odd angles through-out the space, forming a kind of obstacle course. It would be possible to circle through several times and not see someone, if they were moving around too. My eye caught the top of the escalators at the end of the room and I went to look down their vertiginous descending steps – nothing – then crossed the landing to check the boys hadn't gone up the stairs towards the marae. But I didn't want to leave this floor. If I just stood here, and they tried to leave, I would see them. And if they were already downstairs, they would soon come back up and find me. From here though I couldn't see any museum officials, and I should tell someone, that was the thing to do. I called for them again.

Guy Benson said things would be all right. But Guy Benson had said the investigation wouldn't lead to charges. Guy Benson, who was never wrong, had just been crucially, fuckedly wrong.

A museum worker in a teal uniform rose into view up the escalator.

'Excuse me,' I said, 'I've lost a couple of boys.'

'What are their names? We'll make an announcement.'

'Thank you.' I wrote their names on the back of my business card. My hand was shaking. 'I think I should just wait here. In case.'

'We'll call you when we've got them.'

It was so hard to do nothing – to stand still in the hope that they would appear. But I was terrified to move. Sam especially was anxious, and if they were somewhere on this floor, I would eventually see them and yell out, and I didn't want them roaming around looking for an adult who wasn't there.

But there was a sign for men's toilets down a side corridor. Perhaps they were there. What if they were stuck in the loos? Should I run down, call in? They had each other at least – I was just thinking this when the oldest one came out of the bathroom and walked straight to me.

'Where were you?' he said. 'Where did you go?'

'I'm here. Where's Sam?'

He looked at me whitely. 'Isn't he with you?'

'OK.' Was he old enough to leave here? He had to be. 'You stay here. Don't move. I'm going to find him. Don't move.'

'What if he's lost?' He was starting to breathe in that way that presaged a panic attack.

'He's not, he's not. Stay there. Have you got your inhaler? Let's get that.'

I helped him fumble with his backpack.

'I want to call my mum.'

'No, we don't need to do that. Don't move.'

I ran up the stairs to the marae, which was empty, all its multi-coloured carvings shining in the low sun. Soon the museum would close. It would get dark. I remembered a school journal story about a boy who got separated from his class on a museum trip and slept the night in a waka. It had seemed a cosy adventure but this now was a heart attack. I ran across towards the dim hush on the other side of the floor and checked in the waka and in the wharenui, ripping at my shoes to get them off so I could look properly inside, whispering his name.

An announcement came over the tannoy, addressed to the boys – instructions to come to the information desk on the ground floor. I imagined the eldest one hearing his name, stuck in the grip of anxiety, not knowing whether to obey my instructions or the official voice. I stamped my feet back in my shoes, my fingers clumsy with the laces, and whirled through the rest of the top floor, calling loudly now for Sam. On the stairs back down, I skidded and caught myself on the metal banister just in time, my hand burning. The eldest boy wasn't there.

I shouted, 'Fuck.'

A tour guide shepherded her clutch of Europeans out of the way.

I stared down at the section of native bush and the water and thought suddenly of the deep harbour right outside and surely he wouldn't have left the building – but there had been that dog walker with a horde of dogs in the piazza, could he possibly have wandered off to look for him? – I ran down the escalator to the mezzanine floor – why had I taken my eyes off them at the earthquake room, fuck Guy Benson, what was going to happen to Trevor, could he really have made a big mistake, it didn't seem possible or like him at all – why would he need to lie? Outrage bloomed in me, it was a false charge, he would never risk his reputation like that.

Fraud. The word thudded against my skull.

I wanted to call Claire and have her tell me what to do.

I opened the door to the men's bathroom on this floor and shouted for the boys. Nothing. What if they'd been picked up – lured away – abducted. Face down in the sea. Beneath the wheels of an SUV. Crying, lonely, lost. How could I have been so stupid?

I remembered, suddenly, that on the way to the earthquake exhibition Sam had dragged on my hand and looked hungrily at the shop – back up on the floor above – and I'd said we could go in later to buy something. Of course. I ran up the escalator and wheeled through the little store calling his name – but he wasn't there either. I stood outside in the lighting that was somehow dark and too bright at the same time, feeling that my eyes had stopped working.

My phone rang. It was Trevor.

It took me a long few seconds to pick up. The desire to not know, to simply *never be told*, blared through me.

I answered, and asked if he was OK.

'I'm fine,' he said, and it was grounding to hear his voice. 'Sorry about Guy, I should have called you myself, it's flat out here.'

'I've lost the boys.'

'Listen – what?'

'I've lost the boys. I'm at fucking Te Papa and I've lost them.'

'OK, they'll be somewhere. Go, go. We can talk later. I just wanted to say. I will get name suppression. We've applied and there's a hearing next week. So let's keep it quiet. I don't want to tell the kids. Not yet.'

'All right. Of course. I love you.'

'I love you too.'

He hung up. I could feel what hadn't been said sealing over us like plastic. Safe.

Behind me, the shop lights turned out, and I registered that the tannoy was projecting my name. I was being summoned downstairs. Please let them be all right, I prayed, stumbling down to – where was the goddamn info desk, where were they – and then there, at last, a security guard, a woman in a uniform, and Caroline's sons, the youngest streaked with tears, the eldest tight-lipped and angry.

'Where were you?' he said again.

'Are you all right, darlings, you're all right? I'm so sorry.'

I crouched down and pulled them in to me and hugged them till their stiff bodies relented and the little one cried.

'I want my mum,' he said into my shoulder, 'can you tell her to come back?'

We kept occupied for the rest of the weekend: a movie, the zoo, bikes along the seafront, giant milkshakes. The season had turned and I couldn't get warm. The boys were bundles of nerves in their knitted hats, but we laughed at the otters, always so joyful, and I steered them away from the sad bear. It was a blessing having them there, with Trevor being too busy to talk. I do remember reading them a bedtime story while he shouted at Guy Benson from the other room. That was the only time I heard a raised voice.

Sunday came to an end and the boys' parents returned from the forest wedding. Caroline stayed in the car, Trevor stayed in his study and Andy and I did the stairway suitcase bump. On the way down the stairs, I heard music coming from Claire's place – even in passing it filled my chest, imparting strength. When we reached the street Caroline got out and embraced her sons, saying,

'How would you two like to move to the countryside? Would you like to get a horse?'

'We got lost,' Sam said.

'What?'

'Yes,' I said, 'we had a bit of an adventure, didn't we. At the museum.'

'I was scared.'

'Andy,' said Caroline, her voice soft with drama, 'buckle the boys in?'

Come on Teresa, I said to myself. Don't take any shit.

I told Caroline what had happened. 'It gave us all a fright. But they're fine.'

'Why didn't you call me?'

'I didn't want to worry you.'

'I'd have come back, Therese. That's what mothers do.'

'Then you'd have missed the wedding. They were fine.'

'So, what, did they just wander off? Where were you?'

'I had to take a phone call,' I said. 'I'm really sorry.'

'A phone call? Wow. If you couldn't look after them you should have said. I'd have asked one of my mum friends.'

I craved a cigarette.

There was a clatter behind us as Claire, Artan and Jesse tripped out of the building and into the street.

'Hi!' I shouted after them.

Claire turned back over her shoulder to call hi and wave at me before jogging on, with the men, to the pedestrian crossing and around the corner out of sight. Her face left an afterimage, like a bright moon, once she'd gone.

I tried to forget my own feelings – to disappear. When I looked at Caroline again, at her pretty face, puffy from partying, I could see past the anger to her sadness, and her fear. A flush of protectiveness came over me. Was this how parenting worked?

'You seem unhappy,' I said, 'and I'm not sure why.'

Caroline's eyes widened and she exhaled a laugh. 'You lost my kids. Who have anxiety. I'm not unhappy, I'm upset. I can't trust you with them anymore.'

'OK. Fine.'

'Fine? *Fine?*' She couldn't believe it.

'Fine. They're sweet boys. But I don't want to look after them anymore.'

Caroline stared at me.

'You and I need to get along,' I said. 'Especially now.'

'Why? What's going on? Is Dad OK?'

'Everything will be all right. But please.' I took her bangled wrist. She was stunned, now, into a kind of sliding submission. 'Let's be on the same side.'

A squabble broke out in the back seat and she lowered herself into the car, turning to talk to the boys – kindly – then gazed up at me again as Andy pulled out into traffic. I waved them off and found myself walking towards the Therese Thorne flagship store.

The caramel-coloured lights in the window drew you in from the dusk, and the new winter cushions and throws were like so many lush animals waiting to be stroked. As ever you could feel your heart rate settle on entering, the rose-scented candles and lustrous display cabinets working like beta blockers. The Sunday evening shoppers inside moved dreamily amongst the soft sheen of wood cabinetry. Hands stroked velvet nap and picked up smoked glass vases in browns and maroons, turning them to the light. The girls behind the counter greeted me with their priceless smiles. Another girl unlocked a tall vitrine to show a customer a range of pearl-handled knives. The key was so small and delicate. I adjusted the cushions on a bottle-green daybed at the end of the shop.

My phone rang. It was one of the Great Walks women. I hadn't heard from them since the SFO investigation was announced, but we were booked to do the Tora walk together this weekend.

Unfortunately, she said, one of the group now had to have a medical procedure and they had decided to postpone.

I had learned, in the name of discretion, not to ask about people's medical procedures, but couldn't resist.

'Oh...' she sounded vague. 'An emergency... varicose vein removal.'

'Right.'

'How *are* you,' she said then.

'Fine,' I said. 'I'm fine.'

The confidence I'd felt when talking to Caroline left me without warning; my body shook; I was afraid to turn back to the richly shining objects in case they sapped my life force. I felt an overwhelming desire to sit down on the daybed. To pull a blanket around me and bring my knees up to my chest and hide.

Trevor came into our bathroom when I was applying moisturiser. The tools of my elaborate facial routine – a rose quartz roller, a gua sha tool, toner, serum, oil – sat gathering dust on the bench. Who could be arsed? I remembered the sheets draped over the mirrors at Claire's apartment. It was relaxing, to walk around without the risk of encountering your image.

He went to the loo and lifted the seat. Through the mirror I watched him urinate.

'There's another loo down the hall,' I said.

'Oh. Sorry.' He looked hurt. 'I wanted to talk to you.'

He came to wash his hands beside me and I leaned against the heated towel rail, feeling the hot rungs press into my back through the carefully layered towels.

He said, 'Leapfrog.'

'What?'

'That's what I did. I leapfrogged over a step.'

'You skipped a step.'

'Because of time. There's so much red tape. It's a nonsense, has been for years. We all got to the destination with all the necessary elements in place.'

'Which step did you skip?'

'Not so much skip, as did things out of order. We knew the units would sell, so we had to raise the finance on that basis.'

'But they hadn't yet sold.'

'But they did.'

'Well, how bad is that?' I asked. 'Does it count as fraud?'

'If it does,' he said, 'it's a travesty.' He gave a wry smile, but his gaze, as I held it, softened, and I could see the vulnerability. Who else could he show that to? He needed me to believe in him. I just had to get myself over the line.

'They'll have to take into account all the other stuff you've done. Everything that's improved the city.'

'You'd hope so,' he said.

I told him my plans for next weekend had changed and now we could go to a movie, out for dinner, go somewhere that wasn't a regular haunt. Pack a picnic and take a walk by ourselves.

He made that face. 'You know I'd love to, but.' He had counted on working through the weekend. I understood. With how everything was.

'Yes,' I said, 'of course, of course. I just really want to get away.'

He squeezed my shoulder as he passed.

'They've got a gun to my head,' he said.

I thought of Claire's dream.

When he went back into his office, I shook out a towel and clipped it up over the mirror. That was better.

15

I hadn't been back to Martinborough since before our Christmas party, before the council investigation that seemed to kick off our run of bad luck, and was aware of the losses and gains of the past months as I navigated the curves of the Remutaka Hill with Claire in the passenger seat. The back was loaded with boxes of food and booze; gardenia season was over; I'd be returning to the city with only empty bottles. As ever, the hill felt like a portal letting us in to a new, releasing landscape – the muzzy stretches of Wairarapa fields, the extending floodplain. Our house was on the banks of the Ruamāhanga River. I had seen predictive images of the ways the river might move and grow with rising sea levels, a creature absorbing its surroundings.

Trevor and Judith had built the place together in the first decade of their marriage – in fact, they had bought the land the year I was born – and its 1970s modernism – cedar cladding, window seats that looked onto the rolling garden, and a cork-tiled kitchen floor – still comforted me, like an alternative version of my childhood. Forgive me for saying this, but it was my favourite of our houses. In the divorce, Trevor had agreed to give Judith their Wellington home, so that he could keep this place.

Among the exotic trees, Judith had planted an abundant flower garden, which I had maintained and which was tended by a local gardener when we weren't here. I parked on the gravel drive and we stood for a moment by the car, breathing in the misty air and the resiny smell of the liquidambar, which was turning from tawny orange to deep red.

'It's gorgeous,' Claire said, and I relaxed slightly, realising how much I wanted her to like it here. I knew the house was too much, of course it was too much, no one actually lived in it, but I clung to the hope that its beauty would work on her, as it always had on me.

The delphiniums were still going, and some early irises had appeared. We walked around a bit, stretching our legs before going inside, and I showed her the glasshouse, the kitchen garden, and the path to the river. We could hear its steady shoosh.

The housekeeper had opened the windows to air the place, and a fresh fire blazed in the wood burner. A bottle of local wine sat on the dining table next to a corkscrew and two glasses. I slightly wanted to die – this was a routine Trevor and I had set up, but now it looked like I had brought Claire here for a romantic weekend. She and I carried the boxes to the kitchen bench and made a couple of trips back and forth to the car before kicking off our shoes and settling in. I chucked her a pair of sheepskin slippers from the set we kept in a basket by the door.

As she pulled them on, she said, 'This is the fanciest holiday house I've ever been to.'

I didn't know how to reply.

'You're down here.' I picked up her weekend bag and took it down the hall to the guest wing, on the other side of the house from the bedroom Trevor and I shared. Her bed had been made up, and purple-black tulips sat in a small earthenware vase on the dressing table. They struck an incongruous, boudoirish note amidst the mid-century decor.

'There's a bathroom through that door.'

She crossed to the window that looked onto the back of the house, towards the river. 'This place is insane.'

I wished she'd stop talking about it. There was more to show her but I suddenly felt like a docent conducting a museum tour – that is the lawn where the children played on a plastic slip'n'slide, this is the bathroom where Judith told Trevor she was pregnant again, here is the faint stain on the wall where someone smashed a glass, this is the wine cellar the kids nearly drank dry, that is the wood burner that sat unlit all one cold weekend when Trevor learned about the affair, over there is the bedroom where Teresa fell in love with Trevor, where I climbed on top of him on my first morning here and slid him inside me and felt so young, and powerful, and alive, that is the bedroom door Annabel locked herself behind when she wouldn't eat, this is the side of the house where Caroline and Rob staggered back from parties, off their faces on acid, that is the hole in the hedge where Heathcote drove into it, these gouges in the cork tiles are from an unknown source.

'I'll make us a drink,' I said, escaping back down the hall.

'Yes! Open the wine.' She was behind me.

'Or should we go for a walk?' It wasn't lunchtime yet, and the thought of a whole day and a half here with only each other for company sent me into a panic. But if we went for a walk, it would be off with the slippers, back on with our shoes. The fire would die down. It had been a mistake to bring her. I should have come alone.

'Sure,' she said, opening the wine. 'Whatever you want to do.' She poured a glass and pushed it across the table towards me, then poured another and took a swig. 'Relax, Therese. I'm just so happy to be here. To be away! God, I really like Artan but I want my space back.'

All right. The wine warmed my chest. I sat on the floor, leaning against an armchair, and stuck my feet towards the fire. Claire joined me and brought the bottle.

My phone rang, muffled within the handbag I'd dumped on the couch.

'Leave it,' she said. 'It's not going to be anything good. Here.' She got out her phone, and took mine from the bag. 'I'm turning these off.'

'Will Artan be all right?'

'He'll have to be. I'm too far away to help him anyway.'

'What if your family calls?'

'I'm busy,' she said. 'They'll call back.'

She leaned over to the pile of dry logs, opened the wood burner and threw another one in.

'Claire, can I ask you a personal question?'

'Oh my god. Of course you can. Why are you so fucking polite?'

The question felt like a slap. 'Am I?'

'Yes, you're behind a mask the whole time. Stop it.'

I stared at her, then got to my feet.

'What?' she said. 'You're feeling something, say it.'

A thick plug formed in my throat. I poured myself a glass of water. I wanted to throw it on her head, but I drank it. For a second – as if a flashbulb went off, showing everything – I felt incredibly lonely. I tried to speak, but to my horror, my voice broke.

'Therese.' She looked appalled. 'I'm sorry. I didn't mean to make you cry. I just meant. I'd like to know you better. I want connections. That's all.'

'It's OK.'

My reaction shocked me almost as much as her remark. I sat on the floor again and pulled my knees up to my chest.

'What did you want to ask me?'

'About your family. Why Alex doesn't want to see you. What's the deal with you and Mick. How can you be so – shruggy about it.'

'Shruggy?'

'I'm taking revenge for "polite".'

'All right.'

The air between us warmed again. We finished that glass of wine, and another, and another, as she told me her story.

She'd thought of the swap on New Year's Eve 2016, the end of a horrible year. Brexit, the US election, the Kaikōura earthquake. Morale at the fundraising consultancy where she worked was low and the woman she'd hoped would be appointed CEO was passed over in favour of an imported man, which was too on the nose; she'd found herself crying in the car when she thought about Hillary Clinton, who she didn't even like.

'The antidepressants weren't helping so I stopped taking them,' she said. 'I mean, that was meant to be my mother's era. Valium in the suburbs. I started feeling nothing had changed. I'd grown up with "girls can do anything" but my family life was some kind of retrograde throwback.'

She turned the cap of the wine bottle around in her hand. 'It's hard to explain. I hate the phrase *emotional labour*. It's so self-serious. As if human feelings are a transaction.'

I had barely heard that term and had only a vague idea what it meant.

'So I said to Mick, I'll do the bills and the rubbish and the car and the maintenance, and you do the shopping and the cooking and the cleaning. That part was easy. But the hard one is, he's now in charge of keeping in touch with our sons and friends and his own father – which had completely fallen to me – and it's his job to know what's happening with Alex, how she is, friend drama, relationship action, whatever. What she's doing, what she wants.'

I remembered how upset she'd been when Alex called off her planned visit. Perhaps that's why I heard a note of defensiveness creep in to what she was saying.

'I'm still involved – I'm still her mother. It's just for him to take the lead. It's not like I've got some special knowledge he doesn't have in terms of parenting. But somehow I was being treated as the expert.'

'How's it working out?'

'Alex was relieved! This used to be me with her' – she put on a high, probing voice – 'What are you doing, Alex? Do you think your job in that clothes shop will satisfy you? What about this community college course? What about volunteering? What about picking apples or saving to travel or forming a band, you like music, what about those guitar lessons when you were thirteen?'

I laughed, and she kept going.

'My god, look at this room, why don't you paint it, go for a run, so-and-so's kid is a guide at Zealandia, don't you like nature, don't you like birds? A cooking course! A car maintenance course! Get your licence, download the app, what about a scooter, I saw a second-hand pushbike for sale, Alex, Alex, have you read this book, listened to this podcast, have you tried meditation, have you looked at a flat, but don't leave home, stay here to save money, what are you saving for, how about Thailand, London, Dunedin, when I was your age...'

She drew breath. 'I mean, she hated it. Of course. I didn't want to be that person either.'

Being that person. The word 'that' was convenient, I thought, as if these less preferable selves were over there, off to the side of us.

'I just couldn't believe we'd fallen into these roles,' she said. 'That we'd just – succumbed. It had gotten so that any time we went out in the car, Mick drove.'

Trevor did too. I hadn't stopped to think about it. I just automatically went to the passenger door.

'And I was beginning to see us as labels, not as people.'

'Labels?'

'White cis Gen X heterosexual Labour Green middle-class able-bodied tauiwi couple of Anglo-Scots descent. I've probably forgotten something. OK, I know being middle-class and white means I want to be seen as more than middle-class and white so I can continue to enjoy the privilege of being middle-class and white without thinking about it too hard. But still.'

It seemed to me that minding about being middle-class was only something you felt if you'd always been that way. I never minded.

Once they swapped roles, she told me, their sex life heated up. And when she drove them up the coast for weekend walks, she felt elated behind the wheel, surging to overtake trucks as though the only thing she'd ever feared about driving was her own power. She saw how Alex enjoyed the new closeness with

Mick: it was a relief not to be the one trying to steer her daughter's choices without revealing a hidden agenda and generating the opposite effect. She adored Mick's calmness, the baseline assumption of a person with practical skills that things would be all right. On the downside, there were the bills and the rubbish and the car and the maintenance. And he still called her five times from the supermarket to check he was getting the right thing.

'I mean, was I really that controlling?' she said, and drained her glass. 'Rhetorical.'

They were trying, and yet, and yet. She struggled to achieve a similar deprogramming at work. It was hard enough to go cold turkey on exclamation marks, *all good if not*, and nonessential apologies. Her job was to get money for various causes out of high-net-worth individuals. Supplication was an ingrained mode, not easily unlearned. The sight of her emails without the usual emollients made her feel faint.

This I could relate to. I opened the second bottle of wine.

And then, she said, there was age.

It was as if no one else was getting older, Claire told me – only her. No one else was swept up in the river of time. She alone lay awake in the middle of the night as electric currents rippled her limbs, her heart snagging for no reason. Thinking about why she had been a follower all her life. Thinking that all this wide-eyed wonder at the world had been supposed to keep her young. But here she was, ageing anyway. She swam length after length at the local pool, striving to just be a body, to still her mind, to let the little word strings go, but words were everywhere and no good.

Her sister had another take. 'She told me I wasn't depressed, I was angry.'

'Were you?'

She was depressed *and* angry. It was pointless. No, it wasn't! Life was elating, joyous, she was in love with the crystal droplets on the morning twigs before the wind came to shatter them. She loved the glossy birds, the red maple, the bowl of harbour. Her imperturbable husband, their mysterious daughter, who was in the ascendant, who had not yet met time. Mick had gone bald so that was his price paid.

But the rubbish that blew through the streets and the way that it was all wrong everywhere, how did people not go mad, she asked me now, why did they not care why didn't they all just storm something? Perhaps this was menopause but everyone she knew was only in perimenopause, peri, *peri* we said to each other, clinging to those letters as though they were a strand of pearls, sexual relevance, those last four precious pearls.

'Menopause is one of those catch-all diagnoses,' she said, 'like when you have a baby and you blame everything on teething. Because nothing else could be making you cry.'

By now I was drunk and hungry. The only food I had brought was the makings of a fancy salad. I staggered to the kitchen to chop things up. Why did I eat salad, I wondered – did I enjoy salad, did I want fresh vegetables, was it nutritious, or had I just seen it in an advertisement, in a hundred advertisements, this wellbeing, this pose, was I gathering some image in from these projections and performing it as if it were real, even though the women in those fast-forwarded commercials, or in the television shows the ads were interrupted by, hardly touched the sides of what it was like to be me? Claire's way of thinking was infecting me. If that was the right word.

She joined me at the bench to help.

'Ugh. I'm talking too much.'

'It's fine,' I said. 'It's been a long time since I've listened to someone talk.'

'Apart from Trevor,' she said.

'He actually doesn't say much.'

He had used to. Long, looping conversations had been part of our relationship for years – when we were walking, or at dinner, or sitting up late after a movie. When had that stopped? I couldn't think when we had last sat across a table from each other and talked. We avoided restaurants now, and at home we conducted our exchanges about domestic logistics while never looking up from our screens.

We ate the stupid salad and went on our walk, stumbling and dizzy in the pale mid-afternoon light. It felt strange to be walking without my phone. I couldn't remember if I had locked the house properly or closed the vent on the wood burner door. The grass by the river was high and wet, soaking our sneakers and jeans. After about twenty minutes we reached a bridge and took the road away from the river, past rows of tethered grapes, their yellowing leaves edged with crisp red. I felt awake. The low, wide sky stretched over us.

'What are you going to do?' Claire asked.

'What do you mean?'

'About the SFO investigation. Aren't you worried it's going to affect your business?'

'What can I do?'

'Are you angry with Trevor?'

'Angry?'

My mouth was dry from the wine. We should have brought water. But I needed to pee, and I was sweating. I was sick of being this age, even though I knew this was as good as it was going to get, physically.

Claire said, 'Yes, are you angry?'

'Why would I be angry? I'm worried for him. But I'm not angry.' If anything, I was angry with her for asking. In fact, I felt a kind of general anger, an unsettled tension I didn't know what to do with.

'I need a piss,' I said.

It was only the way she looked at me then that made me realise how I sounded. Not like Therese.

'Wow,' she said. 'You're a dark horse.'

We had stopped on the wide, muddy berm. In one direction was the little town, and in the other, where we had come from, were bush-covered hills, strung with wisps of cloud.

'I'm not just some rich lady.'

'I didn't think you were.'

The anger in my chest turned over, warming me. We walked on a bit, back towards the house.

'You could piss here, you know.'

'I'm not going to.'

'Well I am. I'm busting. Keep watch.'

She ducked behind a little rise a few meters away. I could see the top of her head. I thought of the motorbikes that had swarmed my car the last time I was here.

'Come on, Claire!'

'Oh my god, that's better,' she called, laughing, and was still zipping up her jeans as she picked her way back over the gorse stumps towards me. 'Are you sure you don't want to?'

I didn't reply, and we kept walking. The wine we had drunk thumped in my head.

After a while the bridge appeared in the distance.

'Therese,' she said. She touched my wrist, so I stopped again. 'Therese.'

'What?'

I don't think I'd ever been looked at the way Claire looked at me then – it was dizzying – with her goldy-brown eyes. I had to force myself not to turn my head away.

'You're just about as free as a person can be, Therese. You know that. You've got all the choices in the world.'

'Free to do what?'

'I don't know, that's what you have to decide.'

'What about you?'

'I don't think about the future,' she said.

16

Another car was in the drive behind mine, a mid-range green sedan I didn't recognise.

'Damn,' I said. I still needed to pee.

'Who's that?' asked Claire.

'I don't know.'

We peered through its windows as we passed, but the clean anonymous interior offered no clue. It could be the housekeeper, I thought, returned to bring fresh milk. Or – the idea swung in farcically – it could be Trevor, with another woman. That was one thing I had never worried about.

'Hello?' I pushed the door open – the room was empty, the fire blazing, and three big brown bags of groceries sat next to the empty wine glasses and dirty salad dishes that were still on the bench, giving off a smell of vinegar.

There were voices down the hall. I called again. 'Hello?'

I heard, 'Oh, fuck.'

Caroline emerged. She saw me and frowned – I felt her animosity shoot down the hallway like a poison dart.

'Hello,' I said. I found myself going towards her, for a hug that she reluctantly assented to. 'Caroline. Are you OK? Have you talked to your dad?'

She pulled back and nodded. 'Yep. I don't want to talk about it.'

'He'll be OK. He hasn't done anything wrong.'

'Of course he hasn't.' There was an extra stress on 'he'.

I wondered what she meant by that emphasis, but there wasn't time to ask as two other women emerged from that end of the house – Fern, from the gallery across the road from our apartment, who we now heard knew Caroline from the design school, and a younger woman, who was very pregnant. In the flustered introductions I learned her name was Sally. The three of them had the same long, cultivated hair.

'We've come for the weekend,' Caroline said.

Claire and I exchanged glances. 'Listen,' I said, 'I've just got to go to the loo.'

In the bathroom I sat with my head in my hands, feeling all the wine and anticipation run out of me. Now that others were here, I wanted Claire to myself, wanted the uninterrupted hours I'd been afraid of earlier that day. God, this unsettled feeling was running me now, I had no sense of direction. But I knew what should be done.

I cleaned my teeth and brushed my hair and changed into dry clothes – I'd brought the silk jumpsuit, which looked silly with the sheepskin slippers but I'd had a vision of sitting at the table in it, over wine and crackers, maybe playing cards with Claire, maybe the Albanian card game she'd mentioned – it was only now it was no longer possible that I realised I'd even harboured this fantasy, and I thought, who was the part of me that packed the jumpsuit and the wine and the crackers, how did she keep herself secret from the other part of me that was just *going to Martinborough to get away*?

I made my way towards the living room dreading the next conversation with Caroline, let alone the evening ahead. They all turned to me as I entered. Caroline and her friends wore floor-length prairie dresses that looked incongruous next to the fall-of-Communism tracksuit Claire had changed into. Claire, who was inspecting the liquor cabinet, waved. It was like seeing a burning candle across a dim room.

Caroline said, 'I did call, but your phone's turned off.'

'Right. Well, we can all fit. There are enough beds.'

'Oh. Were you planning on staying the night?' she asked.

'Yes.' I willed myself not to say, if that's all right with you.

She sighed. 'It's just, we can hardly ever get away…'

I didn't point out that she had been away just the weekend before.

'…and we've had the chance to take this spontaneous weekend before Sally has the baby…'

'How far along are you?' Claire asked.

'Due in a month.' Sally had a little girl voice that was disturbing alongside her giant pregnant belly.

'We can keep out of each other's way,' I said.

Claire stood, her knees creaking, and said, 'Or we can drink this.' She held up a bottle of ancient tequila. 'Not you, sorry, Sally. Anyone else, though?'

Caroline frowned, but Fern's eyes lit up. 'I've actually brought some cannabis oil,' she said. 'As well.'

I could see the way she looked at Claire – here was something more exciting and weird than the weekend she thought she was getting into. It seemed she was prepared to swallow Trevor's ignominy, as long as she could stay in his house.

'I'm in,' I said.

We all looked at Caroline, but in this little trio it was Fern who had the power. Sally was kept out of it, she would just have to be pregnant and sober all night, and Caroline was going to go along with what Fern wanted.

She caved. 'All right,' she said. 'Fine.'

As Claire was slicing lemons and looking for shot glasses, I tried again to broach the SFO investigation with Caroline.

'What's Trevor told you about it?'

She said, 'That it's centred on your building.' She cut her eyes at me. 'So yeah, let's not go there.' She addressed Claire and got a stool to reach the cupboard above the fridge. 'The glasses are up here.'

'Caroline—'

She ignored me. Could she think because my name was on the building, that it was my fault? Is that what they all thought?

'Here.' Claire lined the glasses up and ran the tequila bottle over them, sloshing liquid over the sides. She bent down to slurp up the spillage. 'Let's go!'

As soon as we'd had our first shot, she connected her phone to the speaker system.

'Sally,' she said, 'I know you can't drink, but can you still dance?' A song kicked in with a pulsing beat and Claire took Sally's hands and drew her into the middle of the room. Fern chucked back her drink and joined them. I pulled the coffee table out of the way.

Candles, dotted around the empty room, threw a flickering light over our bodies. I don't know how long we'd been dancing for. It was dark outside, thick countryside dark. Claire wouldn't let us stop, that was the key — you had to go past exhaustion to reach this new state. The air above us rippled, neon streaks capillarised up from the ground, through my chest and all over the ceiling and I heard the deep click as time unhitched and the joy began to build. The others blurred, wavered like a heat mirage — changing into a new state of matter.

Later, as if on some agreed signal, we all wound down, and Claire lowered the music to a background rise and fall. Caroline had flung herself over the back of the couch, her head on the cushions, her upside-down face open. Fern's arms stretched wide in a pose of exultation, Sally doubled over her bump, hands on knees, wheezing, her chin shiny with sweat. Everyone's eyes shone, slowly blinking in that glassy post-zone state. I felt a wild surge of love, even for Caroline, especially for Claire.

'What *was* that?' said Fern. 'Did you all feel that?'

Caroline said, as if making a discovery, 'I should be with my kids. No. Fuck my kids. Christ! I need another drink.'

The tequila was finished. Fern passed her a golden vial of cannabis oil.

'I'm scared of giving birth,' said Sally.

'You should be. It's much worse than anyone tells you,' said Claire.

Caroline started laughing – a dark, unhinged laugh.

'Really?'

'Think of the worst someone has told you to expect. Multiply it by ten.'

'I don't want to take drugs though. Epidurals can harm the baby.'

'Your funeral.'

I tried to catch Claire's eye – this was a bit brutal – but she was still out there on the other side of acceptability, kicking up the sand under her blazing sun.

It was getting cold, even with the fire. I hauled blankets from the camphor chest in the hallway and handed them round.

Caroline was lying on the floor, her head in Fern's lap. Sally wore the blanket around her shoulders, her hair wild from the dancing. The image evoked a real campfire, and at the same time the artful, constructed images of 'campfire' that we would post to the Therese Thorne social media accounts. A kind of self-consciousness of their own beauty had crept back into the way the women held themselves. Only Claire looked apart from it, scrappy and worn, but vital.

'So cool, if you think about the sacred feminine, we're all represented,' said Fern in a musing way. First she put a hand to her own heart: 'Maid.' Nodding to Sally, Caroline and Claire: 'Mama – well, three different stages of mothering – mama-to-be, mama of small children, and mama of adult children – and,' an airy wave in my direction: 'Crone.'

I checked behind me. No one else was there.

'What *is* a crone?' said Sally.

'Like a hag,' I said, feeling the word exhale from my throat in a hot rush of tequila breath. 'A *hag*. A witch.'

'A wise older woman,' Claire said, before licking closed the cigarette paper on a joint.

'Not so wise,' I said.

'Don't you have children?' Sally asked me.

I shook my head. 'Nup.'

'Do you mind?' Fern asked.

'No.'

'But really?' She was leaning forward on one arm, her face close to mine, dark eyes boring in. 'Never? You never feel like, is this all there is?'

I started to laugh.

'Oh well.' Fern gave a little shrug. 'We can all aim for wisdom, it's a goal, right? I'm following this amazing woman who guides you through a spiritual practice and neural unblocking and she's older but so beautiful, she doesn't wear any makeup, just these oils that she sells online, I've ordered like, a ton. Her whole thing is mama, wanderer, on the path… She's helped me focus on me, and on the gallery, and respect my own needs and I refuse to apologise for that, you know?'

She took Sally's hand and said, 'She's a freebirth advisor as well. She promises it doesn't hurt.'

'Then she's a fucking liar,' Claire said.

Sally ignored her. 'I know it's silly but I can't wait to put "Mama" on my profiles. Caroline, did you have a freebirth?'

'A what now?'

'They used to call it natural birth? No interventions?'

'Oh,' said Caroline. 'Well, I had to have caesareans.'

'Oh no.' Sally gave a bright smile. 'I didn't know that! Well, that's OK, you have to go with the flow I suppose…'

'Yes,' said Claire. 'Or die.' She took a deep drag on the joint, held it in for several seconds then emitted an impressive column of smoke away from Sally's face. 'I had twins via caesarean,' she said, 'and was talked into a vaginal birth for my third kid. Like it was a holy grail of womanhood that I must experience. And by the time I'd changed my mind, I was too far dilated for the epidural, so they just gave me gas and air to suck. I bit down so hard on that mouthpiece I broke a tooth.'

She paused while we all winced, and checked our teeth, then said, her voice thick with tequila, 'There is a creature inside you fighting to escape.'

Sally tightened the blanket across her bump, like a shield.

'It's not that bad,' said Caroline.

'You had an operation,' Claire said, 'you don't know.' To Sally she said, 'It is absolutely that bad. Imagine your bones being dragged out of your body. The aching. The tearing. You think you'll go mad with it.'

'Well this woman says with breathing, and owning your power—'

Claire gave a sharp laugh. 'And oils and affirmations, blah blah blah. The white woman wellness complex.' She was on her soapbox now. I lay down and let the words wash over me.

'Motherhood as a fetish, kids as another branch of ego. Pointless pain because you think it's authentic. The accessory husband, the dried stick in a vase, the hushed voice that suppresses psychotic rage.'

'That's a bit reductive,' Caroline said. A coldness stalked into the room on her private school vowels. 'Sorry, is my voice too modulated for you?'

I felt the reins of the night begin to slip from Claire's hands. Or maybe she was throwing them off.

'Don't you think,' said Caroline, 'that it's good to practise self-care? You know, to put on your own oxygen mask first? So much is asked of us.'

'It's not a war, Caroline,' I said, but she was still speaking.

'We have to step into that power.'

Claire was pacing the room; when she passed, I got a whiff of her sweat. I squinted one eye open and dragged myself up to sitting.

'But what does it mean,' Claire said. 'To "step into your power". Seriously.'

'Are you asking me?'

'Any of us.'

Fern leaned forward, ready to engage. I could see her waiting for someone else to speak first, the 'yes but' forming in her mind, the raptor in her that was hungry. The pregnant girl looked stricken.

'I don't disagree with trying to get free,' Claire said. 'But it's so messy, complicated. Probably impossible. I just think we have to be careful not to make ourselves into some kind of hero.'

Fern took the risk. 'It means I trust myself,' she said.

'To do what?'

Fern started laughing. 'To tell other people what to do.'

'Ha,' Claire said. 'That's honest. But you can't call it a spiritual practice.'

'What do you think it means?'

'I think it depends who it's for. For women like us, who basically are incredibly fortunate, it's a slogan. Meant to make us feel OK about being selfish. And maybe for people who don't have our… proximity to power… it's meant to put the problem of powerlessness back on them.'

'What do you mean, proximity to power?' The edge crept back into Caroline's voice.

Claire looked from her to me and raised her eyebrows. The thought came to me that maybe Claire just wasn't very nice. But I wanted her to keep going.

'What do you believe in then?' Fern asked. 'What's the alternative?'

Claire shrugged. 'I don't know what I'm doing – I don't think there is an endgame. That's why I like the music. The dancing. For a second, there's another way to be.'

'Yes!' I said. That's what I liked too.

'The journey is important,' said the pregnant girl in a small voice.

'Sorry,' Claire said, 'but what does *journey* even mean? It's like it sounds good because maybe it means we're going somewhere good, but actually we're right here. Journey. Journey. We're just scared. I mean, same. I say it too. It is completely debased. I mean, do you want to just be a good little meditator?'

We sold meditation cushions at my shop. Crystals. Incense. We used to sell dream catchers before Rebecca explained that it was wrong.

'I don't go for thin former models hawking natural beauty, I don't go for smoothies as food and bare feet and big sweaters,'

(Claire's own feet were in fact bare), 'self-obsession disguised as ritual, big floppy hats, why are these women always wearing big hats, appropriated tea ceremonies, the word *grace*, the – the fucking word *radical* when applied to self-care, the words *self-care*, *practice*, *wildness*, *mentor*, fuck off, fuck off.'

At the windows she took a breath. Sally had got to her feet and now headed towards the hall.

'Claire,' I said. I patted the air: go easy.

'Not you, Sally,' Claire said. 'I don't mean you fuck off.'

'It's all right,' Sally said in a high voice. 'Excuse me.'

She disappeared towards the guest rooms.

'Caroline,' I said, 'do you want to go and check on her?'

But Caroline was just staring at Claire with disgust, gathering her long mane of hair and letting it drop, then doing it again.

'Look, maybe for some of these saleswomen there's real' – Claire gritted her teeth – 'trauma, they've been exploited or abused and this is how they cope and everyone's trying to make a buck, they seem lonely, I should feel pity for them, but this is all at the expense of other women, they are monetising your feelings of shitness while weirdly, strangely, not solving them. A few drops under your tongue isn't going to solve a lifetime of inequality, including your own part in it. I mean even if you are a rich white lady whose power depends on the subjugation of others, in this world you're still not as good as a man.'

Saleswomen? I'd got stuck on that. Was she talking about me?

Now she fixed an eye at me. The stern eye.

'You're nothing next to a man, you're not even real in this world.'

I put my palms up. 'I'm just going to check on Sally.'

Fern said, 'Have we got any more weed?'

I found Sally in the twin bedroom halfway down the hallway, sitting on a bed with her packed overnight bag beside her.

'Are you OK?'

'I'm fine, I just – why did she go off at me like that? In front of everyone?'

I paused a second, trying to focus. I had thought Claire was talking directly to me.

'Never mind that,' I said. 'Come back to the living room.'

The hand pressed to her belly was plump and young. 'I just want to do the best thing for my baby. It was Fern who said about the face oils. She's been trying to sell them on to me for months. I'm not complicit in anything.'

'Mmm,' I said.

She stood, holding the bag, and scanned the room.

'I always have to do an idiot check,' she said. 'It's even worse now I'm pregnant.'

With an exasperated grunt she collected a large floppy hat from the top of the dresser.

'Skin cancer,' she said, waving it at me. 'That's why we wear them. Skin cancer.'

'Right.'

'I bought this off your website,' she said. She shoved it in her bag. 'I think – I just think I have to go home.'

'Now? In the dark?'

She moved past me up the hall and into the living room.

'I'm going.'

'What, no,' said Fern. 'You can't drive off now.'

Claire looked abashed. 'I'm sorry,' she said. 'I didn't mean to upset you.'

'It's fine.' The long hair was useful in hiding her expression, as she swapped the house slippers for her shoes.

'No, it's awful. Please stay.'

Sally jutted her chin. The high voice had its own kind of power. 'I'm really, really fine.'

'I'll come too,' Caroline said. 'Fern. Let's get our things.'

How had this happened?

Fern didn't move. I followed Caroline back down the hall. 'What's going on?'

Her dark laughter started up again and she said, 'Un-fucking-believable. You've done it again.'

'What?'

'These are family places, Therese. Family. And you just make us so unwelcome.'

'No, hang on. Of course you're welcome. I want you to feel at home here, to be comfortable.'

'Do you understand how that sounds? Of course I should feel at home. It is my fucking home.' She stopped abruptly and spun round so that her face was very close to mine. I took a step back. 'If you wanted us to feel comfortable, this wouldn't be happening.'

'It's just a conversation, people can disagree.'

'I don't think so.'

I stood in the doorway while she gathered her bag and Fern's. She had already placed her nightgown under the pillow – like a little girl – and now she snatched it out and bundled it into her bag as though it was a teddy bear she didn't want me to know she still had.

'Caroline, please don't go.' I felt sober, or at least that it was important to be sober. 'You and Fern can't drive, and Sally shouldn't be trying to do that hill, it's too dark, it'll be slippery and windy at the top, just stay.'

She pushed past me. They were all by the front door now.

'I won't be able to sleep,' I said. 'Please, call me when you get in.'

'You could go,' Caroline said.

'What?'

'You could offer to leave. Rather than the pregnant woman.'

I looked at Claire. She could see, as I could, that this wasn't about her anymore.

'I don't want any of us to leave,' I said.

'I'm sorry,' Claire said again. 'I didn't want to upset anyone.'

'You should have thought of that before you started talking about creatures escaping from inside our bodies,' Caroline said.

Sally burst into tears. 'I just want to be in my own bed. I just want to be with Dan.'

Fern held the door open, having succumbed to the drama, and the cold night air swept in and over us. There would be hell to pay for this, I thought, maybe not now, during Trevor's crisis, but later. Something in me snapped.

'All right,' I said. 'No one wants you to leave, but all right. You're grown women.'

I took their bags of uneaten food from the kitchen bench and stepped past Fern and towards Sally's car, made glossy by the moonlight.

Fern got in the back seat with the bags. Caroline made a show of helping Sally with her seatbelt. I saw her angry white face before she shut the passenger door and the car light went off, and thought of the teenage Caroline I had met, in her phase of running off to party at gang houses, and how what she'd probably wanted was for her parents to come after her, and how sad it was that they hadn't, and that I wasn't going to now.

The car reversed on the gravel and pulled onto the road. I watched it go, and once the sound of the engine had died away, was aware of the rushing of the river.

Claire was inside stoking the fire. I shut the door.

'I'm really sorry,' she said again. 'I went too far.'

'Maybe,' I said. 'I don't know.'

We didn't go to bed. We sat up all night, on the couches, under the blankets, every now and then adding another log to the fire, drifting off, waking up again. I turned my phone on in case Caroline did call, but the only message was the one she'd left on her way up here, checking that no one was using the house.

I probed my heart's corners, as I did every now and then, for regret about not having had children. There was none. Still, it had been a relief when a few years ago I'd had to have a hysterectomy and the question had been put away for good.

It had been done privately, north of the city. They had only taken my uterus: 'We can leave the ovaries, hope to spare you an early menopause,' my surgeon had said. Menopause? At that stage I thought it was something that only happened to frazzled grey-haired women in clompy shoes – yes, please, spare me! She'd added, 'And I'll leave the cervix too, if you like. Some of my male colleagues just whip it all out. But you just let me know what you want.'

I was grateful. The scar was small and neat. The last time I'd thought about it was when I met my personal assistant's mother, at our annual friends and family barbecue, and she told me the reason she couldn't pick her grandchild up was complications from a hysterectomy gone wrong. Her operation had been done by a trainee. When she went home, despite the antibiotics, she developed an infection. The medics didn't listen to her until, after days of agony, she had to have a second surgery. This caused permanent damage to her bowel.

'I'd asked them if they could do that keyhole surgery,' she had told me, 'but the man said it was too messed up in there. He said it would look like something the cat dragged in. A bloodbath.'

'Mum,' said Rebecca, 'Therese doesn't want to hear about your operation.'

'No, tell me,' I'd said. 'I do want to know.'

'It'd be carnage. That was his word, carnage.'

She hitched her T-shirt and pulled down her waistband to show me her scars.

'Oh,' I said. 'Does it hurt?'

'Not any more. Except when I lift things.'

I wanted to reach out and stroke the knotted skin. Between the scar and her bellybutton she had an old, faded tattoo of a lioness's face.

'I like your lioness,' I said.

'You know what though,' she said. 'After I had the second op. It was like when they took out the uterus, they took out something else as well. Like the thing that made me stop from speaking up for myself.'

She had drawn her phone out of her pocket and was scrolling through photos.

'After they messed me around like that, I don't care now what I say. I mean I do, but I used to, you know, stop myself all the time. For no reason, just scared to say what I thought in case I got slapped down. Now I just say it. Here.'

On the phone screen was a photo of a meaty netball encased in a clear plastic bag. The baby batted his hand towards it.

'That's my uterus,' she said.

I laughed out loud. 'You're kidding.'

'No.' She smiled at me. 'That was inside me.'

'It's huge.'

'Yeah, well, fibroids. I lost a few pounds when they took it out, but I put it on again.'

I was suddenly furious that I hadn't asked to see my uterus after they took it out. What an idiot! The fancy private hospital would have brought it in on a silver plate. I zoomed in on the photo to see just how red this flesh orb from her body was, just how much room it must have taken up.

The phone had buzzed in my hand, startling me, and I'd handed it back.

It was sometime in those early morning hours that Claire told me about her night alone on Te Ahumairangi. She said, 'If you hadn't taken me to look through that telescope, I don't know if I would have felt it – even wanted to be there.'

'If that man hadn't been there,' I said, 'to tell us how far away Jupiter is.'

'And that young waitress. Lucy. Don't you wish you could be young again?'

'Of course,' I said, 'and also no.'

Around eight the next morning we were packing the car. Our hair was wet from an early, freezing swim in the river. My body felt the best it had in a long time – not rested, but alive. We'd eaten the bread that I'd stolen from Caroline's grocery bag, torn hunks off the loaf and downed it with coffee. I hadn't heard from Caroline, but nor were there reports of any cars going over the side of the Remutaka Hill in the middle of the night.

I set the alarm and locked up the house and returned the key to the lockbox, Claire leaning against the car, her face to the watery sun, waiting.

'Oh,' I said, 'I should have gone to the loo. Now the alarm's on. What a pain.'

'Go here,' said Claire. 'I won't look.'

I snuck around the side of the house and squatted by Judith's flower beds, fingertips on the grass in front of me for balance. I remembered that Donna, my childhood friend, and I used to pee anywhere on nights out, beside parked cars or in alleyways or behind gorse bushes up in the bleak subdivision hills. It felt dirty and clean at the same time.

From the front of the house Claire called, 'Incoming!' and I heard wheels coming to a stop on the gravel drive – could that be Caroline again? Trevor? – and quickly stood and pulled my trousers up, tripping over the brick flower bed edging so that I came round the corner at a lurch.

A middle-aged man with a pinkly shaved face was getting out of his car. Claire stepped back and made space for me to approach.

'Hello,' I said. 'I'm Therese. Can I help you?'

He thrust out a hand to be shaken. I was acutely aware of my unwashed palm in his bouncy grip.

'I didn't expect to see anyone here,' he said.

'We're just leaving. Are you—'

Now he handed me his card. I recognised a bright red logo. He was a real estate agent.

'Yeah, Trevor's asked me to come and take a look at the property, seeing as it's going on the market.'

On the market? I stared at Claire, open-mouthed. She gestured to my fly. It was still undone. I tried to zip up surreptitiously but caught the man staring, and he ducked his head and persevered with his upbeat tone.

'I've got instructions to put together a presentation plan. He's given me the alarm code, do you mind if I just – there's a lockbox somewhere round here, I believe?'

I pointed to where it was. Trevor had said nothing about selling this place. I felt the wind knocked out of me. It was the first place he brought me to, the first place we made love. I'd

183

been coming here for nearly thirty years. I called them Judith's flower beds but they were mine, now.

On the way back Claire offered to put some music on but I wanted silence. At some point she said, 'It's only a house.'

I wound down the windows and let air rush through the car as I remembered my thought of the night before. That she wasn't nice. I wondered now if that was the same thing as not being kind. Or not being good.

You know those front page photos of tourists sunbathing, drink in hand, while helicopters dump useless water on the forest fire that rages in the hills behind them? I felt as if someone had just shown me that photo, and I'd realised the tourist was me.

17

Guy Benson had arranged for a meeting with an advisor called Marcus Todd, who was white, pink, close-cropped, and moved thickly in his clothes as if made of denser flesh than the rest of us. He had once been a researcher for the SFO and knew the ins and outs.

'Trust me on this,' said Guy.

'It worked so well last time,' I said.

The blonde girl with the coffee tray paused mid-stride.

'What?' Trevor said.

'Just black, thanks,' I said to her.

'Now,' said Marcus Todd, 'Guy tells me the interim name suppression request has been granted.'

'Interim?' I said. 'How long does that last?' It gave me vertigo that there was just that slim little ruling between the press confirming Trevor's mortgage fraud charges and not.

'Until the second appearance. If you're declined after that you lodge an appeal.'

'What are the grounds?'

'There's precedent,' Guy said. 'For high profile people such as Trevor. But that's not a guarantee. One argument would be that as you share a name with the building concerned, Therese, it would be unduly hard on your business. Given you're essentially a bystander here. No offence.'

'I see.'

Trevor leaned forward, impatient to get on. 'And what about the next court appearance?'

The word 'bystander' echoed in my head, and when I tuned in again I'd gleaned something about a two-week stay. Ducks in a row. Story straight. No one actually said 'get your story straight' – that would have sounded like it sounded.

On my return from Martinborough earlier that week, while we were eating the steak I'd cooked, perfectly, because people-pleasing can't stop overnight, I asked Trevor what the estate agent had been doing at the Martinborough house. And why hadn't he told me?

'Shit,' he said. He put down the pepper grinder. 'I'm sorry. I just wanted to get a market value.'

The hotel's new major investor had got cold feet, and Trevor was convinced they'd heard about the charges on the grapevine. There was nothing to stop the press printing this: *Troubled hotel project may halt again.* Public opinion against 'the Hulk' had begun to harden. The hotel was mentioned in an article about the privatisation of public land, though Trevor said the allegation that he would block the public from using the throughway on the water side was untrue. 'It will be part of the hotel, it's an important feature, but of course the public can walk through to get from A to B. Any time they like.'

I wanted to point out that people being able to access the water at Trevor's discretion was not the same thing as it being a public space, but before I could, he topped up my wine and said, 'There's a hole in the bottom of this fucking site and money's draining out of it. I can't go back to John. I need a solution. I'm sorry. I know you love Martinborough. We all do. We've just got to do whatever it takes to plug the thing up.'

'What about the house you just bought for Heathcote? Hasn't the market gone crazy in Auckland?'

'It's all mortgage,' he said. 'The bank owns it.'

'It will have gone up hundreds of thousands even in these few months.'

'Long term,' Trevor said, 'I think the smart move is to hold on there.'

'But why Martinborough? It's so special. There's nowhere else like that place.'

'Darling. It's just one option. Nothing's happened yet.'

This project was ruling our lives. For an oxygenated second, I imagined life without it. I slid my hand across the table towards him. 'Could you let the hotel go?'

'No!' Another man – my father – might smack the table, call me a stupid bitch, but Trevor never lost his temper.

Now, in Guy Benson's meeting room, Marcus Todd said, 'So.'

There was a pause. I sipped my coffee. Here came the moment we had been avoiding. A cool look at the details.

'As Guy will have told you,' Trevor said, 'I maintain I'm not guilty of anything other than leapfrogging a process. I simply don't see the crime. It would be wrong to claim to have committed one. No one was harmed. The bank got their money back and interest to boot.'

'Right,' said Marcus Todd. 'So, what Guy should have told you is that the SFO don't like to lose and they don't file charges unless they know they have what they need to convict. Regardless what your intentions were, the bank maintains that you misled them. My strongest advice is for you to plead guilty and work to secure home detention rather than risk prison time.'

Everyone leaving the burning building. Trevor marching in. Cinders in the sky.

'There's no crime,' Trevor repeated.

'Trevor.' I laid my fingers on the back of his hand. Marcus Todd cast his eyes down to his desk, a form of privacy.

Trevor turned his palm up and squeezed my hand. 'Trust me.'

I wouldn't disagree with Trevor in front of this man. But I wondered at what point preserving his dignity led to neglecting my duty to say what I thought. Outside, the sun caught the glass walls of a finance building, bronze rays twisting the air.

Trevor insisted again. There was no paper trail that led to him forging documents. The move had been strictly expedience, without criminal intent.

'The bank could be asked to provide a victim impact statement,' Marcus said.

Trevor said, 'Ha.' Did he need to repeat the bank had made money? 'Funny kind of victim.'

'The investigators will find nothing with your name on it?'

'Nothing.'

'Then how—' I was stopped by a look from Guy.

In that case there was a tiny chance, Marcus Todd granted, Trevor would ride this out. The process was going to take a long time – we should be ready for that. He advised sleeping on it. The charges, if proved, did merit a possible custodial sentence. He was obliged to say.

'They won't be proved,' Trevor said.

'I'm sorry,' I said, 'but I have to get Trevor to his next appointment.'

They arranged to meet again the next day, just the two of them.

'We can go into more detail then,' Marcus Todd said.

We'd get used to breathing this air, I thought, to being these people. Perhaps I just had to toughen up. Weren't we all living at the edge of a shadow, anyway?

Straight after that meeting Trevor was scheduled to see the oral surgeon for a procedure that couldn't be put off, to remove a cracked tooth over an old root canal. From the waiting room I called Denise, the one person I was obliged to discuss all this with.

'I'm coming down,' she said. 'I've got a pile of stuff on but let me book a flight in a few days. In the meantime, name suppression is our friend.'

I exhaled slowly after hanging up and pressed my palms tight between my knees. A shiver had set up residence in the back of my ribs. I was still waiting for someone to say everything was going to be all right. But that was Trevor's job, and he wasn't there to do it.

As he recovered in a reclining chair, I listened carefully to the doctor's aftercare instructions. From the window you could see the motorway and the impersonality of rushing cars. The doctor had the tooth in a little Snap Lock bag. Trevor told her, slurring, to throw it away.

Who would I look after, if he wasn't there? Sometimes I feared that I didn't appreciate how great Trevor was until I thought about him dying.

We took the antibiotics script into the chemist where Trevor, still loose with Valium, high-fived the pharmacist and drew me to the sunglasses rack to try on ridiculous shades.

'You look good in everything,' he said.

'Yeah right.' I found a pair of heart-shaped frames, red with little white polka dots. I could see in the mirrored aviators Trevor had on that they were too small for my face.

'Sexy.' He kissed my cheek and bounced back, a hand to his jaw. 'Fuck.'

'Careful.'

'Therese.' He had hold of my hand again. His weight shifted, as if he was drunk. 'Where have you gone?'

'What do you mean?' I couldn't see his eyes.

'When I look at you lately, it's like I'm seeing double. I can't make you line up.'

He wasn't being literal. I leaned in to his broad chest.

'I'm here.' I took his arms and put them around me. 'Here.'

'This will blow over. I'll finish the hotel and we'll be in Sydney before you know it.'

'Mm.'

Now, I thought. Now, while he was high on Valium.

'Trevor. If there's no paper trail to you, was it the lawyer who did it? Or the money guy? Are they trying to catch you up in this for some reason? Can you just talk to them, tell them to stop?'

'It's nothing like that. It's nothing. Oh Therese I need you.' He settled his chin on the top of my head. 'You're a good person.'

It was cold there by the door. 'No. I'm not.'

Other customers came and went. We stood like that until the prescription was ready.

'Everything's going to be all right,' I said.

And later, when he had taken a pill and gone to sleep, when the linen sheets became scratchy, when the room spray, from a lavender farm in France, began to smell to me like paint stripper, when I saw that Trevor was still frowning in his open-mouthed sleep, when I walked through the apartment and the cushion fabric that had once told me who I was spoke of nothing, now, but cloth, when the furniture was a mere jumble of shapes, when the talismans from the trips and the galleries and the artisans' studios were just collections of atoms exhausted of their power, I craved the bare boards at Claire's.

18

She'd got rid of her furniture. In one vanload, Claire had carried Mick's things and all the decorative stuff like vases and pots he might miss over to his studio and piled them against a wall. Various organisations – St Vincent's, Women's Refuge, the Sallies – took the books, the couch, the armchairs, all but three of the dining chairs, and the rugs that had already been displaced by the stage.

She was reading a book when I got there, but she knew why I had come.

Without its trappings, the room looked smaller. It felt like being in a strange kind of temple. When Claire put the music on, Artan got out of bed and joined in, his movements still slightly constrained by the surgery – and the energy lifted another notch.

Halfway through a track Jesse wandered in from down the hall. He must have been in bed with Artan. I hadn't seen him since that day in the park. His hair was longer, and out of his security guard uniform he looked even more sprite-like. I felt a flash of guilt that ordinarily would make me want to hide, but he hopped onto the stage and hugged me without any evident bad feeling.

I leaned in and shouted above the music, 'Hey, I'm really sorry about the job,' and he said, 'Why? – *you* didn't fire me.'

I wanted to keep hugging him, but he pulled away and started punching his arms wildly in time to the drums. I punched mine too.

In between zone sessions we lay on the empty floor, in long stretches of silence. Every now and then a phrase would emerge from Claire, like 'the word *woman* is a category error', or 'you still think you can afford to wait', or 'bonsai is for trees'. Something like, 'if you stopped trying to improve yourself, who would you be?' She radiated energy. Her breastbone looked as if it would be hot to the touch.

Heat was in the air too, and crackled between Jesse and Artan, who were physical and loose with each other and delicious to be around, a salty, clean counterpoint to Claire's earthiness. Artan opened up; he was a different person from the serious guy I'd met at the hospital. I wondered if his wife had, after all, abandoned him, or if her leaving him had been an act of love.

Outside, the birds started up. 'What day is it?' I said.

'Sunday.'

At some point he and Jesse went to get food and I drifted off to Alex's old room to sleep. An open shoebox full of polaroids was out on the bed – I couldn't help but look through. At the top were pictures of a naked male torso in different poses. Erect cock. No face. Was it Jesse? Artan? At first I thought the pictures must be theirs – but also there were photo-booth style snaps of Alex, dressed for a school dance, posing with girlfriends, and photos of her smiling and squinting at the camera in the sorts of clichéd beach images that we used in Therese Thorne catalogues – peeking through grass, running away, turning to laugh over your shoulder, that sort of thing. What the fuck, I thought now as I flipped through shot after shot, were these women meant to be running from?

It was hard to imagine Alex, sweet young Alex, taking these polaroids of a posing male body. The torso looked worked, not youthfully slim but gym-toned. The erotic purpose of the pictures was a turn-on in itself. As I was falling asleep, I let myself imagine being fucked by the faceless man in the white frame.

I woke to the sound of voices down the hallway, and went out to find that Artan and Jesse were still not back, but Claire's sister was there. We had been introduced at the dinner party.

Melissa slowly turned around in the middle of the newly bare living room. 'I don't like the look of this,' she said. 'Hi Therese.'

'I should get going,' I said.

'No,' said Claire. 'Stay.'

Something in her look suggested that she needed me there. The stage's black surface gleamed in the afternoon light. Was it afternoon? The red glass bowls were still on the shelf. The lions crouched and stared.

'This is actually nuts,' said Melissa. 'Where's all your stuff?'

'I gave it away.'

'There's nothing to sit on.'

'We can sit on the floor.' Claire perched on the edge of the stage and stretched her legs out. Melissa eyed it as if it might burn.

'I've got a ton of things to do. I can't stay.'

She had come to pick up Alex's hand-me-downs for her daughter. The bags were sitting in the hall, along with a share of the sentimental items she and Claire had inherited from their parents and which Claire had had custody of – blankets, pictures.

'Why don't you stay,' Claire asked, 'and join in?'

'Join in what?' Melissa dug at the floorboards with her sneakered foot. She flicked her eyes to me before saying to Claire, 'Are you having a breakdown? Mick will hate this.'

I poured a glass of water and tried to be invisible.

'Mick isn't here,' Claire said.

'What about your Ukranian?' Melissa craned her neck to look down the hall.

'He's Albanian.'

'Don't you miss Alex?'

What she meant was, who are you if you're not looking after someone? I thought it was a good question.

'Also,' Melissa said, 'is that grey intentional? In your hair?'

'I've stopped dyeing it.'

'But you're going to get one of those tide marks!' she said, as if she were describing self-harm. 'Go online. There are whole Instagram accounts dedicated to growing your hair out properly. Aren't there?' Melissa appealed to me now.

'Properly?' Claire said.

'Look at Therese. She looks great. You look weird with that mixed-message hair. No one else is going to tell you. And you're getting a moustache.' Melissa pointed to the corners of her lips. 'If you uncovered your mirrors you'd know. Claire, I'm sorry, but other people have to look at you. Don't we?'

I laughed. 'Don't bring me into it.' Her compliment had pleased me but I also felt as if *looking great* were pandering.

'Don't be so – *oaty* about all this,' Melissa went on. 'So puritanical.'

She might have meant, don't leave me. Don't travel off into the mad place of witchy women, of scrying and mole hair and middle-distance stares. Stay in the warmth, where we worry about school exams and recycling and the leak in the roof. Don't make me do it alone.

'What about the catering job?' she said now. 'You can't hand out food looking like Baba Yaga.'

'I'm on prep,' Claire said. 'We wear hairnets. Snoods.'

'Snoods!'

Melissa laughed and I could see her relief at still finding the same silly things funny. I thought of Donna – a sharp memory of laughing so hard we both wet ourselves.

I tuned back in to hear Melissa saying, 'The thing is, if we put white men up against the wall, aren't we next in line?'

'That's not what this is about.'

'What is it about? Your "renunciation" or whatever it is.' Here came the air quotes. 'If you're looking to be "authentic" or something, why does that have to mean you abandon looking like a woman? What's so bad about sitting on a fucking couch?'

'What does a woman look like?'

'Oh, don't start that.'

'Mel. I'm just having fun.'

Melissa moved around the apartment, avoiding the stage, nudging the wall, rapping on the head of one of the lions to show how tinny it was.

'Why can't you be one of those long-haired prairie-style witches? The fuckable ones. This is weird, Claire. You've gone weird.'

'How are the kids?'

Melissa was raising her two boys and a girl on her own; her ex now lived in Perth with a new wife and baby.

'He's reneged on his promise to come at Easter. He's given up flying. For the planet. What kind of person has four children *then* starts worrying about the planet? Can't he plant some fucking trees? That's what I said to him, can't you just plant some fucking trees out there in the fucking outback?'

'Maybe he could come once a year. All the celebrations in one visit.'

'Maybe he could step on a poisonous snake.' She slipped into an Australian accent. 'A reely poursonous sniike. Do you know what I realised last night? I always ask my sons to take out the compost. And get my daughter to bring in the laundry. I want to put myself up against the wall. I cancel myself.'

She held a red glass bowl to the light; I wondered if she might smash it on the ground.

'The thing is,' Melissa said, 'not everyone can do a so-called "role switch". Some people have to do the money job and the compost and the car rego and the emotional support because there's no one else to do it. Some people are on 24-7. Like right now, I'm meant to be returning library books and getting eczema cream and finding something I can stand to cook for dinner because if it's pasta with cheese one more time I will grate my own face. And that's before the giant pile of marking that awaits me. It's just life, Claire.' She threw a dismissive hand at the stage. 'You can't opt out.'

'This is life too. Why not? If it makes you feel good. Like...'
She appealed to me, laughing, helpless to justify herself.

'Whole,' I said.

'I don't want to be whole! I like my mind-body split.' Melissa gestured up and down her torso: 'I'm not this lump of meat,

OK? I'm my little whirling thoughts and feelings and I'm fine with that. Meditation freaks me out.'

'It's just dancing,' Claire said.

That wasn't strictly true, but I didn't know how else to explain the zone.

'I don't have time for it.'

'Are you sure?'

'And what's that smell? Patchouli? I mean, fucking patchouli? I'm very, very worried about you.' She was laughing, but she meant it. 'I have to go,' she said, and for a second I thought she was going to cry.

Claire grabbed the remote control for the stereo, hopped up onto the stage, and cocked her head at her sister. She selected a song on her phone – a riot grrrl band I hadn't heard for years – and slowly began to turn up the music. With nothing to absorb it, the sound licked over the walls with the sharpness of fresh paint. I could feel the pull of the zone.

'No,' said Melissa.

'Come on.' Claire moved to the guitar. 'Have a dance!'

'No.' Melissa strode across the room and hoisted her bag over her shoulder. 'I'm not going there with you.' She had to raise her voice to be heard. 'You're having a breakdown. You've got to get rid of your little Albanian prisoner. Get a couch.' Now she was shouting. 'Get a better job. Get a haircut. Get a wax.'

'Melissa, Melissa… There's so much time.'

'No.' Melissa thrust the face of her phone towards her sister. 'Look. I forgot to click the parking app. Fuck. I'll have a ticket.' She marched towards the hall. 'You owe me forty bucks!'

I rounded the breakfast bar to follow Claire into the hallway, where daylight didn't reach. The music was loud behind me. Melissa was by the front door, Claire between us. I couldn't see Claire's face or make out what she was saying over the music, but Melissa shouted – 'You have got no idea about my life' – and a scuffle erupted as Claire tried to prise a rubbish sack from her sister's clenched fist. The clanging music became a soundtrack to a flurry of slapped hands and yanking at sleeves, the door wrenched open then shut again as Melissa lurched sideways, her weight slamming into it. 'Stop it!' I said.

To my surprise they did stop. The next second they were embracing, a fierce hug that Melissa squirmed out of before she swung the door wide open. Claire passed her the bags and picked up a box. 'I'll come down with you,' she said.

'No, don't,' Melissa said. She wiped her face. 'I'll come back for that stuff another time.'

She left.

We came back into the room and Claire turned the music off. In the silence she looked almost porous with vulnerability. I thought then, and would think again later, that our families never really want us to change.

'Are you OK?' I asked.

She said, 'She's right. I am selfish.'

I started to say something, then stopped. My habit, I realised, was to say whatever would make people feel better in a moment, even if it wasn't what I really believed. There had to be another form of kindness. We sat on the edge of the stage. I took Claire's hand and she leaned into me.

'Listen,' she said. 'Artan needs money.'

'What?'

'He needs to get back to Albania but he can't leave till he's paid for his surgery. And he needs to find a new job once he gets there.'

'I thought he was on leave?'

'The guy he works for is corrupt. They're building bridges or something with shitty concrete and he's terrified there's going to be an accident. He's trying to get out of the contract. It's not the worst thing in the world that he's here. Not that we have no corruption.'

Everything I heard in those days seemed like a judgment. Therese. This was not about you.

'You're the only person I know who can afford it,' Claire said. 'He couldn't pay you back.'

'How much does he need?'

'Whatever you can spare.'

What was that amount? What was enough? And was this how Claire saw me – as a mark? I weighed the possibility, and found I didn't care.

'Sure,' I said. 'Let's do it.'

As Claire smiled, a shivery, golden high rushed through me. She kept hold of my hand after hoisting me to my feet. Her grip was light. She smelled earthy, animalistic. I wanted her to put the music on so I could throw myself about again, ragdoll my body, but she said, 'I've got to go to work.'

We were standing close. I could smell toothpaste on her breath.

'Don't say anything to Trevor,' I said. 'About the money.'

'Are you grooming me?'

'Yeah. Our little secret. Is that creepy?'

'You're discreet. Loyal.'

When Trevor and I had first got together he'd asked me not to tell anyone 'about us' until he'd spoken to Judith. Maybe I would have enjoyed confiding in my fellow workers at the hotel, but it was also a thrill to keep the secret to myself. He'd said my discretion was a sign of maturity, and I still carried the praise all these years later, like a barley sugar in my handbag.

'Thanks,' I said.

Claire said, 'It's not a compliment.'

She ran her fingers over my knuckles. The feeling that we were holding ourselves back rose up between us, unsteadying the air, and I didn't know how to act. I thought, people don't do this. I thought, being a good person is not doing this.

When we kissed, a shivery feeling bloomed and rippled through me. The smell of mint, the good wrongness of her mouth. Donna was the only other woman – girl – I'd ever kissed, at a party we held at her house when her dad wasn't there, and that had been for show. Something to entertain the guys. Here we were on the stage but no one was looking now. The outside layer that kept me intact lifted off.

'I've got to go,' she said. The skin around her mouth was pink. She pulled me down off the stage and the normal room rushed back.

'Don't look so worried!' she said. 'This doesn't have to be anything. We never have to do it again.'

Since Trevor and I got together I'd never been unfaithful, not even kissed anyone else: I saw fidelity as something pure, like a crystal bowl, that once chipped was worthless. Not like if you fell off the wagon and had to start your daily count all over again. You could always get sober. No, like if you got a tattoo. Or killed someone. You would always be a person who had killed someone. Keeping a crystal bowl from smashing for thirty-odd years had turned into an endurance task. I'd forgotten the reason, it had just become about the bowl. And that wasn't faithfulness, I realised now, as I stepped off the stage in a daze; it was pride.

19

Denise had chosen a spot outside the café, so that when she needed to smoke she could hover by the table, her cigarette arm extended behind her as though if she couldn't see it no one else would know she was smoking either. It was an e-cigarette, her concession to meeting in person.

I took the bench seat in the shade and, a moment after sitting, shifted into the Claire wide-legged posture as if giving some kind of secret handshake to myself, put my elbows on the table and leaned forward. I kept my sunglasses on.

'Sorry you've had to fly down for this,' I said.

Denise's face couldn't move much, but some rising action happened up near her hairline. 'And to see my mother.'

'Sure. And to see your mother.'

Denise emitted a rattle that could have been a laugh or a cough.

'How bad is it? From your point of view,' I said.

From my own point of view, it was bad to the level of constant nausea. When I did sleep, my dreams were of trying to save babies in choppy seas. Every hour some new consequence would break over me – without Trevor's support my parents would have to move back here – what about my employees – his health – his kids – and those were the things I could give voice to.

Denise gave a dramatic exhale of steam. 'Put it this way. I'm here. And my mother is a stone-cold bitch.'

'OK. I know this is bad. I can't even feel it completely so I know it's bad. But he has got name suppression.'

'So it's only an open secret. Everyone it could possibly matter to already knows.'

'But there's no general publicity, nothing naming him in the news. What about the customers? Have you noticed any change on social?' I had been too cowardly to look at the Instagram account or search *Therese Thorne*.

'You must have spoken to Emalani,' she said. 'What's showing up in the accounts?'

I had euphemised the situation to her, avoiding the word *fraud*. Some trouble with historic paperwork, I'd said. It was a holding position.

'She's hedging her bets,' I said. 'The monthly figures won't be in till next week.'

'New stationery?'

'I don't know.'

The goal was to stock at least three key items that girls had to have at the start of each school term. For the coming winter we'd pinned our hopes on a stainless-steel straw, a clip to hide the camera lens on a laptop or phone, and a giant eraser that bore the legend 'cancelled'.

Denise shrugged. 'The mums do the buying. Their kids won't care about Trevor's problems, but the mothers do.'

'But most of them won't know.'

'I think it depends on where this is all going,' said Denise. 'If only it wasn't your fucking building. Couldn't he have lied to the bank about some other bloody thing?'

I made a face.

'Sorry, sorry,' she said. 'Allegedly lied.'

'He's not guilty.'

'Good.' She gave a wheezing laugh. 'Because if he were to be found guilty of fraud for something called the Therese Thorne building, it's fair to say the Therese Thorne brand would be Therese Thorne fucked.'

A smell of old rubbish wafted over from the street corner.

'What about Sydney?' she asked.

I shook my head.

Holding the front of her blouse away from her chest, Denise bent her head to sniff.

'God, I sweated on the plane. Came straight here so my mother couldn't tell me to change. You know my theory, the more considerate a woman is, the more her mother was a cunt.'

I wasn't sure if Denise was evidence or the exception that proved the rule.

'Sorry you've had to come and clean up after my mess.'

'Is it your mess?'

'Isn't it?'

'Will they call you as a witness?'

'We're hoping to avoid it. But they will, so Trevor's just not telling me much. I mean, he didn't do anything wrong, but it's good that I honestly don't know any details.'

'How's he holding up?'

'Bullish. But I think he's scared.'

'Fair enough.' She lowered her voice. 'Are you likely to be investigated? Separately?'

'There's no reason. All the business stuff is separate, apart from him being on our board.'

Denise nodded, and placed her coffee cup in its saucer with theatrical gravity. We'd arrived at the thing she had travelled from Auckland to say.

'He has to step down from that.'

I gave up on the cowboy posture and crossed my legs. At a table a few feet away, a couple of young women were laughing at something on a phone. When the investigation was first announced Trevor had offered to resign from the board and I had said no and asked him to stay on. It was an easy decision, as simple as taking his hand. He had been so pleased. Now my reasons for refusing his offer had eluded me; I was losing the ability to tell myself the story.

'I don't want to ask him to resign,' I said.

'It's up to you. But listen, the tide has changed, and the optics of a woman staying with her husband at all costs are—'

'Wait. My marriage is not in question.'

'Yes of course, that's not what I meant, I meant publicly standing by him despite any misdeeds.'

'Which still haven't been proved.'

'It's not just about that. He's been charged. That's it, for many people. The way these things are perceived is different these days, and that's what you've asked me to advise on.'

The way this all looked did matter to me. I cared about the so-called optics and not just for the impact on the business, but for my own reputation, such as it was. We lived in a small city in a small country. I had already had a taste of public disapprobation. Even once he was found not guilty, was it going to be easy to walk into restaurants, cinemas, art galleries, the places we considered our habitat, with Trevor, anymore? Political acolytes, these days, invoked 'respect for the position' to explain why they didn't speak out against the sins of those who were unfit and yet held power. The other side of that coin was that if you had no position, your character didn't matter either: disrespect for you. I knew what it felt like to be no one important. Trevor didn't.

'I get that you're devoted to him,' Denise said.

'Devoted's a strong word. Right now.'

'Loyal, then. You're one of those couples, you make sense. And there will be women who relate. But some of them will want you to do what they might not do themselves.'

I couldn't see how looking at my choice through the lens of an impersonal, vague consumer presence would get me any closer to the truth. It was all second-guessing. If a generation ago I would have been expected to stand by my errant husband, was I any freer now, being frowned on if I did not leave, or going down with the ship?

'It's only a board position,' said Denise.

'It's a message,' I said. 'That would be the point.'

'I want you to think about this very carefully,' Denise said. 'Timing is important. There will be such a thing as it being too late to do this and have the right effect. You have to look as though you're making your own decision, not reacting to public or legal pressure.'

The thought of asking him made me feel sick. Not only for the prospect of his anger and hurt, but for what it would reveal of my priorities. I was used to keeping my feelings to myself, my words and actions serving as a kind of shield protecting some other me that no one else, not even Trevor, knew. It had become a habit, and the idea was only just dawning on me that my words and actions, not my secret thoughts, were who I was.

Denise waggled her vape pen. 'I'm going to have a quick think. Then I want to talk about the brand.'

Unlike Denise I was old enough to remember when 'my brand' was a joke phrase, a concept taken seriously only by tragics and wannabes. I watched her pace the street, smoking with one hand and texting with the other. I drew out my own phone and opened up the company website. The first thing that greeted me was a photo of beach grass, the whole family in Breton striped T-shirts, the background in soft focus. It looked like a still from a horror film.

The personal touch had been key to our early success: young entrepreneur with her successful older husband, being a good sport on the yacht. Whether Trevor was there or not, I existed in relation to him. Sun, moon. Oak, sapling. Wife. Of. Had I started the company on my own, no one would have taken any notice. Even my lucky looks, enough to jailbreak me from my child-hood, would not have drawn attention without him.

Denise returned to the table. Here was her plan. Leave Trevor to one side for now. Most consumers didn't look at who sat on company boards anyway. Instead, we could prepare for a worst-case scenario and take the opportunity to refresh the brand, even move the promotions away from the extended family vibe into 'woman alone' or 'solo mother and daughter' imagery. Single women were having a moment.

'You don't have to actually change anything. The images do it all. Striking out. Strong female character. Spiritual. Resilient. Mama bear. A reinvention at a time of change.'

I thought back to Claire's rant against floppy hats. She'd laugh at this idea. It came to me that the available roles were being ruled out one by one. No boss girl, no ingenue, no mama bear, no loyal wife, no triumphant ex, no louche divorcee. Not a maid, thank you Fern, not a nurturer, not a wise crone. I wanted a costume to hide inside, but none of them fit.

Denise didn't want to tread on toes, she said, but we should book a strategy meeting with the design team and finance officer. Scope out some friendly journalists.

'No one's throwing Trevor under the bus. The subtext is, your star rises while his star wanes. A natural result of the ageing process, so if anything, it's respectful. It's your time. Hey – that could be a strapline.'

'Let me think about it.'

'OK.' She patted my hand. 'Not for too long. We need to get things in motion. And,' as she pocketed a breath mint, 'I need to say that I love working with you. You have my absolute commitment. But I need to believe in the brand I manage, OK?'

She studied me, as if trying to see my eyes behind my sunglasses.

'You look rough,' she said. 'Bit of makeup might help. Brush through your hair.'

'I get it,' I said. 'Your reputation matters too. I'm not going to melt down. That's a promise. Good luck with your mother.'

She left the café, laughing until it turned into a cough that progressed into dry retching on the hot, wind-strafed street. When I called out to ask if she needed help, she waved me away with her whole arm.

I sat at the café table for a long time. Denise was paid to think like this. But I could feel my mind straying off course. While I knew the situation was real and consequential, it didn't seem as important, say, as the fact that Denise and her mother would likely never resolve their differences before one of them died, and this would be the only mother Denise would ever have, and for reasons of social indoctrination, denial, and fear, most of their conversations would be play-acted to each other, while Denise told herself that the meaningless content of these exchanges didn't matter as much as the attempt at a loving tone they were able, with great effort, to employ.

Then there were Rebecca, Emalani and the other employees. If Therese Thorne went under, would they be tainted by association? What was happening in the employment market? How would Rebecca and her fiancé get ahead? What would my years of working amount to? What else could I do?

Across the road a familiar portly figure, a rival property developer, strode towards an office block and was swallowed by its massive plate glass doors. Late at a party one night, years ago, that man told me – bragged to me – that he had done the very thing Trevor was now being investigated for. He tossed it in while reeling off his latest success, emphasising the risks he was prepared to take.

'You can't wait for the pen pushers.' He was drunk, and he had taken my hand in his prawny fingers and said, 'Can tell you're pushing forty.' He nodded around the other women in the room. 'Younger than these trouts though. The hands never lie.'

At the time I had thought, of all of it, Trevor would never do that. Now I looked at the back of my hands and saw how freckled they had grown. Why hadn't I snatched my hand away?

20

I was on my way to a meeting at the university when Claire came up the stairs towards me. Her hair was wet from a swim, and she smelled of chlorine. She looked somehow dimmed. We hadn't seen each other since the kiss. I felt a sudden crisis of etiquette – what did we owe each other?

'I'm in a rush,' I said. 'But – shall I come over later, shall we do something?'

'Yes, sure,' she said.

'What?'

She shook her head. 'I feel bad saying it.'

My stomach lurched. I didn't like being above her on the stairs, but couldn't press past. 'Tell me,' I said, trying to keep my voice light.

'It's been great having Artan here but I want my space. This year was meant to be about me being on my own. And he's just always there, and now Jesse is too. Did I tell you he had to move out of his flat? I've got this loved-up couple around 24/7. It wasn't the plan.'

'When's Artan going back?'

'I don't know, never at this rate. There's nothing stopping him but he just extended his visa. I hate the young.'

I was giddy with relief that her problem wasn't me.

When I started the engine my petrol light came on with a little ding, but I was in a rush, so ignored it, and besides the warning always sounded too soon. I found a park by the university bookshop.

The fundraising officer was still in another meeting. Someone showed me into her office, where a tray of tea and biscuits was laid out on the small round table. On the wall behind the desk hung a tapa cloth and I got briefly lost in the pattern. Last time I was here, it had been an oil portrait of a man with a pipe. A third chair, Trevor's chair, sat empty at the table; the office was small and there was nowhere else to put it. The fundraising officer gave it a glance as she crossed the room to shake my hand.

'Kia ora. Therese? Sorry to keep you waiting. The VC likes to talk. Please, sit down.' Her name was Hana.

'I have a friend who was in fundraising,' I said. 'Claire?'

Hana gave a small nod. 'Oh yes. I know her.'

Her tone was less than warm, which surprised me.

'Are we expecting your husband too?'

'No,' I said, 'just me, sorry.'

She rolled right on. 'I hope you've received the letters from last year's prize winners?'

I had. I read them every year, sometimes more than once – they were a little well of nourishment. Of course, some were dashed off, or had come from students so groomed by the private school system that the tone was more one of accepting their dues than of genuine enthusiasm, but a few made me cry. No matter how sophisticated the language and ideas, you could almost smell the youth coming off the page. They were not cynical. I wanted to live in the future they imagined.

'I don't know how much you've been told,' I said, 'but Trevor and I are keen to make a similar sum available for scholarships towards living costs. No academic requirement, just needs-based. I know the first year is free now, but people still have to work or take out loans and we want to make it easier for even a handful.'

Trevor didn't, in fact, know I was here. But it was his money too, so it seemed only right to include him.

Hana put her coffee cup down. My lipstick had left a little print on the rim of mine, which I thumbed off.

'Thank you for coming in,' Hana said, 'because we value your contributions very much. When I started working here, everyone talked about how great your support has been. And your husband's.'

'It's both of us,' I said.

'And can I ask how things are going with Trevor's business? The investigation.'

This took me by surprise. I should have anticipated it – as far as she was concerned, he was still being looked into by the SFO. She couldn't know about the charges, but she'd think it possible some would be laid.

'It's a pain,' I said. 'They're just doing their job, but he hasn't done anything wrong.'

That wasn't strictly a lie.

She nodded, dry and implacable, and as sweat formed in my armpits I thought, lucky her, she must be on the other side of menopause.

'It does mean we are in an unusual situation,' she said.

'What's unusual?'

'I'm sure that there hasn't been any wrongdoing, but while Trevor is under investigation, we…'

The words floated to me out of order. Investigation, complicated, generational attitudes, students, no rush, certainty. She came to an end and let the silence sit.

'We're not funding an opioid crisis,' I said, trying to laugh. 'Trevor didn't rape anybody.' Rape! I was making things worse.

She looked startled. 'No one's saying that.'

'It was a joke. Sorry. Obviously, obviously he didn't,' fuck, I was going to say it again, 'rape anyone. He isn't a rapist.'

'This is very awkward,' she said, 'please don't be offended. We're just suggesting we hold off, for now, on setting up new scholarships. They wouldn't come into place until the end of this year anyway. So we can wait.'

'What about the Thorne Family prizes?' I asked. 'Do you want to can those too?'

'I'm sure it will all have cleared up by the time we're looking at those.'

I laughed, then realised she was serious. 'Is any student going to turn down free money?'

'I'm new to the tertiary environment,' Hana said. 'As your friend Claire knows. But we're finding that students – they take an interest in where the money comes from.'

'Isn't it more important what they do with it?' I said.

'There's a lot of discussion around names, for instance, associations.'

'Associations. I don't know what you mean.'

She looked at her hands. It dawned on me that she felt sorry for me.

'If it's a question of values,' I began, and to my embarrassment my voice cracked. I shook my head. 'Sorry.'

Hana topped up my water glass. They're very lucky people, Claire had said of the donors she had worked with: 'they get to have and they get to give.'

I took a sip. What would Trevor do? Would he be outraged, would he make light of it, would he ask to speak to some-one higher up? Any of these responses were beyond me. I could understand what Hana was saying. It just made me so sad.

On the desk behind her was a photo of a boy in a school uniform, a broad, wonky grin showing missing front teeth.

'Is he your…?' I asked.

'My grandson. He lives with me.'

'He looks like a great kid.'

'Yeah, he's a crack-up. Have you got kids?'

I shook my head. 'Trevor has. Grown up now.'

She nodded. 'They're easier when they're little.' Then she gave me a wink, and it felt like the kindest gesture anyone had ever made. It also made clear there was nothing more to say.

I got lost on the way out of the building. Walls had moved, and a new mezzanine level seemed to have appeared. As I walked along its corridor, the open atrium below, a grey-haired man walked towards me. I felt a heave of rage towards older men.

The grandfather clock in the atrium chimed the first stroke of the hour as the man neared. I hated them at the gym, with their aftershave. I hated them on bush walks, panting. He wore a shirt and jumper over suit trousers and from the way he carried himself, had once been important. The clock struck again. I pressed back against the wall to give him passing space. I hated them in restaurants, with their voices, and in movie queues, talking, coats over their arms, and I hated them in cars and grocery shops, and I hated the ones who had been beautiful and were now floury in band T-shirts and the ones that stood in waiting areas and loudly discussed roads and travel routes and weather, confident in their right to be boring.

The clock chimed the third time as the man reached me – I could push him over the edge of the banister right now – then he had passed. As I descended the stairs, I looked up and saw that Hana had come out of her office to talk to him. She nodded, and glanced down at me – I waved, then realised she hadn't seen me, and because another person coming up the stairs witnessed the whole non-exchange, I stretched my arm higher in the air as if I had a dicky shoulder and said, 'Ooh, this weather.'

The smell of petrol mingled with the harbour air; the unleaded pumped through the nozzle into my car. I marvelled that the sensor stopped the flow before it came splashing out all over my shoes. I didn't know how anything worked. Under the fluorescent lights I paced the service station shelves. There was something I needed but what was it?

I got into the car with a cellophane-wrapped steak and cheese pie warm in my hands and tossed a packet of cigarettes onto the passenger seat. Two things I hadn't bought for thirty years. Eating the pie was chaotic, somehow filling was left over once all the pastry had gone and when I turned the bag inside out to lick it, I got meat sauce all up my wrist and on my shirt. Instead of returning to the car once I'd put the wrapper in the rubbish bin, I found myself back at the counter paying for a second pie – chicken this time. This one I ate standing over the bin.

I texted Rebecca to say I'd be out of the office for a bit longer, and pulled onto the motorway. I'd forgotten that my car didn't have a cigarette lighter in it, and had to wait till I reached my old neighbourhood to buy matches from the dairy. My heart thumped as if I were going to be caught smoking on the street corner.

The head teacher of my old school was in a meeting. I waited in the foyer, with a view onto the open door of the sick bay, where a small boy lay on the bed clutching a hot water bottle. What did he love, I wondered, who were his enemies, where were the secret places he liked to go? My phone beeped – a series of texts from Rebecca that must have come through while I was driving, reminders that we needed time to prepare for a video call with the latest potential investor in the Sydney boutique. I sent back fire emojis.

My stomach made a loud growling noise and I tried not to think of the pies. I wanted that hot water bottle. That sick bay bed. The taste of the cigarette I'd smoked leaning against my car, outside the school, still prickled in my mouth.

'Therese Thorne?'

'Yes.'

When I'd gone here, I had been Teresa Holder. That was a thousand years ago and I didn't tell the youthful head teacher my old name, as, still spinning from the nicotine, I sat opposite him – he could give me five minutes – and explained that as a former pupil at the school I would like to make a donation. Anonymously, please. There wouldn't be a name attached, not mine, not my husband's.

My phone pinged with a text and I set it to do not disturb, then named the amount I wanted to donate. It was my share of the trust fund. It would mean cashing in. No strings, no agenda. The school would decide what they were going to do with it. Maybe a van to get to sports competitions, classroom supplies, special needs support, the library... I was rambling.

The head teacher had a deacon-like appearance, and didn't react with any surprise or delight but kept his eyes on me while he noted the amount on a scratch pad in front of him. While I talked, explaining my connection with the school, the importance of its library, my desire to give back, he patted the figure with a fingertip as if to make sure it stayed put.

'We never turn down money,' he said. 'And yep, there's a long list of things we need.'

'Great. I mean, that I can help.'

We talked logistics, which was really him sounding me out to make sure I knew how these things worked and wasn't a delusional random off the street, and he asked his secretary to set up a meeting with their treasurer.

Although the five minutes were soon up, I didn't want to move from my seat and sat smiling at him, feeling cleansed. In the silence, my stomach creaked. 'Excuse me.'

The head teacher's face twitched, but he controlled it. 'All good.'

He was rearranging things on his desk but I ignored the signals that the meeting was over. I wanted this moment to last. It was like the feeling after being in the zone, only not for my body, but for my soul.

I asked after teachers who had been at the school in my day, and he reckoned a couple of them had only just retired.

'Do you know the journalist Haimona Scott? He went here.'

'Oh, yes. We still have Scotts coming through, awesome family, very involved. I think he was here not so long ago, giving a talk, careers day. Is he a friend of yours?'

'We're neighbours,' I said. My stomach roiled again and I focused on holding still.

'Should I know what you do?' he said. 'Apologies for not knowing your name, but it's a very generous donation and I assume there's...'

'Nothing special,' I said. 'I have a homeware business.' My hand closed around the car keys in my pocket. 'Thanks so much for your time.'

'Well really,' he said. 'Thank you.'

As I stood up, a tearing fart escaped me. The head teacher stared.

'Oh my god,' I said. 'I'm so sorry. I – you don't want to know.'

'No, no,' he said, and he let himself laugh, shoulders shaking like a boy, 'you've made my day. Twice.'

His giggling was infectious. I was standing in the midst of a terrible smell.

'Stay there. Don't come any closer.'

'I – oh man, whoo—' He lurched backwards and opened the window beside his desk. 'We really, thank you for your—' the attempt to regain seriousness failed and he put a hand to his breast with a grin running free on his face. 'Thank you so much.'

Sweating, I clung to the shred of me that could still function in a normal social way. 'I'm going now,' I said, 'I have to go.' A sound like a dog whine came from my guts.

'Can you leave your details for a thank you from the Board of Trustees? I'll get one sent to you. I'm so sorry—' he could hardly speak for laughing.

'No, I'm sorry.' I wasn't slugs and snails and puppy dogs' tails. That's what I'd been taught here. I was Little Floss skipping across the asphalt. But my top lip was sweating and my bowels seized and before it could happen again, I left the room and walked quickly and tightly down the corridor, opened a door onto the staff loo but it had an Engaged sign and seemed too public, and now at a half jog I scanned the hallway for any student toilets and there they were, just as I suddenly remembered.

I sat in the cubicle in my own stink for a long time. What was I doing here? Why had I come to this place when it all could have been done with a phone call? Was it to reach across the distance for that smaller me, the girl who sat in the library with Donna when the others were at the zoo, reading a child's version of the Greek myths? Donna liked stories about girl detectives. We threw them all over for sex and shopping. With that memory came the feeling that all of those years were waiting for me here, that I'd turn the wrong corner – or the right one – and Teresa would be there.

I wasn't ready to drive home. I sat in my parked car, wound down the window, lit another cigarette and absorbed the smoke. After a minute I got out.

216

Two blocks away, Donna's house was recently painted, with scrubby agapanthus on the verge. The suburban afternoon silence held me in suspense. Was it possible her dad still lived there, over thirty years on? Donna herself was long gone, I knew that, and no amount of Facebook searching had found her.

It was hard to imagine Steve in his late seventies, retired. He must be at least that age now, must have been early forties when I was seventeen.

It was a mistake to have followed my feet here; the car I'd left back by the school appeared in my mind's eye, shiny and vulnerable; it would be stripped for parts, or hotwired, gone. But that was Therese thinking, Therese who had the luxury of remaining girlish and unhardened, who made a fucking fetish of it.

Someone appeared at the end of the street, approaching from the direction of the shops, and to the left my eye caught a flicker – the reflection of a bird across a window, or a movement from within Donna's house. I crossed the scraggy verge. A bin on the concrete steps was filled with beer bottles, empty cereal boxes and washed tin cans. I knocked on the door.

There's that science, isn't there, that says we're not in charge of our actions like we think. That first our bodies move of their own accord, and our minds only make sense of the gesture a microsecond later – put a story to it. Same with physical sensations. Your stomach burns, and depending on the situation you interpret that as excitement or fear or a service station pie.

A smell of stale beer wafted up from the empties. I didn't remember this bubbled glass on the door. Perhaps I had the wrong house. Next door a rectangle of earth had been turned into a veggie garden – a few grey pumpkins nestled between leaves.

The sound of the door opening, a teenage girl: cami top, tracksuit pants, bare feet. She had a phone in her hand.

'Hello?' She glanced me over as if my purpose would be obvious – to spread the word of the Lord, or recruit for a multi-level marketing scheme.

I asked, knowing it was impossible, if Steve or Donna were there – like someone gate-crashing a party and pretending to know the host. My voice sounded foreign to this place and I tried to relax into the way I used to speak.

She didn't know who I was talking about.

'They used to live here,' I said. 'I used to come here. When I was about your age, so like, couple of years ago!'

She didn't laugh. 'Sorry,' she said, going to shut the door.

'Is this your place? Could I come in?'

An indistinct query came from within the house, and over her shoulder she called, 'Pause it.' To me she said, 'Have you got an ID?'

'No.' I plucked at my shirtfront, as if an invisible lanyard hung there. 'I was a friend of theirs.'

She yelled again to whoever waited for her, 'It's no one! I'm coming!' and began to close the door again. 'I've got to go.'

I put a hand on the door and said, 'Just a quick look? I've been away a long time and you know, tour of the old neighbourhood.'

Another once-over. I must have seemed weird, but no real threat. 'OK.'

The space she left in the door was only wide enough for me to see a bit of wall. I pushed the door open wider and saw the short hall-space with doors leading off it, all closed except for one to the living room, beyond which was the kitchen. All so familiar.

There was no point thinking now about how it started. In mine and Donna's last year at school, we got boyfriends. I quickly broke up with mine, but I was looking for someone new and her dad – Steve – noticed me in a new way and I noticed him noticing. He was a grown-up. Good-looking. Funny. It was like having warm water poured on me, bringing all my surfaces to life. I was the first person it had ever happened to.

Now I walked towards the open living room door, to the sound of talking: 'I don't know, some old white lady,' and another girl glanced up from the couch as the first girl emerged from the kitchen with a glass of water in her hand and they watched me look around, hands on their phones.

'Could I have a water too?' I asked.

'Are you OK?' said the girl beside the couch. She wore track pants and a bikini top. On the television screen an anime was paused on two androgynous young people with spiked eyelashes going in for a kiss.

'Yes, thanks,' I said. 'Just having a hot flush. Sorry to interrupt your show.'

The first girl came back with another glass and I took it.

The one on the couch started up the anime again. The perfect characters kissed and drew apart, eyes wet.

The other girl nodded at my silent question, and followed me slowly as I touched the walls – all in the same place, no renovations here – and walked from room to room.

I felt dizzied by the number of choices it had taken, to become what I thought a woman was. Growing up as a series of acceptability tests. Can you laugh, can you flirt, can you listen, can you resist. For so long, none of it was real, until one day it had formed you, even as a faint voice told you this was just what you'd learned, not who you were. Once, after we kissed, Steve said he was in love with me, but a small, honest part of me didn't believe it, even if he thought it was true. He was smitten. I knew there was a difference.

Somehow a rumour started about me and Donna's dad. Perhaps Donna told someone her suspicions, and they soon hardened into accepted, slutty fact. First she stopped speaking to me, then everyone did. That was the worst part.

Now I thought of Haimona – how when he'd mentioned he knew where I was from, my first feeling was that same, old, shameful one, of being found out.

From then on I kept to school and home, and walked the long way to the shops to avoid this house, but Steve stopped me by the dairy one afternoon and said, if you want to get out of here you should try for university. It was the kindest thing he could have done.

I'd left home for a cold flat in town with girls whose jokes went over my head, and tutorials where I couldn't speak, and I was lost for the first year but I never came back, and I hadn't seen Donna since.

We were back in the living room. The anime soundtrack stopped. Here in this house where I'd spent hours, months of my life, I realised Steve was not the point. It was Donna I missed.

In the slow voice of someone talking to an idiot, the girl said to me, 'Do you know what your name is?' To her friend she said, 'I think she's having a stroke. Should I call an ambulance?', and the youth in her voice brought me to.

'No,' I said, and gave them my best smile. Therese was back. 'Thank you so much. Sorry to bother you.' I ducked into the kitchen to deposit the empty glass in the sink, at home here. 'That was just what I needed.'

They saw me out and leaned in the doorway, arm in arm. They had matching toe rings. Because they were watching me leave the property, I couldn't peel off a bit of wallpaper or pick up a stone or agapanthus stalk or run back for an empty beer bottle. When I looked back from the street, they had disappeared inside.

Now the street looked pretty – the pale pinks and blues of the houses against the white and purple agapanthus, the lion's face on a slinky blanket draped over a windowsill, the rusted letter-boxes and peeling cars.

I checked the time on my phone. I'd forgotten to turn off the do not disturb function, and had missed seven calls from Rebecca. With a flick of adrenaline I broke into a jog, almost elated at the thought of what trouble I was going to be in. On the way to the motorway I detoured to the old block where I used to live. The flats had been replaced years ago by a superstore, as I already knew. Despite how late I was, I sat in its carpark, and looked on my phone again, in vain, for any sign of who Donna had become.

21

I emailed Heathcote there was a leak in his apartment and to stop renting it out until I fixed it. Then I gave the master key to Artan and Jesse and told them to move in.

Claire spun through her apartment, over the stage, around the kitchen island, down the hallway, in and out of the bedrooms, while I watched from the balcony, laughing. She stuck her head out the door and said, 'You're a genius.'

'I can't believe I didn't think of it sooner.'

Around and around she spun, head flung back, palms to the sky.

I asked Trevor if he would mind stepping down from the Therese Thorne board. He said, 'Not at all. Probably a good idea.'

But the cleansing high from the school donation quickly faded. I replaced my nightly reading of online advice columns with community donations websites, and cried over other people's tales of children's surgery and a bucket list trip to Stewart Island and overseas tuition fees and funeral costs and taxi cab break-downs and assaults, robberies, truck accidents, picking one at random, adding my anonymous drop to the chasm of need. I donated to a group of protestors occupying land that an international conglomerate wanted to use for a golf course. Poured another glass of wine and sent funds towards the air tickets for a fringe theatre company going to New York.

None of it worked, not the pies or the wine, not the donations, not the renewed vigour with which I went over the
Sydney proposals and made phone calls setting up meetings,
working late with Rebecca to refine the pitch; not the early
morning runs I went on to counteract the wine and the pies,
wheezing from the cigarettes, stopping after a few blocks to
light another cigarette which would give me the spins as I
walked past Trevor's abandoned hotel that looked like a ruin
in a phase of deconstruction rather than something on its
way to being complete, stopping by the sea to marvel at the
water's rosy sunrise surface, at the investment bank building
that pulled sun into its glass walls and sent it back into the
air in gold shards that you wanted to hold onto, not while
skateboarders and workers on scooters floated past me; not
giving Trevor a back massage and a foot massage, none of that
quieted the feeling that the real world was distant from me,
on the other side of a veil. The only place it shifted – where
I felt myself unzip the air and walk through – was in Claire's
zone.

'What,' Claire asked, as we walked down the stairs together
towards the bus stop, 'is going on with you? You look like a deer
in the headlights of your own life.'

I knew exactly what it was. 'I'm worried my motives are
wrong.'

The problem was, I said, that it seemed very convenient to be
changing my views on things right now. To doubt Trevor just
as his power was on the wane. To decide looks were unimpor-
tant as my own were fading. To rethink my beliefs on marriage,
money, family because these conventions were now, socially, in
question.

'I don't know where I end and the world begins,' I said. 'I'm
just a sheep.'

'Stop worrying,' she said.

Stop worrying? It was all I did! All the television shows I
watched, the articles I read and all the podcasts I listened to

were worried, worried about the climate, worried about injustice, worried about how to be good, what was good, whether this person or that was good, whether one could ever be good enough. The answer was nearly always no. I knew it wasn't enough to just be aware of the problem, but that was where I'd got stuck. Part of me longed for the dumb, rich days of not knowing. A large part.

We had reached the bus stop outside the hipster café. Young people drank the new kind of coffee, which was the old kind of coffee with a different name. On the corner, a strip club advertised itself with the round, pink thighs of a blonde girl in that kneeling pose, as if she was about to tie someone's shoelaces.

Claire put her glasses on to read the bus timetable.

'What should I do?' I asked.

'Three minutes,' she said.

She sat down on the bench next to me and held my hand.

'Therese,' she said, and she wasn't not laughing at me. 'You're still trying not to be wrong.'

My mind rang at this – a physical reverberation more than cogent thought. Another woman ran up to the stop and checked the timetable. She clocked our held hands and gave me a quick affirming smile.

'I'm wrong all the time,' Claire said. 'It's impossible not to be.'

'You don't seem it.'

'I'm a hypocrite for a start.'

'How?'

'Well, I grew up in a middle-class nuclear family,' Claire said. 'So I always thought the problem with the world was middle-class nuclear families. I mean, I held that belief like a jewel. My secret wish for the destruction of everything I knew.'

The woman glanced down at us again and stepped slightly away.

'I thought our kind of socialism was too easily distorted by capitalism, that really the best system would be anarcho-communism, but then I realised that until someone actually makes me share all my property, I'm living a life of total compliance with the current regime.'

'Regime?'

'My point is, I think I hate it, but judging by my behaviour I fucking love it. I've got my comforts, my husband and children, and you know that package comes with social acceptance and tax benefits. My choices, so many choices about plastic and veganism and public transport, here we are at the bus stop, I always vote Green or Labour, I voted Mana before that crypto guy freaked me out, but it's not like any of them are about to collectivise my apartment or return the stolen land this city stands on. It's like, yes I want that, or I think I do, but also could someone else please enforce it?'

'Do you really think communism's better?' I hadn't given this much thought.

'Than late-stage capitalism? Yes.'

Despite her beliefs, Claire said, when it came to it, when at her consultancy she and the other two fundraisers who worked there had been given the choice of having their hours cut, or one of them losing their job, she was the second of them to cave.

'We thought we were rock solid. A unit. Together we'd go down to three days a week. And then, on our own, we did our maths and looked at our mortgages and our children's educational needs and − I don't even want to try and justify it,' she said. 'We sold each other out. Of course I thought the young one would get the chop, and she thought it would be me. But it was Hana, the best of us. The most experienced. Whose husband had just had a stroke.'

'Oh no.' I thought back to the meeting in Hana's university office, the way the air had crisped up at the mention of Claire's name.

As well as the regret, Claire said, and the guilt, the galling part was that until then the solidarity, burn-it-all-down part of her had felt like her inmost self.

'I thought it was me. My core. What I had thought of, for a long time now, as my *personality* had been constructed around this idea that I've done nothing to bring about. I mean, if it never feels the air, is it me? Or is it a delusion?'

'Why do people call it *late*-stage capitalism?' I asked. 'It always sounds like wishful thinking.'

A bus came, but it wasn't hers. The woman got on and a bunch of schoolgirls got off. I watched them walk past the strip club billboard, showing each other something on a phone.

'I don't mean there's no point,' she said. 'We have to act. Of course, this whole line of thought should be a spur to action. Self-criticism only gets you so far, I mean we've got a moral duty to enjoy what we can. I just don't want to spend my life thinking I'm someone I'm not.'

'What, though,' I said. 'Are we just meant to accept reality?'

She shrugged. 'It's harder than it sounds.'

After she boarded her bus, I crossed the road to gaze in the Therese Thorne shop window. The under-shelf lighting gave its depths a delicate pink tinge. A trailing plant spilled over the counter by the money card reader, which sat next to a Himalayan salt lamp and a hunk of selenite. Crystals and plants and promises of cleansing: cleansing what? I hadn't been only after comfort, I realised. Not just shiny distractions, like Atalanta's golden apples. I wanted these things to tell me who I was, to give me absolution and courage too. Could a cashmere throw do that, a faux-fur cushion, the jumbo corduroy beanbag in nostalgic colours? The wall hangings, the enamel cookware, the vegetable peelers and the blond wood toilet stools? Perhaps – I borrowed the formulation from Claire – the nice things were there to make people who had nice things feel less bad about having nice things.

The Wairarapa estate agent promised Trevor the figures he wanted to hear, and the Martinborough house was put on the market. He gave me the news over dinner.

'We'd have had to sell it eventually,' he said. 'Would have been mad to keep it once we're in Sydney.'

'Yes,' I said. 'We've got too much stuff. It's just a house.'

He got up to clear the table and I raised my juice-smeared plate to my face and licked it.

'What the…?' he said. 'Do you mind?'

I wiped my chin and handed him the dish. He shuddered.

I remembered a book I'd read some years ago, about a woman who'd fallen in love and agreed to do everything the man said, even when she knew it was stupid. She'd gone along as they'd got lost in foreign cities, as the house they built sprung leaks, as the pets had run wild. It had started off sexy then taken a turn, and ended with their untrained dog attacking the man and his death from the infected wounds. Blood poisoning is a horrible way to go.

Trevor went to his study and I paced the room, back and forth over the rug. I wanted not to care about Martinborough, I wanted to lick my plate like an untrained dog, but why did I feel this tugging sense of loss? I didn't want to be an accommodating ninny but I didn't want to be a brutal person either, and I could see that Claire was sometimes brutal, that she let other people take care of their own feelings. You had to be careful. She was dangerous. On the other hand, that was exactly why I wanted to be near her.

When I got there Artan was riffing off a Balkan DJ and everyone was on the stage jumping, heads flung back. Fern was there in the zone, fucking Fern, and her art gang, a loose group of seven or eight young people she squired around as if they were social currency. A couple of them had already adopted Claire's look: the op shop tracksuit, the home-cut hair, the thickening brows, but others dressed in Little Bo Peep smocks and porn star shoes. I'd seen them before, at the bar across the road. Trevor had said, 'The way they're dressed makes me uncomfortable,' which I thought was probably the point.

I joined them, and lost myself. I was quicker at it now.

The silence at the end of a song extended and we reached that tacit agreement it was over. People collapsed, slow motion, on the stage, panting. Claire and I were the only ones still on our feet. She breathed hard, her face sweaty. I wanted to be alone with her.

'Let's go down to the sea!' said Fern. 'Let's get in the water.'

Through the others' excitement, gathering of shoes, coats, I tried to catch Claire's eye but she jumped lightly off the stage to pull back the balcony door and stood with the cold night air flooding over her, knuckles rapping at the lioness's head.

'Are you going to go?' I asked. 'To the beach?'

'I've been thinking about you,' she said.

My body tingled. 'What?'

'You're part of things, Therese. Just as much as me, Fern, Jesse, the guy who runs the corner shop. You can't just pay a tax and be separate.'

Impatience ran through me. 'I don't want to be separate.'

Behind us, the others were arguing over which beach to go to and whether the wind was coming from the north or the south.

'Come on, Claire,' Fern called. 'Lead the way!'

'I'm not in charge,' she whispered, making a face. 'I don't want the responsibility.'

'Well,' I said. 'You fucked that up.'

That made her laugh. Her eyes snapped onto mine then and she squeezed my wrist hard and I wanted to skull a glass of vodka, or crush her into me, or run to the unlit city beach, to strip naked and immerse myself in that black, sharp water.

Shit it was cold. The shallow water bit my ankles as I stood shivering in my bra and knickers. Fern strode in at a steady pace, her incredible pride drawing her forward till she suddenly dropped under and came up a few meters away, gasping. Artan and Jesse wrestled each other in and the art girls screamed and fell through the surface, face down and arms out cross-wise in a self-induced baptism. Hoarsely whispered shouts, 'It's cold! Jesus!' filled the air, and I recalled Trevor's family in the Sounds, stumbling in the warm shallows. That had been months ago.

From up the beach behind me Claire finished getting out of her clothes, ran past, grabbed my arm and dragged me with her, splashing noisily, swearing as we pushed through the dense water till our whole bodies were in. The only way to do it was all at once, like tearing off a giant plaster. We held ourselves down in the thumping cold that set me alight and at the same time, I thought, might kill me. It didn't smell great – fishy, boaty, full of whatever got let into the harbour. Everyone else was back on the beach now, shaking like dogs, scrubbing at themselves with the inadequate towels we had brought, fighting with their jeans. I turned away from them to face the harbour, every movement making water ripple icily over my skin. The red and yellow container dock lights were like embers against the massed hills, as if we were twigs cradled in a giant, dormant hearth. When the wind picked up, the water felt warm by comparison. I sunk my shoulders under.

My breathing settled into a slow rhythm, and my heart pounded, but steadily. Claire had struck out towards the pontoon and was already nearly there, about forty meters across the dark water. The brain freeze was like being stoned. It felt amazing to be a speck. The metal handrail on the pontoon caught the moonlight and I wondered if once there, Claire would turn the raft into a zone.

Cheers and whoops burst out behind me – Artan and Fern waved from the shore at Claire, who had got to the raft and was waving back. I pushed off to swim towards her. I wanted to go past the pontoon, past the buoys, round the island and out through the heads to the Strait. But my body would not transform, it was weak and human, and when I thrust a foot downwards to feel how deep the water was, and couldn't touch the bottom, panic broke through and activated a scrap of mind that wanted to turn my limbs around and plow back towards the beach. Salt water was in my eyes, burning up my nose. I couldn't see the pontoon, or Claire. But the shore was more distant too – I'd swum further than I'd thought. My arms ached, the bottom half of my body was a ridiculous weight. I felt that weakness turn over inside me – that insistent little floss that had sat at the controls for years and years and years – and I crushed it, kicked at the water, and swam on.

The pontoon was empty, creaking, small waves splashing its edges. For a second I panicked that Claire had disappeared, then saw her halfway back to shore and realised we must have passed in the water without seeing each other.

I clung to the metal rungs to catch my breath. Zones were just waiting, I thought, all over the city, on traffic islands and in entry lobbies, in car parks. On government lawns. I remembered the times we emerged from the trance, how when everyone breathed together it really did sound like trees. 'Organise your breath,' my old yoga instructor used to say. Disorganise me, I thought now, and shoved my head under the water.

When my eyesight cleared, I saw Claire emerge ahead from the shallows and stagger up towards Fern, who thrust towels over her and held her close, then helped her into her clothes. My teeth began to chatter. Once Claire was dressed Artan and Jesse hoisted her onto their shoulders and they all began to parade down the beach. I was colder now than I'd ever been, and unsure I could prise myself from the rung and make it back. Could I stay here till I warmed up? But the wind had sharpened and I knew I would only get colder. I crouched at the top of the ladder and yelled for Claire. What did I expect her to do? They were near the other end of the beach now, by the band rotunda, and the distance and darkness transformed the group into a big blob, Claire riding on the top. No one was coming to get me. The realisation made me laugh. The animal in me kicked in at last and plunged back into the water.

22

A burble of male voices came from the living room. It was half-dark, early evening. For the past week I'd sweated out a fever in bed, in the grip of a cough that wouldn't be satisfied. Trevor had come and gone, bringing lemon honey drinks, paracetamol, and cold facecloths, which he called flannels. My laptop lay cold and unopened beside me. Rebecca had called – her voice washed through the cell phone speaker and over the pillow, over my mind – I lay inside a display cabinet in the new boutique in Sydney as purple jacaranda shadows dropped softly across the floor and the smell of eucalyptus carried through the cabinet's glass. Trevor hovered above the cabinet, looking down at me. He was speaking French to a moon-faced nurse. I coughed and coughed and the cabinet clouded with my breath – I wanted them to open it, but the nurse was busy fluffing flowers from the Limoges market into a vase.

'She had a seizure,' Trevor said, the words magnetic. 'I thought she was going to die.'

Sometimes I knew I was in my bed at home and he was sitting in the armchair, in the corner, just as he had in the hospital in France. 'Are you awake? Do you want anything?'

One bad night he wanted to take me to a doctor, but I didn't want to go to the emergency waiting room. All the comforts I needed were here.

A day later, in the morning, I felt his weight settling beside me on the bed. He was still in his pyjamas, having come from the spare room where he went to catch a few hours of sleep each night. He'd wrapped his arms around me, spooning, and I'd pressed back against him.

'Feeling a bit better?' he asked. 'You don't seem quite as hot.'

'Yeah,' I said. 'I'm good. What time is it?'

'About ten.'

'Why aren't you at the office?'

'I'll go soon.' He tensed up – the tiniest amount, but I felt it.

'Has something else happened? Trevor?'

'No.'

I flipped over to face him and held on, the length of my body against his, my forehead pushed into his solid chest. I could feel his heartbeat.

'I've been worried about you,' he said. 'Don't do that again, OK? Gadding about. Midnight swims. Whatever you get up to with Claire.'

I shifted so his pyjama button didn't jab my cheek. This was good – this was normal – not coming out of the sea in the middle of a cold night to have to run after the group, clutching my clothes, calling for them to wait while I caught up. Not Fern's triumphant eyes sliding towards me, not Claire's startled face at noticing I'd been gone, her sudden, lunging kiss on my mouth. Two of Fern's friends hoisted Claire onto their shoulders and carried her up the parade towards town. I let them go ahead. I wanted to be with the group, but I didn't want to lose what I'd felt in the water, when no one was coming for me. The feeling that despite being scared, I was equal to this.

We'd got back to her place and that was when I'd begun shaking, a shiver I couldn't stop. The others ran for her hot shower, laughing and pushing each other like kids, but I felt a powerful homing instinct and took the stairs to my apartment on leaden legs, clutching my pile of clothes. They were laundered and folded on the armchair now, the one in which Trevor had been watching over me.

'I won't do it again,' I said. 'But Trevor. What were you going to say?'

He took a breath as if to speak, then hesitated, and I pressed in tighter.

'Tell me.'

'I fucked up,' he said. 'The bank thing, your building, your brand. I get it. I shouldn't have done it. I'm sorry.'

He was staring at the ceiling. I felt a giant rush of love and relief, like seeing someone in a crowd when you think you've lost them. I took in the sun scars on his skin, the crows' feet reaching towards his temples and the long lines that ran from his nose to the corners of his mouth, his whitish stubble: the himness of Trevor, not whoever I wanted him to be.

'What are you going to do?'

The court appearance where he would enter his plea was just a few days away. He shook his head. 'I'm furious with myself.'

We lay together without saying anything more, and though I had to turn away to cough, and sit up and take the painkillers that Trevor passed me, the room seemed airier, the sun fell in soft folds across the pale blue sheets and I felt able to breathe properly for the first time in ages. Soon Trevor, who never liked to be still for long, patted my arm and rolled out of bed.

'Shall I get up and have breakfast with you?'

'Go back to sleep,' he said. 'You're nearly better. No point risking it.'

I did, blank with relief, and didn't wake until the voices from the other room broke through my sleep and I realised the day had passed.

Heathcote was sprawled on a sofa in the living room, across from his father, both laughing as I walked in. They caught themselves, as if the joke had been private. The table lamp's light gleamed in two glasses of beer.

'You're up!' Trevor stood and we hugged each other tight. 'God, you were sick.'

'Thanks for getting me through.' My hair, still wet from the shower, left a dark streak on his shirt.

'Cup of tea?'

'Rum and Coke, please.'

'Begorrah, Therese,' said Heathcote in his fake Irish accent. 'You've been poorly I hear.'

I sat across from him. 'Self-induced.' Trevor handed me the drink and I said, 'Your dad's been a great nurse.'

Heathcote smirked. He was tanned, noticeably so next to Trevor's pale skin, but discomfort was detectable beneath the surface, like cells squiggling under a microscope. Whenever I saw him I had two conflicting feelings: compassion, and the conviction some people were just shits. Now, though, with the sense that Trevor was returning to me — that whatever happened, we would be together, and all right — I felt expansive, and said, 'Nice to see you back in town.'

'Heath's moving home,' said Trevor, clapping his son's shoulder.

'Downstairs?' I would have to explain about Jesse and Artan.

'Yeah. I've invested in a new bar.'

'Down here? I thought you were involved with one in Auckland.'

'Yeah, nah, that didn't get off the ground, the people were...' he made a sour face. 'They didn't have a real vision, you know? This one, this is being set up by a very cool guy, I'm the major investor. We're going to be the hottest spot in the city. Then Auckland, Sydney, Hanoi.'

'Have you talked to Andy?' Caroline's husband had struggled to make a profit with his suburban bar for three years now.

Heathcote shrugged. 'Andy's cool. We're in different markets.'

'What market are you going for?'

'Jaysus, Therese. You're breaking my balls.'

'Just curious.' My good mood was draining under his presence; I chucked back the rest of my rum; its instant effect, a soft punch inside my brain, reminded me I hadn't eaten properly for days. I went to pour myself another.

'I'll connect you with the hotel's restaurant people,' Trevor said, 'and hey, there's a new gin distillery out in Trentham you should look into, your uncle Paul's leasing them the land, you could—'

'Yeah, perfect.' Heathcote placed his glass back on the table, the foam vestiges sliding to the bottom. 'When's the Martinborough money coming through for the hotel? Your bridging finance must be costing a bomb.'

Why did he know so much of our business? The objects in the room overlapped under the power of the rum. I squinted at Trevor to hold him in one place.

'I've been talking to the kids,' he said, on his way to the bathroom. 'About the charges, what it might mean, the investors, all that. Family meeting tomorrow, they're coming here.'

'OK. So we can…?'

'Approach this as a family.'

'Great.'

He left the room, and it was just Heathcote and me.

'I take it the leak's sorted out,' he said. 'Downstairs.'

'There's someone staying there.'

'Eh?'

'Yes,' I said. 'Two guys are staying there.'

'Are you renting it out to them?'

'No, they're not paying anything.'

'I've been turning people down. Paying guests.'

'Sorry,' I said.

'Sorry! It's hundreds of dollars I could have made. Thousands.'

'Get a job,' I said. Oh, the bliss of saying it.

'I've got a job. I work.'

'What do you do?' The air was very thin now. My heart beat fast.

'What do *you* do? You dick around with your shop, do you think that would fund your lifestyle? Dad does everything for you, Therese, haven't you worked that out yet?'

'Grow up,' I said. 'It's not too late.'

'You're a parasite on our family.'

The extremity of this sent me to the sink for a glass of water. 'Heathcote.' My hands were shaking. 'People like you and me, who don't fight much, we're not good at it. We can easily say things we'll regret. Things that are hard to recover from. I think we should stop.'

'Stop what?' Trevor was back.

Heathcote shrugged, and stretched ostentatiously. 'Apparently my apartment's in use, Dad. So I'll be staying here.' He levelled his gaze at me: see.

'Oh good. I'll make up the spare room.'

'Right. I'm off to poker. Very cool new spot by the yacht club. Ah, I still miss that yacht. Remember, Dad, the sailing holidays?'

The yacht had been sold thirty years ago, in the divorce.

I stripped the dirty sheets from the spare bed while Trevor pulled the pillows from their cases.

'Heathcote should pay rent,' I said. 'On the apartment downstairs.'

'We don't need the money.'

'He's a grown man, he's got a trust fund, he can get his own place.'

'He'll be using the trust fund for his bar.'

'Oh my god.' The fresh bottom sheet snapped as I shook it from its folds.

'Why should he pay rent if he doesn't have to?' Trevor sounded as if he genuinely wanted to know. 'Why do I do all this? What's the point of having money if you can't support your children?'

I burst out laughing. 'Are you serious? He's an adult. It's about his dignity.'

'Your parents are adults and I cover their expenses.'

I hoisted the last corner of mattress to tug the fitted sheet over it. 'I do too.'

'This is one flat,' said Trevor. 'My kid. Maybe it's wrong to keep propping him up. But Heath is vulnerable.'

Again and again Trevor tried to return to that unreachable place where Heathcote was eight years old and nothing had been broken.

'It's not working for him,' I said. 'You can't go on in this same pattern.'

Trevor chucked the pillows on the bed. 'It's a bottomless pit. I know I'll never fill it up but I can't stop trying.'

236

'Maybe you trying so hard is what makes him feel like there's a hole to fill.'

At that he shrugged. 'Have you got this? I'll do the dishes.'

In the living room my phone pinged – a notification for a voicemail from earlier in the day. It was Rebecca, her voice high with stress. 'Sorry, I know you're not well. But someone just came up to the office and asked me if I knew anything about... some kind of... fraud allegations? Like, something to do with our building, Therese Thorne House? I just said no. I mean, of course not. But yeah if you could give me a call? I'm sure it's nothing! But yeah, just, could you call me?' There was a brief pause and then she said, 'Sorry, they mentioned something about Trevor. Sorry.'

I could hear the name suppression splinter like an ice cube in a drink. There was no way it would hold.

To Trevor's back I said, 'I just want to know why you did it.'

He raised his voice over the running tap. 'What?'

'Why did you rush the process? With the building. Why? What was the hurry?'

Without turning around he reached for the chopping board and knife and squeezed detergent over them. I truly didn't know if he had heard me or not. My bowels turned and for a second I imagined pushing back from the table, raising my dress, squatting to my haunches and shitting in the middle of the rug.

23

At noon the next day Annabel joined us by video call from Singapore, where it was eight in the morning. Heathcote and Caroline sat around the laptop at the kitchen table, and Judith came too – I was surprised to see her, then felt stupid for being surprised. Rob texted to say he was on his way.

The old me would have baked a cake and laid out seasonal fruit. Warmed the teapot, freshly ground the coffee. I would have lit a candle and blown it out before everyone arrived so that its scent lingered but didn't cloy. Removed smears from water glasses. Sliced lemon, shaken out the pips. Cheese to room temperature. Baguettes in the oven. Muffins. Pastries, glistening. Bubbles on standby. Whoops! No orange juice. Trevor would offer to run down to the convenience store and the old me would say don't, their juice is made from concentrate.

Part of me would have known this was nuts. Too much. That no one really liked persimmons, that there were other ways to show love. But then – I'd smell the yeast, prod that pillowy dough, and the warmth would spread through my sternum. I'd feed the family.

That morning, I'd got Claire to drop me at a service station on the way home, and smashed a pie into my face on the forecourt. It dulled the jitters my few hours of sleep had left me, having woken at 4 a.m. and driven in a van to the moonlit hills above the South Coast with her and the others, where we'd drunk wine and danced ourselves into a frenzy. We'd had no music, just Claire's drum and her fierce eye and the sweeping wind to scream into. When the sky turned pink, we'd run jaggedly down the hill into the golf course and clawed ruts in the turf to scatter seeds – flowers and pumpkins and greens, I don't know, it was Fern's idea. At the gas station I remembered the family was coming over and bought two bags of corn chips. These I now ripped open and dumped on the table, spraying orange dust everywhere.

'No bowl?' Judith asked.

'Pardon?' I said. I could see Trevor wince. 'I mean, what?'

'Oh Trevor,' Judith laughed, 'you've been Enry Igginsing again.' To me she said, 'It's only because he's so hopelessly middle-class. Say whatever you like.'

I swallowed a gob of anger. 'Trevor, can you make the coffee?'

When we'd got home Claire and I had climbed the stairs to her door, where we hugged goodbye. 'We should light a fire next time,' she said, picking dried grass and flakes of dirt from my hair. 'But not in my flat!'

She'd asked if I wanted to come in, but my business was with Trevor. In our bedroom I turned on the bedside lamp and woke him. As we fucked, the bed shook against the wall and the cloth fell from the long mirror with a whump – we both turned and caught our reflection, the woman in a dirty T-shirt on top of the naked man, his hands gripping her hips. We could have been fighting; for a second I was floored by how much humans still trusted one another. I bent forward to kiss him, slowing everything down.

Now the kettle bubbled, and Trevor spooned coffee into the plunger. My eye caught the dirt still crescented beneath my fingernails. An image of hands raking the earth flashed and subsided against the silver gleam of teaspoons and the pink mugs Caroline had lifted down from the shelf. Her face was subtly different since I'd last seen her, a new flatness between her brows and lift in her cheeks – the expensive kind.

Trevor wanted to wait to begin our discussion until Rob arrived, and there was an edge in the air. As he stood behind me and set the milk down, I reached my hand back and ran it up his inner thigh. He squeezed my shoulder.

'How's Margaret?' I asked Judith.

'She's got a cold,' Judith said. 'Heath, you have to drop in. She's been asking after you.'

He nodded. 'Will do, Ma.' He huddled over his coffee, looking like hell; when I'd left at four that morning the spare room door had been open, the bed untouched.

Caroline spoke up. 'I went to visit Granny last weekend.' She looked to her mother for praise, but her mother was frowning at Heathcote.

'Dad,' said Annabel through the screen. 'Dad. Ugh, can someone angle the screen better, I can't see Dad.'

'Just getting something from my study,' Trevor said, as he crossed the room.

'Can someone just tell me this isn't him breaking the news he's going to jail?'

'Annabel!' said Judith. 'Of course he isn't.'

Heathcote said, 'Do you know how long this is going to take? I've got to get my girlfriend from the airport.' He flicked his eyes to me. 'Do you need the car?'

'Girlfriend!' Caroline and Annabel said in unison. 'Who's your girlfriend?'

Heathcote grinned. 'Nope! No way.'

Amidst their chiming questions – what does she do, how old is she, how did you meet – all of which Heathcote dodged – Trevor returned, carrying the architect's scale model of the hotel. We cleared a space on the marble island and he set it down between us.

'It's like a wedding cake,' Caroline said. 'There you go, Heath, you can marry her at the hotel.'

'I am going to take her for a look round,' he said. 'If I can get access to the site, Dad? I could take her on the way back through town.'

Trevor raised an eyebrow. 'That depends.'

Finally, Rob arrived, giving us all his long-suffering face as he crossed the room. He kissed his mother on the cheek and lifted a chair over from the dining table. He sat down, shorter than the rest of us on our stools.

'Sorry,' he said. 'I've been downstairs talking to Haimona.'

'The journalist?' Trevor said. 'I should bloody hope not.'

'Can we start?' Annabel's voice was tinny through the computer screen. 'John's in London and I have to get the boys to basketball soon.'

'He's an environment journalist, Dad. He's got more to worry about than this family.'

'My boys are at drama,' Caroline said.

Heathcote said, 'Of course they are.'

'What's that supposed to mean?'

Judith patted her daughter's hand. 'It's not a competition.'

'OK,' Trevor cut across her. 'Here's the thing.'

As we all knew, he said, the latest loss of a hotel investor had left the project stalled again and haemorrhaging money. The sale of the Martinborough property would plug the gap, but more was needed. At the mention of that house Caroline glanced at me, a mini death stare, before exchanging glances with her siblings; I knew they'd always felt it should have stayed in Judith's hands, and wasn't his to sell. Judith was unreadable. I wondered how she felt about her garden.

Trevor continued, oblivious. He said a tipping point was approaching and if we didn't act right away the whole thing could fall out of his hands. All he'd have to show for it would be the debt. Now he was proposing a deal: to liquidate part of the family trust and transfer the funds to the hotel project. We would all become investors.

It was strange, I thought, it never stopped being strange, that Trevor could live with me, sleep with me, eat with me, but often the first I would hear of what he was thinking was when we were with other people. And then I thought, no – I wanted it to be strange, because that promised mystery, the chance of being new to each other. When I used the word *strange*, it was to cover up the real word, which was *sad*.

Annabel went first. 'Hang on. Who's "we"?'

'You four kids. And Therese.'

'How much are we talking about?'

'Probably half the trust.'

'Half!' Annabel pushed back from the computer screen, whipped her phone out and began calculations.

Trevor slid papers across the table to the children and told Annabel to check her emails.

'Have you got another set?' I asked.

'I thought you and I could go over it later.'

I reached for the originals.

Annabel looked up from her phone. 'Our monthly income would drop by a lot more than half.'

'At first, yes, but the hotel will make a profit. It's an asset. Who knows, there could be a chain. It could be a family thing, a legacy – your kids could be part of it one day.'

Rob wanted to know about the building's carbon footprint. 'If I were to agree, this is hypothetical, OK, I'd have to insist on the latest green tech. There's fantastic new stuff out there.'

'That would be brilliant,' said Caroline. 'A selling point.'

Trevor listed the materials that were already being used: he pointed to the model and showed how the building design maintained a moderate temperature, where the green walls would go, how the roof worked, how the concrete was manufactured using recycled water and renewable energy. He passed over photo mock-ups of the locally sourced furniture and fittings.

'I can bore on for hours about water recycling but it's all in there. We're aiming for top level Green Star certification.'

'You never told me that,' said Rob, and Trevor raised an eyebrow.

'You never asked.'

He was enjoying this, drawing them in. An aura began to hover over the family group as they discussed further details, including Annabel from her little rectangle of screen, and Judith, whose habitual dryness fell away as she joined the discussion.

'You know what,' Annabel said, 'obviously John's one of the financers already, but I think we could invest more. Put some of our own money in.'

Caroline said, 'Let's keep it fair between us siblings, eh? If you've got more invested, you'll want more say.'

'What about your share of the trust?' Annabel asked Trevor. 'That's not here.'

'I'm no longer a named beneficiary.'

As he looked away from her I caught his eye, and saw something calculating there. I wondered if he had known how soon he would be in this position. He had signed his part of the trust over to Heathcote in case charges against him would restrict his access to his own funds. And here we were. As if he had seen it coming.

Heathcote, oozing hangover, flicked through the proposal like it was the instruction manual for a new dishwasher. 'Baller,' he said.

I hated that word.

He said it again, drawing it out. 'Baaallerrr.'

'Baller.' A heavy click sounded inside my head. 'Baller.'

People were looking at me. I felt the tight grip of the mask. All my attempts to tear it off. Where had they got me. Right here.

I had to do it now. To say something true that I couldn't take back.

'Well,' I said, 'seeing as Heathcote's taken over Trevor's share, out of all of you he'd be the majority investor. In terms of who would have more say.'

Beside me, Judith stiffened. Trevor stared at me as if I'd farted.

'Share of what?' said Caroline.

'Therese,' Heathcote said, soft, Irish.

I remembered seeing them in the upstairs office at Judith's, discussing real estate. What was this really about, this insane overproviding for Heathcote?

'It doesn't say that here,' Rob said. 'What do you mean, Heathcote's got Dad's share?'

'Your dad signed his interest in the trust over to him.'

'Why?'

'Why not to all of us?' Caroline said. 'Why not spread it out?'

I shot a glance at Heathcote, expecting him to be glaring at me, but he was looking into his lap, and he didn't look pleased with himself, or defiant, he looked like a kid waiting to be hit. I felt a swoop of shame.

Judith spoke, kind but careful. 'The rest of you don't need it.'

A tiny pause as they took this in, then Annabel scoffed down the video line, Rob said something unintelligible, shaking his head, and Caroline scraped her stool back, her face pink and betrayed.

'Heathcote doesn't even have children!'

'Darling,' her mother began, but Caroline slapped her away.

'"It's not a competition!"' She had Judith's tone pitch-perfect. 'Yeah right. Stop gaslighting me.' She stalked towards the sofas then turned back. 'Were you just sitting on it,' she asked her younger brother, 'your little extra pile, hoping no one would notice?'

'I thought Dad had told you,' he said. He sounded mortified.

'Just admit you've got a favourite,' Caroline said to both her parents. 'Just say it. This would all be so much easier if it were out in the open. He's the baby, Annabel's perfect, Rob's some weird alien who doesn't belong in this family and doesn't even give a shit, and I'm the one with the loser husband and the mental kids. I'm the difficult one. I always have been.'

'Andy's great,' said Rob. 'What's wrong with Andy?'

'It's nothing to do with favourites,' Trevor said, 'it's not love, it's just money.'

'Ha!' Caroline slapped the countertop and grabbed her bag, magnificent in her hurt. 'Ha! Ha! Ha! Ha! Ha!'

Each *ha* was delivered into one of our faces by turn, the last one into the screen, where Annabel recoiled as if Caroline had the power to burst through.

She made for the door.

'Don't go, Caro,' said Rob. He went after her and stalled her.

'Seriously though, what the hell,' Annabel said, her face framed tightly now, enormous, 'why should Heathcote get double? He's not that much of a fuck-up.'

Judith leaned towards the screen. 'Because I worry about him all the time!'

A cold little silence bloomed. I felt my heart crack for Judith.

'Ha.' Heathcote tried to laugh. 'Cheers, Ma.'

Judith spread her hands as if she could take back the moment. 'Heathcote, I don't really. I don't, I don't. You're, you're doing really well—'

He spoke over her. He was red-cheeked, tense in a new way.

'Yeah, Dad – I mean, of course I said yes to the money, I'm not an idiot. But why give it to me? You know the SFO might come for me next. And then what? Then it would be frozen just like yours.'

Rob and Caroline made their way back to the island.

'The Fraud Office? Why would they come for you?' Judith asked.

Heathcote looked at his dad, who shook his head.

'No they won't, Heath. They won't.'

Judith held herself very still. 'Trevor? Why would they come for Heathcote?'

The pause, as we waited for Trevor to explain, was broken by a racket erupting through the computer as Annabel's sons leapt into frame, jumping around behind her, making faces and long burp noises. She turned and shouted, 'Shut the fuck up! You fucking gross little morons! Leave me the fuck alone!'

Caroline leaned over the counter, pressed the mute button on the keyboard, and sat down again on her stool.

Heathcote waited until everyone was silent and said, 'It was my idea to lie to the bank. About the pre-sales in the Therese Thorne building.'

His idea? My name in his mouth made me feel raw, naked. Like I was part of something wrong. What did he mean? I glanced at my dirty fingernails but they were not a sign of secret power. Just ordinary dirt.

'Dad was in a rush,' he said. He spoke to me now. 'You'd been in France and I don't know, you'd had a brain problem or nearly died or something. So he wanted to push the development through, secure the loan, and the financial crisis had just started, no one knew how bad it was going to get. He really wanted to make the deal happen.'

'No, no. You weren't even working for your father then,' Judith said. 'During the GFC. You'd left to start your member's club.'

'That's why—' Heathcote broke off. 'Ah, shite.' The Irish brogue was back. 'I need a drink.'

'Stop talking in that accent,' I said.

'That's why what?' Judith's eyes lasered at Trevor.

'It got the job done,' he said. 'We sold the units in the end.' But his voice was paper-thin.

'That's why what?'

She stared at me now, and I said, 'I don't know what they're talking about.'

A third time, slowly, she would not be stopped. 'That's why what?'

Neither man wanted to answer her. I fetched the whiskey from the drinks cabinet and pushed it towards Heathcote. Walking around, moving, felt surreal, as if we were all captured in this bubble.

'Who forged the documents?' Sweat circles had appeared under the arms of Judith's blue cotton shirt.

Everyone's phones pinged at the same time. Annabel: *get me off mute.*

My eyes met Caroline's as she obeyed, and we briefly held the connection, her own gaze watchful, stripped of any anger.

'Fucking thank you!' Annabel bellowed through the screen, and Caroline gave me a smooth little smile before our focus returned to Heathcote.

'I did,' he said. He couldn't look at his mother. 'I forged them. I organised it and I did it. And I don't want Dad to get in trouble, I don't want him to plead guilty to something he didn't really do, but I'm just – scared – that if they go to trial, they'll dig all this shit out and...'

He and his father stared at each other in helpless silence. They were so physically alike – the boyish good looks.

Rob had his hands to his face, shaking his head. His phone buzzed with a text that he started replying to until Judith snapped, 'Would you mind not doing that!'

She looked at Trevor as if she might murder him.

'So,' Annabel said. 'You're going to plead guilty, right, Dad? You're going to protect Heath.'

I couldn't really believe he had taken so long to decide. Perhaps he had just been delaying the inevitable. Trying to bend the world to his will, again.

He shook his head. 'I suppose I am.'

Caroline said, 'But you didn't do it.'

Annabel said, 'Yeah, but Heath did it for him.'

'No one should have done it,' Judith said, her voice tight and her body almost swaying with rage. 'Or let it be done.'

'But hang on,' said Rob. 'Isn't there some way round this? If you plead not guilty, Dad, and go to trial, they can't pin it on you because you didn't do it. There won't be any evidence. And maybe they'll be satisfied with a couple of scalps, the lawyer, the money guy, maybe they won't ever find any proof that Heath was involved, sorry bro, but are you really going to let Dad take the rap for you? – he's a 73-year-old man, for fuck's sake.'

Heathcote said, 'I know.'

The skin around Judith's mouth was completely white. She poured a glug of whiskey into her coffee cup and drank it with such need that I felt the scalding, smoking liquid in my own throat as she swallowed. She couldn't want her son to go through this. But what if Heathcote never went through anything? It was impossible.

'Trevor,' I said. I wanted to grab the wheel of time and haul it back a decade, to before all this started. 'Why did you do it?'

He lifted his head from his hands to meet my gaze. 'Why did we rush it through? Because you wanted it.'

Ice water trickled down my back. 'I wanted it?'

'You'd nearly died. You wanted the store. You *needed* it. Don't you remember?'

'No – we talked about it, yes we talked about it, Trevor, but – not like that. I probably did say I wanted it, like, like I want a coffee, a new pair of sneakers, I want to watch my show on TV. I didn't mean for you to...' I was babbling.

'You couldn't wait,' said Judith. 'I remember. You were desperately worried he would lose the site. Your lease was up and you needed momentum and you wanted the flagship store to open so there would be an Auckland store and a Christchurch store and you would continue to get whatever you wanted.'

Each *you* was like an alarm bell on a plane. Ding. Ding. The seatbelt light coming on. The metal seized, buffeting. The steep rise and sudden drop. Where was the oxygen mask? Where was the girl to sing 'Amazing Grace'?

'Heathcote,' I said. 'I would never have wanted you to do this.'

He gave a small shrug. 'I didn't do it for you.'

I could feel the shaking come over me again, an echo of the fever, and gripped my arms to make it stop. The time for being weak was over. That little internal bit of fluff I thought I had killed in the cold sea, her filaments were still there, embedded in my guts. She was so tiny, and so hungry. That was where the burn came from, the wanting that drove me forward, that's what had lit up when I saw the Darling Point site before Christmas, and a decade ago when I told Trevor I wanted the Therese Thorne development. It's what had sparked into flame when I first saw Trevor. Little, savage floss.

The family was talking. How had the SFO got onto this in the first place? Was it Trevor's scandal with the city councillor, did that trigger an alarm, or was it through one of the other men, the financial consultant or the lawyer, they were complicit, did they know Heathcote was involved, no, Trevor had shielded him, they'd helped with the documents but neither of them would trace it to Heathcote, Trevor had gone through all that at the time making sure...

'But you were still prepared to use him,' Judith said. 'Why didn't you say no? Why did you let it happen? Why didn't you do the fucking forgery yourself?'

Rob barked a laugh. 'How about not doing it at all?'

'I wish I hadn't let it happen,' Trevor said. 'I wish I hadn't. He knows how sorry I am. I know I'm a bad father.'

Caroline was crying. 'No, you're not.'

'Mum,' Annabel said. 'Mum, what should we do?'

'There's no one I can talk to.' Judith stared at the patterns in the marble, as if speaking to herself. 'There's no one.' I knew what she was thinking. Her social clout, her old connections, counted for nothing here. Even if she had a cousin high up in the SFO. Even if she knew the judge. In a case like this, in this country, it wouldn't make any difference.

'Heath, come and stay with me,' Annabel said. 'Come to Singapore. Until it all blows over. They can't get you if you're out of the country.'

'No one's going to get him,' Trevor said.

'But Dad,' Heathcote said. 'I can't let you take the blame – I can't.'

'How bad even is it!' Annabel cried. 'People do worse shit than this all the time. There's so much corruption in John's world – I mean Dad you must know stories – the fast lanes, the backroom deals, the insider trading, the grey area that bleeds into actual crime constantly, this is nothing.'

'Humans are terrible,' Rob said. 'The sooner we wipe ourselves out the better.'

Judith stood up, knocking over her stool. 'I hate that argument. It's just despair. It's morally wrong. If you don't love people, you can't love anything and if you don't love the planet, you won't bother saving it. It's not radical to wish humans gone, it's a cop-out.'

Rob's jaw worked, like he was going to fight back, but he subsided on his chair and said, 'Right. I'm the one who's morally wrong.' He poured himself a drink.

I picked up Judith's stool and pushed it towards her – we exchanged a brief, burning glance. The girls started arguing.

I wanted a whiskey. I craved one. But I had to remain clear. My wanting things was part of all this – I saw that now. I looked around the apartment. A month ago I had toyed with the idea of clearing out, as Claire had done. Letting her do my thinking for me. I'd taken a vanload of stuff to the Women's Refuge. But those were the things in cupboards, the extra crockery, the spare blankets and pillows, the belongings that had come here in boxes from our last place and never been unpacked. They had been easy to let go. When I'd come home and seen what was left to give away – the plum-coloured sofa, the rug, the paintings and ceramics and silverware and side tables and lamps – I'd lost my nerve. These things were my clothes, my skin. At the time I'd told myself Trevor would never accept living without those comforts, but it wasn't him, it was me.

The artificial savoury smell of the corn chips made me feel sick. I screwed up the bags and took them to the bin. The bin smelled too and I began to empty it into a council bag to take downstairs. Wanting things was the engine that ran me, and even once I had them, I couldn't turn it off, I wanted more. Safety. Love. My own things. A line of goods, a shop to sell them in, another shop, another. A building. Another one. I used wanting like a rope to pull myself forward, hand over hand. As if it was what got me from one moment to the next. That was what I loved about the zone: the wanting went away.

'Therese!' Trevor's voice cut through and I realised he'd been saying my name. 'I'll do the rubbish later.'

'What do you think, Therese?' Caroline asked. 'If this all comes out it'll be bad for your company.'

'Her company!' Judith said. 'It's her company that started all this. Fuck her company.'

She was right – in the context it hardly seemed to matter what happened to my company, but I made myself think it through. If Trevor fought the charges, there was a chance that his lawyer could sow confusion around exactly who falsified the documents, and that might lead to an acquittal. That way, even if his name came out in public, there'd be a not guilty verdict to point to. Therese Thorne might survive.

But if he pleaded guilty, that would be that. People his age, convicted for the same category of fraud, did get custodial sentences; I hadn't just taken Marcus Todd's word for it but had looked it up. Four years, five, seven.

Even if the SFO found out the truth about Heathcote's involvement, Trevor would be convicted of enabling, abetting, profiting, whatever. Therese Thorne, with its sunlit beach grass and its promise of goodness, would be permanently tainted. But that wouldn't be the worst of it. Whichever way this unravelled, whether it was Heathcote or Trevor or the lawyer and accountant I'd never met, someone would have to pay for lying to the bank. And even though I had not asked anyone to do that, it had been done because of what I wanted.

Annabel had frozen on the screen, mid-blink, but her voice came through. 'I'm still here. Can you still hear me?'

'We can hear you,' Caroline said. 'I just asked Therese what she thinks.'

'What did she say?'

I knew what Claire would say. Claire would mow them down in one sweep of her eye. But this wasn't her family. It was mine.

'I think Trevor—' I stopped addressing the static computer image and turned to him. 'I think you have to plead guilty to your part in it all. Tell them what happened. And Heathcote. You should tell them about the rest. Just tell the truth. It gets so complicated if you don't.'

Trevor rocked back on his stool. 'Ha.'

I pressed on, feeling the implications of what I was saying close in. 'You trust Marcus Todd. This is what he's advised. There might be home detention, or in a couple of cases I've looked up there's just been community service and a fine, it's a slim chance but now that you're both involved… especially if neither of you are entirely responsible.'

'We're both responsible,' Trevor said, his voice dull.

'You think they should both go down?' Rob was incredulous. 'How do you square that?'

'They might not "go down", whatever that means – look I don't know. You asked me what I thought. Isn't it better to face into it?'

'Your brand will be fucked,' Caroline said. 'Therese Thorne, prison furnishings.'

'I have been trying to prevent that.' Trevor levelled his gaze at me.

'I know. But I don't want you to do that anymore. You know, protect me.'

'OK.' He stood up. 'That's one for both of us going to jail.'

'It's not what I mean, Trevor,' I said, trying to talk over him, 'of course I don't want that!' but he continued,

'Annabel, you're for just me going, Rob votes for Heathcote, Caroline, I think you're the deciding vote? Judith.' Their eyes met. 'I won't make you choose.'

'It's not like that,' I tried again, the kids joining in, 'for fuck's sake, come on, no one wants anyone to go to prison' – but our protests slid off the bubble that encased Trevor and Judith, the intimacy that still held them together: the golden young couple, the kids, the betrayals, the weathered détente. She loved him, I could see that, but would kill him to protect her son.

'That's not fair,' I said to Trevor, 'you know what she'd say.'

Judith looked away, and Trevor went over to the fridge, where he stood facing into the open door, like someone who'd forgotten what he was looking for.

Annabel was frozen still on her screen, and Caroline was telling Rob to stop mansplaining.

Heathcote said, 'I'll do it. I'll tell them what I did. But Dad – only if you plead not guilty.'

No one heard him but me and Judith. I watched Judith reach towards the model of the hotel, pull it across the marble countertop towards her, lift its unwieldy weight off the kitchen island and smash it to the ground.

Rob left after exacting promises that nobody would make a decision before they'd all had the chance to sleep on it. On her way out the door Caroline gripped my arm and said, 'I know about you and that woman. Fern told me.'

'What?'

Her face was being held in place for her, but the tips of her nostrils were white. 'Don't you dare. Don't you dare do that to my father.'

I couldn't believe it. 'There's nothing to know.'

She was fighting through the crap in her bag for her car keys and I had a sudden image of Claire doing that, so long ago now, on the landing, when she told me her dream. Why didn't women just fling their bags upside down and throw all the shit to the wind? I wanted to wrench it off her myself and chuck it out the window – phone and lipstick flying.

Judith was on the balcony, talking to Heathcote, but watching us.

'Are you thinking of your own mother?' I asked.

Caroline gave a low growl. Just like an animal. 'Just look after my dad,' she said as she was leaving.

I wanted to leap on her back, flip her on the ground, and roar in her unlined face.

For a long moment I faced the empty living room. Trevor had retreated to his study with the broken hotel model and a hot glue gun, and no further mention of the trust fund. On the balcony, Judith and Heathcote were finishing their business. I watched her bend to light a cigarette, a signal he was dismissed.

Heathcote moseyed towards me, his face crooked, and I wondered what Judith had said. He told me he was going to collect his girlfriend from the airport.

'Will you bring her back here?' I asked.

His smirk returned. Maybe, I thought, he was in love. 'She might come to this building.'

That was an odd thing to say. We were more than the building. But I let it go. He tossed the car keys in the air and caught them with the same hand.

'My life's quite fucked, Therese. I do know that.'

I nodded. 'I don't know what I'm doing either.'

Judith saluted a goodbye to him through the plate glass balcony doors, and exhaled an elegant stream of smoke. I leaned against the sliding door frame.

'Shit,' I said.

She took another drag, leaning her elbows on the balcony railing, looking into the middle distance above the street. 'Be a big sacrifice for you.'

'What, the company?'

'There's a chance he'd beat the charges,' she said. 'And that they'd never find out Heathcote's involvement. If he pleads not guilty.'

'But a trial could lead them to Heathcote,' I said. 'It's a massive risk.'

A strange noise came out of her as she turned away from me. I thought of Claire and Alex – that unstoppable love.

'Trevor listens to you,' I said.

'Hmm, does he.' She turned and gave me her full attention. 'Tell me how you see it, Therese. Is this a moment for Trevor to redeem himself? To do the noble thing, face it like a man, wear the consequences, even for something that is – frankly – a victimless crime?'

She was mocking me.

'All that would be taken into account. Weighing up this thing against everything he's done for the community.' I had a flash-back to my little speech at our Christmas party, and cringed. It occurred to me there wasn't an impartial figure out there, keeping a ledger book of our sins and virtues. It was a frightening thought.

'Right,' she said. 'Everything he's done.'

A green sludge seeped through my stomach. A kind of know-ing something was about to be said, and not wanting to know what it was.

'Trevor, Trevor, Trevor,' she said. 'Trevor this, Trevor that.' A quick smile. 'He is pretty extraordinary. All that creative energy. But you're creative too.'

'Me? No. Not really.' That wasn't how I saw myself. A sparrow hopped on the railing and came to investigate Judith's ashtray.

'I've got a cocktail party to go to tonight,' she said. 'Another fundraiser for the hospital, god knows I should make the most of the invitation.'

'Judith, no one will—'

'I don't care.' She cut me off, her face pointed with anger. 'They will. And I don't care. I have other ways of doing the things I need to do.'

She ground out the cigarette. 'I actually admire your optimism. That Trevor will do the right thing. Of course I'll murder him if anything happens to Heathcote. I'd rather see Trevor go to jail. But I don't think he will. I mean, nothing touches him, does it? Look at that thing with the council.'

'About the hotel? The building permits?'

A little pause told me that what was about to follow was a thing she had been dying to say.

'About the social housing. He scuppered that proposal just as it was about to get passed. And now, the *irony*, they've given him the public right of way to the water and it doesn't matter if he "lets people use it" as he's promised to, the point is why should it be up to him? Something that only a month ago belonged to everybody?'

'He actively worked against the social housing?'

'They didn't even investigate that in the end. I'd call them dozy bastards but it wouldn't be fair. Trevor's good at covering his traces, and it's just the usual network in operation.'

'But he's pro social housing. I mean, he developed that block of units years ago, for nothing.'

'Yes, that was rather my influence, I'm afraid.' She gave a wry smile. 'Trevor responds to a nudge in the right direction. If someone's willing to give it.'

There was moss growing inside the groove of the sliding door frame. I picked at it, understanding now why Judith had stuck around to have her cigarette here. A long strip came away. I ran my fingers over its fuzzy greenness. My mouth was dry, and I saw us both, him and me, from a long way away, and we were so small.

Trevor was trying to fit the roof of the hotel back on, but the east wall had buckled in the smash and wouldn't stay in place.

'Judith's gone,' I said from his study doorway. 'I'm on my way out too.'

He glanced up over his glasses, then went back to his model. 'OK.'

'Of course I don't want you to go to jail, you know I don't. I feel ridiculous even saying these words.'

'I know.' He nodded. 'It's just that you'd like things to be simple.'

'That sounds like an insult.'

'Well it's not.' A brief smile, half at me, half down at his project. 'I love you, Therese.'

'I'm sorry,' I said, 'that I've expected you to be a certain way.'

'Hm? What do you mean?'

'Like, a leader. In control. Infallible. I feel like we haven't always shown each other who we really are.'

'Of course we have. Who else would we be?'

'Not that we're not us, but—' I hated that phrase, *this is not who I am*. It was cheating.

'We're working people,' he said. 'You've got your business, I've got mine. We're not those types who live in each other's pockets all day long.'

'I mean – I think there's a way we both could be more free. If we didn't have these habits of mind.'

He laughed. 'I'm about as free as a person gets,' Trevor said. 'I'm well aware of that. I'm just trying to keep it that way.'

Wasn't that what Claire had said of me, on our walk in Martinborough? Why had I needed someone else to tell me?

The little people, plastic models that the architect had used to show scale and which were no bigger than a matchstick, had come off the base and lay beside the hotel parts. I picked one up – a female figure with a red dress and dark hair. Caroline

was right, it could have gone on a wedding cake. I saw myself
open my mouth to exhale a jet of fire at it, exploding the hotel,
scorching a blaze up the centre of the room.

'Would you ever have told me,' I said, 'about Heathcote?'

'It probably would have come out.'

'And what about the hotel land being meant for public housing, would you have told me about that?'

'What?' He paused, roof in hand.

'Judith said the first enquiry, your pet councillor rushing the
permits and that. That it did happen, you got special treatment.
And she said you persuaded them to approve the hotel instead
of a social housing project.'

'That's my job,' he said. 'Steering the ship.'

'So the social housing's just abandoned, or shunted out to
miles away to be built on top of some rubbish dump.'

'It's a prime location,' he said. 'The waterfront. It should be a
site for everybody.'

That was so audacious it almost made me laugh. I ground the
head of the figurine into the tabletop. 'But your hotel isn't for
everybody.'

'You know what I mean. They were never going to put social
housing there, come on.'

'Why shouldn't they? Why shouldn't it be where the golf
courses are, or the fancy hotels? It would have been amazing.'

'The people in those units aren't going to be the ones buying
three hundred dollar cushions and room sprays from your shop,
are they. Shit.' He'd found a piece of mezzanine that he hadn't
stuck in and now it wouldn't slide into place unless he took the
roof off again. 'Worse than a bloody flat pack bookshelf.'

'How did you swing it with the councillor? Money, a job for a
kid, the use of a holiday house? Some old bit of dirt from when
you were at school together?'

'Therese.' He leaned back against the edge of his desk and put
the hotel roof to one side. 'You are not this naïve.'

'Or do you not need to do anything? Do you just need to be
you? Is that good enough.'

'I've been good enough for you for a pretty long time.'

If Judith hadn't already broken the hotel I would have done it then and there. He was right.

'You must think there's something wrong with it,' I said, 'in a tiny part of you. Or you would have told me.'

He turned to the mezzanine level and angled it into place.

I snatched it and threw it across the room. 'Look at me.'

'Hey.' He did – down his glasses, his face closed.

'Look at me! Me!' I bared my teeth. I pointed to where my crooked eyetooth used to be. 'I fixed this. I learned how to speak. What to like. How to be. Everything I've done in the last thirty years has been shaped for you – I've spent more of my life with you than without you and I've loved it, I've loved you, you're brilliant and loving and so generous, and you know the world, but I don't want to be in that world any longer. I don't want it. I can't stand this stupid smile.'

'It's all right.' He was calm. Trying to calm me. 'I understand, it's been a really hard time, you've put up with a lot.'

'This is the kind of phrasing I hate! It's meaningless. It's just more words that get trotted out, *put up with a lot, wonderful, supportive, gorgeous*, it's all just another way to keep things as they are. Our words have meant nothing for *years*. We may as well not speak.'

He put his fingertips to his forehead and looked away. 'Well, I don't know what to say in relation to that. You've painted me into a corner.'

'You're not in a corner. Neither am I. You're not doing this to me. I am.'

'Doing what?'

'Selling me this drug.'

'Are you using drugs?' A brief dawning came over his face, like, of course, that explains it, followed by concern.

I laughed, 'No,' and he laughed too, with relief. 'Drugs! I wish.' Again I thought of Claire with her antidepressants, her family liking her better that way. 'Do you know what I'm saying, Trevor?'

He thought for a moment and said, 'I know you want me to be honest. So, no. No, I don't.'

I knew there were people who were happy like that. Who lived in parallel and that was enough. But I had to try to push this through. I felt closer than I ever had. I was holding his hand.

'If I were to change,' I said. 'Like I'm trying to. If I were to be somehow different from how you've known me to be, from who I've become because of you. Do you think you'd still love me?'

He looked perplexed. 'It would depend. I love you as you are, Therese. I'm not sure I would like you another way.'

'OK,' I said. 'Thanks for being honest.' I squeezed his hand. And then I gave up.

'Oh, come on, don't cry.'

'I'm going out.'

'Downstairs? I can hear that music all hours of the day and night. What the hell do you get up to down there?'

'Just – I can't explain.' I didn't want to. I was as guilty of not talking as he was.

'Seems like some kind of cult. Guy I went to school with became a cult leader, but then he turned out to be a sex pest, I don't think it ended well.'

He was trying to make me laugh, and it worked. We were reaching an understanding. Unless I did something, we would go on like this, I saw. The arrangement would continue as if that deal we had struck right at the start could never be broken.

'It's nothing like a cult.'

'Are you sure?' Trevor stood back to assess the model. 'She hasn't given you all new names? That's what my old school mate did. What's your cult name?' he asked.

I stared at him and said, 'Therese.'

24

After I left his office I paused outside his door for a moment, but standing still I felt sadness begin to unbutton me. In the hall I yanked on my sneakers and lifted the enormous ring of keys from the hook. I wasn't sure which were the ones to unlock the padlocks around the hotel site's door, so I took them all.

I rattled down the stairs and knocked on Heathcote's apartment door.

'Artan! Jesse! Are you there?'

Jesse answered, shirtless, in jeans.

'What's up?'

'Get Artan, I've got somewhere for us to go.'

While they got ready I darted back up to my place for some blankets. As I lifted them out of the hall cupboard, I heard Trevor talking quietly, reasonably, on the phone in his office.

Jesse and Artan had already crossed the landing to Claire's. She was in her hallway with them, putting on her coat. I loved them all for being up for it.

'Can you bring the speakers?' I said. 'And candles. And the firelighters.'

Claire said, 'Are we going to have a fire?'

'Yes.'

'What about the others?' Jesse asked. 'Fern and that.'

'Let's message them on the way. I warn you. We'll be trespassing.'

'Wait up then.' Jesse let himself back into Heathcote's apartment. We drifted back into Claire's living room, where the
balcony doors were open.

'Aren't you going to shut those?'

'No one could climb up here,' she said. 'It's fine.'

I thought of the hairy, stripe-tailed creature of my nightmares
that had scaled the building to prise open my apartment's outside
doors and hunch over my rug. I supposed if it tried to break into
Claire's place the lions might scare it off.

There was a football game on at the stadium across town, and
through the balcony doors we heard a faint cheer, the whole
crowd really sounding like one voice. A few years ago Trevor
sponsored the football team, and the kit bore his name. On the
first big match night after the sponsorship deal, I was laid out
with the flu. He gave his seat away to stay home with me, and
we turned off the stereo and sat in the dark with our doors
and windows open, listening to the crowd. The team won, and
Trevor danced around the coffee table clapping his hands above
his head like a boy. For a second, remembering, I felt dizzy, and
wondered if I should return upstairs.

'All ready,' said Jesse, coming down the hall. He was dressed in
his security guard uniform.

Artan whistled.

'Let's go.'

Outside the protective white plastic sheeting, the harbour slapped
the wharf and boats rasped against their moorings. Here in the
half-built hotel atrium, nīkau fronds rustled in the wind. The lights
on the cranes glittered above us like planets through holes torn by
weather in the plastic. The building's frame creaked as the wind
wrestled it and sent little eddies of leaves scuffling in the corners.
On the living walls, long strands of ferns and grasses swayed back
and forth, and the sharp scent of Jesse's cigarette drifted over from
the door he leaned against in his security gear.

We had trooped through the streets like any group of people
going to a picnic, blankets under our arms, a sports bag holding

our things. When we reached the Hulk itself, spread over the block, the sea black and sparkling behind it, I had another moment's doubt. If real security came, or the police, it would be one thing for me and Claire, but another for Jesse and Artan.

'Maybe we should just go to the beach,' I said.

But they all wanted to go in. Jesse went first with the keys, as we hung back on the corner, admiring his convincing nonchalance. The door was made of the same jib board that protected the entire ground level at the street front, and it took him a long time to get the padlocks off and unhook the chains. If anyone had come past I don't know what they would have done – but we were far enough from the nightclubs and bars, and the street was dark, and nobody did.

Inside, we worked quickly by the light of our phone torches to set up the zone, marking it out with rows of fat candles on the polished concrete. We found a brazier and cleared a space for it in the middle of the building site, and gathered wood and rubbish to burn. I was amazed, and slightly afraid, of how close parts of the interior looked to being finished. From the inside, it didn't look at all like a ruin in decay. It looked like a creature about to take its final form.

Beyond our zone, past the palm trees, was a hazard course of loose tiles, reinforcing rods poking up in places through the concrete, piles of corrugated iron and a few small metal bars. Half a dozen concrete blocks sat at angles like a giant child's discarded toys. A fence of steel pipes screwed together blocked the stairway. Unfinished stairs led to a honeycomb of corridors and rooms.

I remembered there were no operating elevators yet, there was no roof garden, no swimming pool, no restaurant, that all these things were to come.

Claire's phone flashed and she went to the door to let Fern and her crew in. There were more of them than we'd seen before, and again I felt scared, like this wasn't in my control. They entered in a little stream and soon the torchlights from their phones were dotted around in too many places to count.

Beyond the crane lights above us, the sky was fully dark. Fern and her gang breached the fence by the stairs and climbed up to the floors above — I heard them calling to each other and watched them clamber through tangrams of wooden wall frames, bare legs, hoodies and thick coats, their phone lights bobbing.

Down here Artan and Claire got the fire lit, and flames quickly leapt above the rim of the brazier, casting shadows against the polythene. I didn't want to burn the place down. I just wanted to know, whatever happened, that a zone had been here.

Claire started the music — the same track she'd put on the first time we entered the zone together, that early morning in the middle of summer. I ran to her like we were at a party or in a club, and pulled her by the wrists into the area bounded by the candles. That feeling when the beat enters your body and you disappear, when a force other than your stupid mind is moving you. The concrete was hard, I knew it would kill our legs by the morning.

Fern and the others flowed down from the upper levels to join us, their lights bleeding fluid lines into the darkness. Around me the group pulsed, buoyant, high. There was Claire, her loving eye catching the light. I felt a rolling sense of wellbeing under her gaze. Jesse was in post by the door and I went to bring him into the group. 'Come on, no one else is going to turn up.'

'I'll give it a bit longer.'

'You're the best.'

'This is cool,' he said, casting his gaze around. 'I like it.'

Just then there was another knock on the wood behind him and he widened his eyes at me, grinning. 'Who's this?'

It was a small group of women I recognised from Claire's dinner. 'Hello, hello.' I led them over to the music. Fern did the rounds with her gold vial of cannabis oil. It flared warmly in my bloodstream and moonlight streaked down in shafts through the holes in the roof, catching us tiny creatures in its beam.

One of Jesse's favourite tracks came on and he flicked out his cigarette and pushed himself off from his post at the door to join Artan, holding his waist, and Claire pulled me in with them. We sang loud in each other's faces, we swayed and buckled towards the blankets on the ground and though we'd landed there through clumsiness, everything slowed, there was a mood change. The zone gave permission, I realised – to tell the truth, to apologise, to show our love for each other. We should do that all the time, I thought stupidly, a kind of starburst going off in my head as I watched Jesse kiss Artan, then look at me with his considering gaze. He kissed me on the cheek, then laughed. He was joking, I thought, but anyway I kissed him back. Then Artan, heavy-lidded, held my face and kissed my mouth. He pulled away and kissed Jesse again, and I saw Claire watching us, and couldn't get the smile off my face. I touched her cheekbone, rubbed my thumb along her jaw.

Beside me Artan had his shirt off and he reached for my jumper and I raised my arms and he pulled it up over my head. Jesse and Claire kissed, we were all moving in the heat from the fire together, slowly peeling off items of each other's clothes.

It was funny, amateur, sexy, awkward. My knee crunched into the concrete, we had bad blanket management. Beyond the range of the fire's warmth, my skin froze. Jesse ran his fingers up the back of my neck into my hair, and I tipped my head back and he kissed me, Claire kissed my throat, we rolled over, I could see Fern and her crew douse their phone lights, close in and reach for each other, you could tell by their moves they were much more practised at this.

Time stretched, the music went on, we were just skin and sensation. Colours melted down the walls – I held Claire down, feeling it in my own body – the holding down, the hard floor at her back.

I'd so often stopped myself doing things because I was worried I'd regret it. Because I didn't know how I'd find my way back to safety. The fear rose off me and vanished up through the open roof like a veil being pulled off by a giant invisible hand.

'Claire.'

She stopped laughing and for a second we just looked at each other – that click – before we shut our eyes. My fingers felt sweat slipping between her legs, she smelled sharp and sandy. Through blurred eyes I saw in slow motion someone's flick of dark hair, a scrape of stubble, Claire's hot breastbone, her breasts. For a moment Jesse and I broke away to kiss each other then I moved over her body, Jesse beside me.

Without warning, a light passed over our faces and Jesse jerked his head away, squinting. On a delay, like when real-world sound enters a dream, I registered that I'd heard the scrape of an opening door and Jesse was here with us, not on guard. Torchlight – a strong white beam – struck us again and stayed. We sat up. In a split moment I felt the shocking individuality of the others in the space – Artan, Jesse, Fern, everyone – and followed Claire's blinking gaze as we all heard,

'Mum. What the fuck?'

Alex, her daughter, stood just meters away, her face frozen with disbelief. Next to her, aiming his torch at us, was Heathcote.

'Hi Fern,' he called across the space. 'Caro said you might be here.'

Fern. The little narc.

'Hi,' she said, 'how *are* you?' – as if we were at a fucking art opening. I could have flown across the room and murdered her. She caught my look, and raised an eyebrow back.

Claire had grabbed a blanket to cover herself and pushed herself to her feet. She went towards her daughter but Alex stepped back.

'What the fuck are you doing?'

She was the centre of the room. In the firelight, against all of our unkemptness, Alex looked startlingly glossy. She was dressed in a white turtleneck, boots and denim shorts, like an image off the Therese Thorne website; her waxy legs were perfect according to the beauty standards of our age. She was not the girl who'd moved to Auckland a few months ago.

Jesse cut the music and the group milled closer, catching up. Heathcote's face was a picture of shock and glee. Alex reached for his hand.

It was clear that he and Alex weren't just former neighbours. They were a couple. I saw Claire see it too.

Claire tried to take Alex's hands and talk as if normal questions were warranted.

'When did you get here? Are you coming home?'

But her daughter clung to Heathcote.

I had groped for a blanket and now sheltered under it, pulling my clothes on. Heathcote. Alex. A series of connections flashed through me: they'd arrived home together after our Christmas party. The rich friend Alex lived with in Auckland – that was Heathcote. The shoebox of photos in her room, polaroids of a half-naked man – that, god help me, was Heathcote. But he's nearly forty and Alex is a child, I thought, then realised what I had thought. Well. It looked different from the outside.

'Alex,' Claire said, 'come on. Let's go home.'

Alex couldn't move and wouldn't speak, but you could see on her face: she was torn between hating her mother and adoring her, scorning her and wanting to be like her. She had clutched tight to her secret life but longed for her mother to find out. She had never, not for a second, thought her mother might have one too.

I knew in that minute – looking at Alex and Claire and how they were undone by each other – that the zone, as we had known it, was over.

It wasn't Claire's fault. That force, motherhood, had only let her out of its grip for so long. Now she was answerable again. I wished she'd find another way, but there was no point objecting. Alex called the shots, as daughters do. She made her mother come home. First to the apartment, where Alex walked around, Claire told me, in shock at the lack of furniture, the spreading stage. Then to where Mick lived, in Auckland.

That was to come. For now, I waited with the keys while everyone gathered their belongings and left. The fire in the brazier still burned hot and yellow; I carried a bucket of water across the atrium to put it out. Heathcote sat on a giant concrete block, elbows on his knees, and watched me blow out the candles and drop them back in the sports bag. I had to pass him to collect one of the speakers.

'You'd better tell Trevor,' he said. 'Or I'll have to.'

'Whatever.'

'Excuse me?'

'He's got other things to worry about,' I said, 'this is nothing.'

'Didn't look like nothing.'

'What do you see in Alex?' I stopped to face him. 'Apart from the obvious. I'm sure she's a great girl, but she's hardly lived. How can she have anything to talk about? Or is it not about talking?'

He picked at his shoelace. 'No, it is,' he said. 'I'm not just some lech. She's not dumb. It's not like I can tell her what to do, I thought you of all people would know that.'

Now he stood and shone his torch around the cavernous interior. 'This place is going to be amazing,' he said. 'He's done it again.'

I felt sorry for Heathcote then, and that the question really was, what did Alex see in him.

'I suppose Dad won't complain,' Heathcote said, inspecting the nīkau palms. 'About you and your orgies.'

'Oh for fuck's sake.' What a ridiculous word. What, I thought, a ridiculous scene. I wanted to laugh at it, and cry about it too. The smell of salt water blew in through the gaps in the walls. What were we trying to break through to? Was it so hard to just be where we were?

'He'll never hear a bad word against you. And he's got his own cheating past.'

I slung the bag over my shoulder. It was heavy, the straps cut in. 'You should ask him about that,' I said, 'and ask your mum.'

'No thanks. Why?'

'Just ask her. Trevor's a good man. In that way.'

We took a last look around the atrium and stood on the other side of the door, in the faintly lightening street, while I locked the stiff padlocks one by one. It took ages. Heathcote leaned against the wall and watched.

When I'd done the last one I picked up the sports bag again, ready to walk home.

'Are you sure you put that fire completely out?' Heathcote asked.

He was smiling, mischievous. He'd been waiting to say that. I pushed him in the chest, not entirely friendly – I did want to hurt him. He pushed my arm, and we walked up the street together. I tried to give him the sports bag, but he wouldn't carry it.

*

I drove Artan to the airport and while he and Jesse said their goodbyes in the terminal, I wandered off past the currency exchange stands to look in the concession store of a rival home-ware company.

When I thought about what would happen to Trevor, I took strength from the way Artan had recovered from his wife leaving him. Who knew what Amina's life was like now – she'd have returned to Tirana long ago, she'd be at her job discussing policy and political structures with other informed young people, she'd be living the irony of talking about democracy and misinformation in a café in the old dictator's residence. I still envisaged her in the mountains of the South Island alone – doing the Routeburn Track, making coffee outdoors on a portable gas stove, drinking in a ski town bar. Perhaps I just liked imagining a woman with a middle-distance stare.

'Can I help you?' the sales assistant asked.

I had a snow globe in my hand. Inside it was a gingerbread cottage, surrounded by trees. I shook it and the globe filled with a white blur, before the house slowly emerged from the swirl. 'All good,' I said, 'just looking.'

She ducked her head swiftly and I realised I recognised her. It was the girl Heathcote had brought to the Sounds. The one who'd been so affronted by my telling her to leave. The one I had seen before, on the stairs in our building.

'I know you,' I said. 'Bella, right?'

'Yes,' she said. She set her chin at me.

'You came on holiday with us in the Sounds. And I've seen you in my building.'

'I'm a friend of Alex's,' she said.

Of course. We're friends of Heathcote's girlfriend. She's in Auckland right now.

'And Heathcote's,' I said.

'Yeah.'

'You thought I was rude to you.'

'You were.'

We held each other's gaze. I didn't need to ask her. She and Heathcote had returned to Wellington a day before us, and he'd let her into our apartment and she had left a shit on the rug. I was surprised to find I admired her for it.

'What do you want, Bella?'

She blinked at me with what might have been false eyelashes – either that, or she was lucky. 'What do you mean?'

'Do you like working here? Are you putting yourself through uni or something?'

She shook her head. 'I'm the store manager.'

I glanced around. The style owed a lot to Therese Thorne Homewares, but I had to admit, it had a kind of edge. 'Nice,' I said. 'Good job. Don't get stuck.'

'Don't worry,' she said, her voice only a tiny bit derisive. 'That won't happen to me.'

Jesse found me by the card carousel, and I gave him a hug. 'All right?'

'Better start saving for a ticket,' he said.

I nodded. 'You will.'

Since we'd been inside the terminal it had started raining, and we crossed the parking lot to my car into horizontal sleet.

I turned the car heater up and while we waited for the windscreen to clear I looked for a song to put on – something different from what we'd listen to in the zone. Jesse pulled a piece of paper out of his damp satchel and spread out the creases.

'This is for you.'

It was a sketch of Claire and me, lying back on the boards of the stage, my hair spread out against the black wood grain, Claire staring up at the ceiling. It looked like a moment from just after the music had stopped, when we were slowly coming out of our inner selves and into the everyday world. He'd captured her free, open expression – the life and amusement in her face that made you want to go wherever she was going. And me – I was in profile again, as I had been in the sketch he'd made of me and Trevor, looking at her with the same devoted gaze.

I felt a churning in my solar plexus.

He was looking at me like he knew what he had shown me.

'It's amazing,' I said. 'You've got us.'

We pulled out of the carpark. I stuck my hand out the window in the rain to wave the parking ticket at the machine. The barrier lifted and I drove us towards the harbour, windscreen wipers sluicing the rain that was so heavy it muffled the music. The sketch sat on my knees and I glanced at it again when we stopped at the traffic lights. That gaze of mine was something to think about.

*

Trevor's trial date was set for August 2019, eleven months from that night at the hotel. In mid-June the financial consultant would change his plea. He would plead guilty to making false statements and the lawyer would plead guilty to obtaining by deception. In July they would both be sentenced to home detention. Neither of them would take Trevor's calls. They would still be serving their sentences when we went into the first pandemic lockdown, and still under detention when the lockdown was lifted; I thought of them often, but especially then.

Trevor called to tell me he was pleading guilty.

'I was planning to come to court,' I said, 'if you want me there.'

He hesitated, then said, 'No. Thanks, but I'd actually rather you didn't... have that image of me.'

I understood. We'd held a dream mirror up to each other for so long. I didn't mind pretending to still hold it.

'I'm so sorry,' I said. 'I'm really sorry, Trevor.'

'Yep,' he said. 'Me too.'

His conviction was made public, and the papers reported the details of the mortgage fraud. If you searched the internet for Trevor Thorne or Therese Thorne, that was the first thing you would find.

After I was faced with losing my company, I remembered how hard I'd worked for it. Sure, there were things more meaningful and useful to do with my life, and I would rather look for those than open a branch in Sydney, but for now I could at least try to do a good job.

Given Trevor's age, his otherwise good record, and because he helped the SFO with an enquiry into another developer, the man who at that party had taken my hand and called the other women trouts, he was granted home detention too. He elected to spend it at Judith's. They were still together when Annabel returned home from Singapore with her boys; her marriage to John had foundered, some final straw, or perhaps she just got tired of propping it up. They would move into the unfinished apartment below Claire's, and finally make it habitable. Trevor and Judith rented a room in Rotorua while they were quarantined there, and stood outside the fence every day at exercise hour, to wave and blow kisses. I heard it all from Caroline, when we ran into each other one day at the park.

'You know,' Caroline said to me while the dog she'd got for the boys' anxiety strained at its collar and barked and barked and barked at gulls, 'we've known each other a long time, but I don't think you ever let me get any closer to you than when we first met.'

'Did you want to be?' I was surprised. In the harsh wind her face looked old; I'm sure mine did too.

'I used to look up to you.' She squinted at me. 'When I was young.'

I laughed. 'Cheers.'

We stood together for a bit longer in the grey light, until I said, 'So how's Andy?' and she made a scoffing wave of her hand and said, 'Andy? He's fine!'

Trevor did give an interview where he made it clear I'd had nothing to do with the mortgage fraud – Haimona had suggested a receptive journalist. I kept my head down and looked at ways to absorb the anticipated losses, but they were, oddly, not that bad. Being associated with a grifter wasn't the career ender it might once have been. I didn't take comfort from that. Denise has to be credited with rehabilitating the brand – the charity work, transitioning to an employee stock ownership plan, increasing our efforts towards sustainability. Then of course there was the pandemic. Online sales have been good.

*

I didn't remove everything from the apartment, but not long after that hotel night I removed myself, and took just a few things with me. The plum-coloured sofa, a lamp, and of course the rug, the shit rug, as I called it now.

'Are you sure you're not over-correcting?' Judith asked when we crossed paths on the stairwell, on the day I moved out.

Judith had her own anger – anyone could see it, if you knew how to look. I recognised it everywhere now, on the streets – each woman like a storm in a body, a weather system on a leash. Female rage was breaking the surface, swiftly being packaged by the culture and commodified, appearing in slogans on cushion covers in my shop, Fierce Bitch or Strong Female Character taking the place of Live Laugh Love on the bib of an apron. As the rage was paid lip service and neutralised, I wondered what lay underneath it. Anger, I had read on a self-help website, was a secondary emotion. So what was it a reaction to? Fear? Sadness? Humiliation? How Judith would hate the idea of that.

She was dropping a birthday cake off for Heathcote. She and Trevor had convinced him not to hand himself in to the SFO, to just continue with his life as if he'd never had the idea to lie to the bank, had never gone to the trouble of falsifying documents to compound the lie and please his father. Rob would not forgive Heathcote, but his sisters would. I don't know whether they all went back to the Sounds for Christmas, with Judith too. I was gone by then.

Claire said it was Heathcote's punishment just to be Heathcote, to know in his soul that he hadn't earned his own freedom. To continue getting older without facing himself. But I'm not sure he would swap that arrangement even if he had the chance. He has, in fact, had plenty of chances.

It came out that it was Heathcote and Alex together who posted Claire's apartment on the letting site, because Alex wanted some quick cash and Heathcote, king of the bad idea, had suggested it. They'd thought Claire was away for New Year but she had stayed home with a flu. She was never meant to meet Artan and Amina, never meant to know. Which meant I would never have met them either. Claire's life would not have taken that unexpected turn. And perhaps there wouldn't have even been a stage on which to find the zone.

I hoped Heathcote would get on with his life too, but also that he wouldn't forget what he'd done. The thought of forgetting what I'd done kept me up at night. I didn't want to forget, ever, that I'd said, without even thinking, 'I want that place' to Trevor, and started a chain reaction.

I'm going to go and visit Claire in Auckland – not to recreate the zone, that would be impossible – and not to seduce her away from Mick either. Maybe some of us need to keep close to the thing we fight against, to help us feel our own outlines. It is certainly weird out here where I am, knowing now I've got to start my new life, where there are other things to work for. Gives me vertigo if I think about it too hard; better to get on with it and do something. No, I just want to go up to spend a bit of time with her. Claire's an interesting woman.

Before she moved, I bumped into her one last time. I had been passing the old building on my way to the chemist, and couldn't help pausing to look up at it. Just then she emerged from the foyer.

'Therese,' she said. 'Are you going in?'

As she spoke, an estate agent came out and put a pole bearing a teardrop flag on the steps. A middle-aged guy approached us and walked through the doors into the building.

'Is it your place that's for sale?' I asked.

She nodded. 'I want to see who's interested. Have you got a minute?'

We walked to the little park along the block, and perched on a bench with a view of the building's entrance.

She sat with her legs wide apart, her hands on her knees, staring up the block at our old front door. A young couple neared the steps and she turned to me excited, eyebrows raised.

Claire watched the building, and I looked at the people in the park. Birds strutted on the grass. A group of students rose up off the benches and disappeared into the design school. A dog sniffed around the base of a rubbish bin while the human on the other end of its lead talked on her phone. Posters promoted bands and safe sex. A man sat against a wall in a sleeping bag, with a hand-written piece of card and an ice cream tub by his side. Cars slowed as they approached the lights, because people always jaywalked here, and you couldn't rely on the traffic signals.

By now I had taken in the impact of Jesse's sketch. I had fallen under Claire's spell, just as I'd fallen under Trevor's. I didn't blame myself — it was wonderful to be in thrall to something. But reality, I was beginning to find, was more enlivening.

The other day I was walking down by the waterfront when I rounded a corner and Trevor's hotel reared up in front of me, finished now, glittering as if covered with a billion green paillettes. It's not really Trevor's hotel, another developer took it over when he became untouchable. I don't know who stays there, given what's happened to tourism.

As I stood there looking at it – honestly, marvelling at the achievement – Claire rang from her back garden, launching straight in, as she usually does.

'God it's hot. The humidity's off the chart today. I can't wait for you to get here, I've found a secret spot to go skinny-dipping. Alex won't come with me, she's horrified by the idea. Or by me. Anyway, I'm working on it.'

'Nice.' At an angle, if you squinted, the hotel looked like a colossal fish, bucking up out of the sea.

'Oh,' said Claire, '—did you hear that?'

'No.'

'Weird, like a short, heavy vibration. I felt it all through me. Maybe it was a truck.'

I imagined her looking around, up the side of the weatherboard house, with a hand over her thumping chest. The road at the front of the house would be dazzlingly empty.

'So I'm reading the show notes for the second series of this Atalanta shit,' she said. 'And get this, they've got her hunting down wild creatures, going after the Golden Fleece, all that. Choosing her husband in a rigged race. But they're missing what happens next, when they have sex in a temple and get turned into lions as punishment. Don't you think that's the best bit?'

The fish twisted and flashed, green scales catching the light.

'I do,' I said. 'I just can't see it as a punishment.'

I had changed before, I thought as I kept walking; I could do it again.

Acknowledgements

I am deeply grateful to my editor Emma Herdman for an enriching and enjoyable editing process.

To my agent Georgia Garrett, thank you as ever for your insight, skill and patience.

To Greg Heinimann for the brilliant cover, and to Theodora Danek, Francisco Vilhena, Hermione Davis, Clare Meldrum, Helen Upton, Meenakshi Singh, Cristina Cappelluto, Paul Baggaley and all at Bloomsbury, heartfelt thanks. Alexandra Pringle, thank you for connecting us.

Thanks to Sue Orr, Anna Smaill and the Glen Road Writers for valued feedback and support. Thanks to Elizabeth Knox for the table we sit around, and for recommending the fascinating book *Ecstasy in Secular and Religious Experiences* by Marghanita Laski.

Thanks to Rachel Davies and Alison Manning for working your life-changing magic.

Thanks to readers Suzy Lucas and Gillian Stern for your astute responses, and to Pip Adam for helpful comments on an early chapter.

Thanks to Brita, Robyn and Catherine, especially for the Queenstown trip, and to Suzy, Janine, Becky and Sophie, for being on the road at the same time.

Thank you to the people I spoke to for research purposes; although the story may have taken a different form, those conversations have influenced this novel. Rick Christie, Tim Stewart, Philip Stevenson, Rob Flanagan, Paul O'Neil, Ralf Gjoni, Adam

Goldwyn, Altin Raxhimi, Shpresa Raka, Edlira Babamusta, Keiti Kondi, Ilva Tare, Andrew Mueller and others in Wellington, London and Tirana. I'm grateful for your generosity and expertise – any mistakes I've made are mine alone.

I loved the book *The Rich: A New Zealand History* by Stevan Eldred-Grigg, which informed the way I thought about Judith's family and her marriage to Trevor, and recommend it to anyone who wants to know about wealth accumulation in Aotearoa New Zealand.

Thanks to Creative New Zealand for a grant that helped me write an early draft of this novel, to the New Zealand Arts Foundation Te Tumu Toi for their generosity, and to Te Herenga Waka Victoria University of Wellington and my former colleagues and students at the International Institute of Modern Letters, for teaching me so much.

And finally, love and thanks to Veronica, Cass and Mary, and to Karl for your constant kindness.

This novel is set largely in Wellington, but its streets, buildings and institutions are invented.

The exhibition Therese visits in Sydney was by artist Pipilotti Rist, entitled *Sip My Ocean*, at the Museum of Contemporary Art Australia, 2017–2018. Specific works described: *Ever is Over All* (1996), *Pixelwald* (Pixel Forest) 2016.

A Note on The Author

Emily Perkins is the author of a prize-winning collection of short stories, *Not Her Real Name*, and four novels, including *Novel About My Wife* (winner of the NZ Book Award and the *Believer Magazine* Book of the Year), and *The Forrests* (longlisted for the Women's Prize for Fiction). Her work for stage and screen includes co-writing the film adaptation of Eleanor Catton's novel *The Rehearsal* (directed by Alison Maclean), an adaptation of Ibsen's *A Doll's House*, and the original play *The Made* with the Auckland Theatre Company. She lives in New Zealand.

A Note on the Type

The text of this book is set in Bembo, which was first used in 1495 by the Venetian printer Aldus Manutius for Cardinal Bembo's *De Aetna*. The original types were cut for Manutius by Francesco Griffo. Bembo was one of the types used by Claude Garamond (1480–1561) as a model for his Romain de l'Université, and so it was a forerunner of what became the standard European type for the following two centuries. Its modern form follows the original types and was designed for Monotype in 1929.